MR MIDSHIPMAN
HORNBLOWER

C. S. FORESTER

LONGMANS

LONGMANS, GREEN AND CO LTD
6 & 7 CLIFFORD STREET, LONDON W1

THIBAULT HOUSE, THIBAULT SQUARE, CAPE TOWN
605–611 LONSDALE STREET, MELBOURNE C1
443 LOCKHART ROAD, HONG KONG
ACCRA, AUCKLAND, IBADAN
KINGSTON (JAMAICA), KUALA LUMPUR
LAHORE, NAIROBI, SALISBURY (RHODESIA)

LONGMANS, GREEN AND CO INC
119 WEST 40TH STREET, NEW YORK 18

LONGMANS, GREEN AND CO
20 CRANFIELD ROAD, TORONTO 16

ORIENT LONGMANS PRIVATE LTD
CALCUTTA, BOMBAY, MADRAS
DELHI, HYDERABAD, DACCA

First published 1950

Published by arrangement with Messrs Michael Joseph Ltd
in the Heritage of Literature Series 1957
Second impression 1957
Third impression 1959
Fourth impression 1960

PRINTED IN GREAT BRITAIN BY
NORTHUMBERLAND PRESS LIMITED
GATESHEAD ON TYNE

CONTENTS

CHAPTER		PAGE
I.	THE EVEN CHANCE	I
II.	THE CARGO OF RICE	35
III.	THE PENALTY OF FAILURE	64
IV.	THE MAN WHO FELT QUEER	85
V.	THE MAN WHO SAW GOD	105
VI.	THE FROGS AND THE LOBSTERS	126
VII.	THE SPANISH GALLEYS	164
VIII.	THE EXAMINATION FOR LIEUTENANT	189
IX.	NOAH'S ARK	209
X.	THE DUCHESS AND THE DEVIL	231

CHAPTER ONE

THE EVEN CHANCE

A JANUARY gale was roaring up the Channel, blustering loudly, and bearing in its bosom rain squalls whose big drops rattled loudly on the tarpaulin clothing of those among the officers and men whose duties kept them on deck. So hard and so long had the gale blown that even in the sheltered waters of Spithead the battleship moved uneasily at her anchors, pitching a little in the choppy seas, and snubbing herself against the tautened cables with unexpected jerks. A shore boat was on its way out to her, propelled by oars in the hands of two sturdy women; it danced madly on the steep little waves, now and then putting its nose into one and sending a sheet of spray flying aft. The oarswoman in the bow knew her business, and with rapid glances over her shoulder not only kept the boat on its course but turned the bows into the worst of the waves to keep from capsizing. It slowly drew up along the starboard side of the *Justinian*, and as it approached the mainchains the midshipman of the watch hailed it.

'Aye aye' came back the answering hail from the lusty lungs of the woman at the stroke oar; by the curious and ages-old convention of the Navy the reply meant that the boat had an officer on board—presumably the huddled figure in the stern-sheets looking more like a heap of trash with a boat-cloak thrown over it.

That was as much as Mr Masters, the lieutenant of the watch, could see; he was sheltering as best he could in the lee of the mizzen-mast bitts, and in obedience to the order of the midshipman of the watch the boat drew up towards the mainchains and passed out of his sight. There was a long delay; apparently the officer had some difficulty in getting up the ship's side. At last the boat reappeared in Master's field of vision; the women had shoved off and were setting a scrap of lugsail, under which the boat, now without its passenger, went swooping back towards Portsmouth, leaping on the waves like a steeplechaser. As it departed Mr Masters became aware of the near approach of someone along the quarterdeck; it was the new arrival under the escort of the midshipman of the watch, who, after pointing Masters out, retired to the mainchains again. Mr Masters had served in the Navy until his hair was white; he was lucky to have received his commission as lieutenant, and he had long known that he would never receive one as captain, but the knowledge had not greatly embittered him, and he diverted his mind by the study of his fellow men.

So he looked with attention at the approaching figure. It was that of a skinny young man only just leaving boyhood behind, something above middle height, with feet whose adolescent proportions to his size were accentuated by the thinness of his legs and his big half-boots. His gawkiness called attention to his hands and elbows. The newcomer was dressed in a badly fitting uniform which was soaked right through by the spray; a skinny neck stuck out of the high stock, and above the neck was a white bony face. A white face was a rarity on the deck of a ship of war, whose crew soon tanned to a deep mahogany, but this face was not merely white; in the hollow cheeks there was a faint shade of green—clearly the newcomer had experienced seasickness in his passage out in the shore boat. Set in the white face were a pair of dark eyes which by contrast looked like holes cut in a sheet of paper; Masters noted with a slight stirring of interest that the eyes, despite their owner's seasickness, were looking about keenly, taking in what were obviously new sights; there was a curiosity and interest there which could not be repressed and which continued to function notwithstanding either seasickness or shyness, and Mr Masters surmised in his far-fetched fashion that this boy had a vein of caution or foresight in his temperament and was already studying his new surroundings with a view to being prepared for his next experiences. So might Daniel have looked about him at the lions when he first entered their den.

The dark eyes met Masters', and the gawky figure came to a halt, raising a hand self-consciously to the brim of his dripping hat. His mouth opened and tried to say something, but closed again without achieving its object as shyness overcame him, but then the newcomer nerved himself afresh and forced himself to say the formal words he had been coached to utter.

'Come aboard, sir.'

'Your name?' asked Masters, after waiting for it for a moment.

'H-Horatio Hornblower, sir. Midshipman,' stuttered the boy.

'Very good, Mr Hornblower,' said Masters, with the equally formal response. 'Did you bring your dunnage aboard with you?'

Hornblower had never heard that word before, but he still had enough of his wits about him to deduce what it meant.

'My sea chest, sir. It's—it's forrard, at the entry port.'

Hornblower said these things with the barest hesitation;

A*

he knew that at sea they said them, that they pronounced the word 'forward' like that, and that he had come on board through the 'entry port', but it called for a slight effort to utter them himself.

'I'll see that it's sent below,' said Masters. 'And that's where you'd better go, too. The captain's ashore, and the first lieutenant's orders were that he's not to be called on any account before eight bells, so I advise you, Mr. Hornblower, to get out of those wet clothes while you can.'

'Yes, sir,' said Hornblower; his senses told him, the moment he said it, that he had used an improper expression —the look on Masters' face told him, and he corrected himself (hardly believing that men really said these things off the boards of the stage) before Masters had time to correct him.

'Aye aye, sir,' said Hornblower, and as a second after-thought he put his hand to the brim of his hat again.

Masters returned the compliment and turned to one of the shivering messengers cowering in the inadequate shelter of the bulwark. 'Boy! Take Mr Hornblower down to the midshipmen's berth.'

'Aye aye, sir.'

Hornblower accompanied the boy forward to the main hatchway. Seasickness alone would have made him un-steady on his feet, but twice on the short journey he stumbled like a man tripping over a rope as a sharp gust brought the *Justinian* up against her cables with a jerk. At the hatchway the boy slid down the ladder like an eel over a rock; Hornblower had to brace himself and descend far more gingerly and uncertainly into the dim light of the lower gundeck and then into the twilight of the 'tween-decks. The smells that entered his nostrils were as strange and as assorted as the noises that assailed his ears. At the foot of each ladder the boy waited for him with a patience whose tolerance was just obvious. After the last descent, a few steps—Hornblower had already lost his sense of direction and did not know whether it was aft or forward—took them to a gloomy recess whose shadows were accentuated rather than lightened by a tallow dip spiked on to a bit of copper plate on a table round which were seated half a dozen shirt-sleeved men. The boy vanished and left Hornblower standing there, and it was a second or two before the whiskered man at the head of the table looked up at him.

'Speak, thou apparition,' said he.

Hornblower felt a wave of nausea overcoming him—the after-effects of his trip in the shore boat were being accentuated by the incredible stuffiness and smelliness of the 'tweendecks. It was very hard to speak, and the fact that he did not know how to phrase what he wanted to say made it harder still.

'My name is Hornblower,' he quavered at length.

'What an infernal piece of bad luck for you,' said a second man at the table, with a complete absence of sympathy.

At that moment in the roaring world outside the ship the wind veered sharply, heeling the *Justinian* a trifle and swinging her round to snub at her cables again. To Hornblower it seemed more as if the world had come loose from its fastenings. He reeled where he stood, and although he was shuddering with cold he felt sweat on his face.

'I suppose you have come,' said the whiskered man at the head of the table, 'to thrust yourself among your betters. Another soft-headed ignoramus come to be a nuisance to those who have to try to teach you your duties. Look at him'—the speaker with a gesture demanded the attention of everyone at the table—'look at him, I say! The King's latest bad bargain. How old are you?'

'S-seventeen, sir,' stuttered Hornblower.

'Seventeen!' The disgust in the speaker's voice was only too evident. 'You must start at twelve if you ever wish to be a seaman. Seventeen! Do you know the difference between a head and a halliard?'

That drew a laugh from the group, and the quality of the laugh was just noticeable to Hornblower's whirling brain, so that he guessed that whether he said 'yes' or 'no' he would be equally exposed to ridicule. He groped for a neutral reply.

'That's the first thing I'll look up in Norie's *Seamanship*,' he said.

The ship lurched again at that moment, and he clung on to the table.

'Gentlemen,' he began pathetically, wondering how to say what he had in mind.

'My God!' exclaimed somebody at the table. 'He's seasick!'

'Seasick in Spithead!' said somebody else, in a tone in which amazement had as much place as disgust.

But Hornblower ceased to care; he was not really conscious of what was going on round him for some time after that. The nervous excitement of the last few days was as much to blame, perhaps, as the journey in the shore boat and the erratic behaviour of the *Justinian* at her anchors, but it meant for him that he was labelled at once as the midshipman who was seasick in Spithead, and it was only natural that the label added to the natural misery of the loneliness and homesickness which oppressed him during those days when that part of the Channel Fleet which had not succeeded in completing its crews lay at anchor in the lee of the Isle of Wight. An hour in the hammock into which the messman hoisted him enabled him to recover sufficiently to be able to report himself to the first lieutenant; after a few days on board he was able to find his way round the ship without (as happened at first) losing his sense of direction below decks, so that he did not know whether he was facing forward or aft. During that period his brother officers ceased to have faces which were mere blurs and came to take on personalities; he came painfully to learn the stations allotted him when the ship was at quarters, when he was on watch, and when hands were summoned for setting or taking in sail. He even came to have an acute enough understanding of his new life to realize that it could have been worse—that destiny might have put him on board a ship ordered immediately to sea instead of one lying at anchor. But it was a poor enough compensation; he was a lonely and unhappy boy. Shyness alone would long have delayed his making friends, but as it happened the midshipmen's berth in the *Justinian* was occupied by men all a good deal older than he; elderly master's mates recruited from the merchant service, and midshipmen in their twenties who through lack of patronage or inability to pass the necessary examination had never succeeded in gaining for themselves commissions as lieutenants. They were inclined, after the first moments of amused interest, to ignore him, and he was glad of it, delighted to shrink into his shell and attract no notice to himself.

For the *Justinian* was not a happy ship during those gloomy January days. Captain Keene—it was when he came aboard that Hornblower first saw the pomp and ceremony that surrounds the captain of a ship of the line—was a sick man, of a melancholy disposition. He had not the fame

which enabled some captains to fill their ships with enthusiastic volunteers, and he was devoid of the personality
which might have made enthusiasts out of the sullen
pressed men whom the press gangs were bringing in from
day to day to complete the ship's complement. His officers
saw little of him, and did not love what they saw. Hornblower, summoned to his cabin for his first interview, was
not impressed—a middle-aged man at a table covered with
papers, with the hollow and yellow cheeks of prolonged
illness.

'Mr Hornblower,' he said formally, 'I am glad to have
this opportunity of welcoming you on board my ship.'

'Yes, sir,' said Hornblower—that seemed more appropriate to the occasion than 'Aye aye, sir', and a junior
midshipman seemed to be expected to say one or the other
on all occasions.

'You are—let me see—seventeen?' Captain Keene picked
up the paper which apparently covered Hornblower's brief
official career.

'Yes, sir.'

'July 4th, 1776,' mused Keene, reading Hornblower's date
of birth to himself. 'Five years to the day before I was
posted as captain. I had been six years as lieutenant before
you were born.'

'Yes, sir,' agreed Hornblower—it did not seem the occasion for any further comment.

'A doctor's son—you should have chosen a lord for your
father if you wanted to make a career for yourself.'

'Yes, sir.'

'How far did your education go?'

'I was a Grecian at school, sir.'

'So you can construe Xenophon as well as Cicero?'

'Yes, sir. But not very well, sir.'

'Better if you knew something about sines and cosines. Better if you could forsee a squall in time to get t'gallants in. We have no use for ablative absolutes in the Navy.'

'Yes, sir,' said Hornblower.

He had only just learned what a topgallant was, but he could have told his captain that his mathematical studies were far advanced. He refrained nevertheless; his instincts combined with his recent experiences urged him not to volunteer unsolicited information.

'Well, obey orders, learn your duties, and no harm can come to you. That will do.'

'Thank you, sir,' said Hornblower, retiring.

But the captain's last words to him seemed to be contradicted immediately. Harm began to come to Hornblower from that day forth, despite his obedience to orders and diligent study of his duties, and it stemmed from the arrival in the midshipmen's berth of John Simpson as senior warrant officer. Hornblower was sitting at mess with his colleagues when he first saw him—a brawny good-looking man in his thirties, who came in and stood looking at them just as Hornblower had stood a few days before.

'Hullo!' said somebody, not very cordially.

'Cleveland, my bold friend,' said the newcomer, 'come out from that seat. I am going to resume my place at the head of the table.'

'But——'

'Come out, I said,' snapped Simpson.

Cleveland moved along with some show of reluctance, and Simpson took his place, and glowered round the table in reply to the curious glances with which everyone regarded him.

'Yes, my sweet brother officers,' he said, 'I am back in the bosom of the family. And I am not surprised that nobody is pleased. You will all be less pleased by the time I am done with you, I may add.'

'But your commission——?' asked somebody, greatly daring.

'My commission?' Simpson leaned forward and tapped the table, staring down the inquisitive people on either side of it. 'I'll answer that question this once, and the man who asks it again will wish he had never been born. A board of turnip-headed captains has refused me my commission. It decided that my mathematical knowledge was insufficient to make me a reliable navigator. And so Acting-Lieutenant Simpson is once again Mr Midshipman Simpson, at your service. At your service. And may the Lord have mercy on your souls.'

It did not seem, as the days went by, that the Lord had any mercy at all, for, with Simpson's return, life in the midshipmen's berth ceased to be one of passive unhappiness and became one of active misery. Simpson had apparently always been an ingenious tyrant, but now, embittered and humiliated by his failure to pass his examination for his commission, he was a worse tyrant, and his ingenuity had multiplied itself. He may have been weak in mathematics, but he was diabolically clever at making other people's lives a burden to them. As senior officer in the mess he had wide official powers; as a man with a blistering tongue and a morbid sense of mischief he would have been powerful anyway, even if the *Justinian* had possessed an alert and masterful first lieutenant to keep him in check, while Mr Clay was neither. Twice midshipmen rebelled against Simpson's arbitrary authority, and each time Simpson thrashed the rebel, pounding him into insensibility with his huge fists, for Simpson would have made a successful prize-fighter. Each time Simpson was left unmarked; each time his opponent's blackened eyes and swollen lips called down the penalty of mast heading and extra duty from the indignant first lieutenant. The mess seethed with impotent rage. Even the toadies and lickspittles among the midshipmen— and naturally there were several—hated the tyrant.

Significantly, it was not his ordinary exactions which roused the greatest resentment—his levying toll upon their sea chests for clean shirts for himself, his appropriation of the best cuts of the meat served, nor even his taking their coveted issues of spirits. These things could be excused as understandable, the sort of thing they would do themselves if they had the power. But he displayed a whimsical arbitrariness which reminded Hornblower, with his classical education, of the freaks of the Roman emperors. He forced Cleveland to shave the whiskers which were his inordinate pride; he imposed upon Hether the duty of waking up Mackenzie every half hour, day and night, so that neither of them was able to sleep—and there were toadies ready to tell him if Hether ever failed in his task. Early enough he had discovered Hornblower's most vulnerable points, as he had with everyone else. He knew of Hornblower's shyness; at first it was amusing to compel Hornblower to recite verses from Gray's 'Elegy in a Country Churchyard' to the assembled mess. The toadies could compel Hornblower to do it; Simpson would lay his dirk-scabbard on the table in front of him with a significant glance, and the toadies would close round Hornblower, who knew that any hesitation on his part would mean that he would be stretched across the table and the dirk-scabbard applied; the flat of the scabbard was painful, the edge of it was agonizing, but the pain was nothing to the utter humiliation of it all. And the torment grew worse when Simpson instituted what he aptly called 'The Proceedings of the Inquisition' when Hornblower was submitted to a slow and methodical questioning regarding his homelife and his boyhood. Every question had to be answered, on pain of the dirk-scabbard; Hornblower could fence and prevaricate, but he had to answer and sooner or later the relentless questioning would draw from him some simple admission which would rouse a peal of laughter from his audience. Heaven knows that in Hornblower's lonely childhood there was nothing to be ashamed of, but boys are odd creatures, especially reticent ones like Hornblower, and are ashamed of things no one else would think twice about. The ordeal would leave him weak and sick; someone less solemn might have clowned his way out of his difficulties and even into popular favour, but Hornblower at seventeen was too ponderous a person to clown. He had to endure the persecution, experiencing all the black misery which only a seventeen-year-old can experience; he never wept in public, but at night more than once he shed the bitter tears of seventeen. He often thought about death; he often even thought about desertion, but he realized that desertion would lead to something worse than death, and then his mind would revert to death, savouring the thought of suicide. He came to long for death, friendless as he was, and brutally ill-treated, and lonely as only a boy among men—and a very reserved boy —can be. More and more he thought about ending it all the easiest way, hugging the secret thought of it to his friendless bosom.

If the ship had only been at sea everyone would have been kept busy enough to be out of mischief; even at anchor an energetic captain and first lieutenant would have kept all hands hard enough at work to obviate abuses, but it was Hornblower's hard luck that the *Justinian* lay at anchor all through that fatal January of 1794 under a sick captain and an inefficient first lieutenant. Even the activities which were at times enforced often worked to Hornblower's disadvantage. There was an occasion when Mr Bowles, the master, was holding a class in navigation for his mates and for the midshipmen, and the captain by bad luck happened by and glanced through the results of the problem the class had individually been set to solve. His illness made Keene a man of bitter tongue, and he cherished no liking for Simpson. He took a single glance at Simpson's paper and chuckled sarcastically.

'Now let us all rejoice,' he said, 'the sources of the Nile have been discovered at last.'

'Pardon, sir?' said Simpson.

'Your ship,' said Keene, 'as far as I can make out from your illiterate scrawl, Mr Simpson, is in Central Africa. Let us now see what other *terræ incognitæ* have been opened up by the remaining intrepid explorers of this class.'

It must have been Fate—it was dramatic enough to be art and not an occurrence in real life; Hornblower knew what was going to happen even as Keene picked up the other papers, including his. The result he had obtained was the only one which was correct; everybody else had added the correction for refraction instead of subtracting it, or had worked out the multiplication wrongly, or had, like Simpson, botched the whole problem.

'Congratulations, Mr Hornblower,' said Keene. 'You must be proud to be alone successful among this crowd of intellectual giants. You are half Mr Simpson's age, I fancy. If you double your attainments while you double your years, you will leave the rest of us far behind. Mr Bowles, you will be so good as to see that Mr Simpson pays even further attention to his mathematical studies.'

With that he went off along the 'tweendecks with the

halting step resulting from his mortal disease, and Hornblower sat with his eyes cast down, unable to meet the glances he knew were being darted at him, and knowing full well what they portended. He longed for death at that moment; he even prayed for it that night.

Within two days Hornblower found himself on shore, and under Simpson's command. The two midshipmen were in charge of a party of seamen, landed to act along with parties from the other ships of the squadron as a press gang. The West India convoy was due to arrive soon; most of the hands would be pressed as soon as the convoy reached the Channel, and the remainder, left to work the ships to an anchorage, would sneak ashore, using every device to conceal themselves and find a safe hiding-place. It was the business of the landing parties to cut off this retreat, to lay a cordon along the waterfront which would sweep them all up. But the convoy was not yet signalled, and all arrangements were completed.

'All is well with the world,' said Simpson.

It was an unusual speech for him, but he was in unusual circumstances. He was sitting in the back room of the Lamb Inn, comfortable in one armchair with his legs on another, in front of a roaring fire and with a pot of beer with gin in it at his elbow.

'Here's to the West India convoy,' said Simpson, taking a pull at his beer. 'Long may it be delayed.'

Simpson was actually genial, activity and beer and a warm fire thawing him into a good humour; it was not time yet for the liquor to make him quarrelsome; Hornblower sat on the other side of the fire and sipped beer without gin in it and studied him, marvelling that for the first time since he had boarded the *Justinian* his unhappiness should have ceased to be active but should have

subsided into a dull misery like the dying away of the pain
of a throbbing tooth.

'Give us a toast, boy,' said Simpson.

'Confusion to Robespierre,' said Hornblower lamely.

The door opened and two more officers came in, one a
midshipman while the other wore the single epaulette of a
lieutenant—it was Chalk of the *Goliath*, the officer in
general charge of the press gangs sent ashore. Even Simpson made room for his superior rank before the fire.

'The convoy is still not signalled,' announced Chalk. And
then he eyed Hornblower keenly. 'I don't think I have the
pleasure of your acquaintance.'

'Mr Hornblower—Lieutenant Chalk,' introduced Simpson. 'Mr Hornblower is distinguished as the midshipman
who was seasick in Spithead.'

Hornblower tried not to writhe as Simpson tied that label
on him. He imagined that Chalk was merely being polite
when he changed the subject.

'Hey, potman! Will you gentlemen join me in a glass?
We have a long wait before us, I fear. Your men are all
properly posted, Mr Simpson?'

'Yes, sir.'

Chalk was an active man. He paced about the room,
stared out of the window at the rain, presented his midshipman—Caldwell—to the other two when the drinks
arrived, and obviously fretted at his enforced inactivity.

'A game of cards to pass the time?' he suggested. 'Excellent! Hey, potman! Cards and a table and another light.'

The table was set before the fire, the chairs arranged, the
cards brought in.

'What game shall it be?' asked Chalk, looking round.

He was a lieutenant among three midshipmen, and any
suggestion of his was likely to carry a good deal of weight;

the other three naturally waited to hear what he had to say.

'Vingt-et-un? That is a game for the half-witted. Loo? That is a game for the wealthier half-witted. But whist, now? That would give us all scope for the exercise of our poor talents. Caldwell, there, is acquainted with the rudiments of the game, I know. Mr Simpson?'

A man like Simpson, with a blind mathematical spot, was not likely to be a good whist player, but he was not likely to know he was a bad one.

'As you wish, sir,' said Simpson. He enjoyed gambling, and one game was as good as another for that purpose to his mind.

'Mr Hornblower?'

'With pleasure, sir.'

That was more nearly true than most conventional replies. Hornblower had learned his whist in a good school; ever since the death of his mother he had made a fourth with his father and the parson and the parson's wife. The game was already something of a passion with him. He revelled in the nice calculation of chances, in the varying demands it made upon his boldness or caution. There was even enough warmth in his acceptance to attract a second glance from Chalk, who—a good card player himself—at once detected a fellow spirit.

'Excellent!' he said again. 'Then we may as well cut at once for places and partners. What shall be the stakes, gentlemen? A shilling a trick and a guinea on the rub, or is that too great? No? Then we are agreed.'

For some time the game proceeded quietly. Hornblower cut first Simpson and then Caldwell as his partner. Only a couple of hands were necessary to show up Simpson as a hopeless whist player, the kind who would always lead an ace when he had one, or a singleton when he had four trumps, but he and Hornblower won the first rubber thanks to overwhelming card strength. But Simpson lost the next in partnership with Chalk, cut Chalk again as partner, and lost again. He gloated over good hands and sighed over poor ones; clearly he was one of those unenlightened people who looked upon whist as a social function, or as a mere crude means, like throwing dice, of arbitrarily transferring money. He never thought of the game either as a sacred rite or as an intellectual exercise. Moreover, as his losses grew, and as the potman came and went with liquor, he grew restless, and his face was flushed with more than the heat of the fire. He was both a bad loser and a bad drinker, and even Chalk's punctilious good manners were sufficiently strained so that he displayed a hint of relief when the next cut gave him Hornblower as a partner. They won the rubber easily, and another guinea and several shillings were transferred to Hornblower's lean purse; he was now the only winner, and Simpson was the heaviest loser. Hornblower was lost in the pleasure of playing the game again; the only attention he paid to Simpson's writhings and muttered objurgations was to regard them as a distracting nuisance; he even forgot to think of them as danger signals. Momentarily he was oblivious to the fact that he might pay for his present success by future torment.

Once more they cut, and he found himself Chalk's partner again. Two good hands gave them the first game. Then twice, to Simpson's unconcealed triumph, Simpson and Caldwell made a small score, approaching game, and in the next hand an overbold finesse by Hornblower left him and Chalk with the odd trick when their score should have been two tricks greater—Simpson laid his knave on Hornblower's ten with a grin of delight which turned to dismay when he found that he and Caldwell had still only made six tricks; he counted them a second time with annoyance. Hornblower dealt and turned the trump, and Simpson led—an ace as usual, assuring Hornblower of his re-entry. He had a string of trumps and a good suit of clubs which a single lead might establish. Simpson glanced muttering at his hand; it was extraordinary that he still had not realized the simple truth that the lead of an ace involved leading a second time with the problem no clearer. He made up his mind at last and led again; Hornblower's king took the trick and he instantly led his knave of trumps. To his delight it took the trick; he led again and Chalk's queen gave them another trick. Chalk laid down the ace of trumps and Simpson with a curse played the king. Chalk led clubs of which Hornblower had five to the king-queen —it was significant that Chalk should lead them, as it could not be a singleton lead when Hornblower held the remaining trumps. Hornblower's queen took the trick; Caldwell must hold the ace, unless Chalk did. Hornblower led a small one; everyone followed suit, Chalk playing the knave, and Caldwell the ace. Eight clubs had been played, and Hornblower had three more headed by the king and ten— three certain tricks, with the last trumps as re-entries. Caldwell played the queen of diamonds, Hornblower played his singleton, and Chalk produced the ace.

'The rest are mine,' said Hornblower, laying down his cards.

'What do you mean?' said Simpson, with the king of diamonds in his hand.

'Five tricks,' said Chalk briskly. 'Game and rubber.'

'But don't I take another?' persisted Simpson.

'I trump a lead of diamonds or hearts and make three more clubs,' explained Hornblower. To him the situation was as simple as two and two, a most ordinary finish to a hand; it was hard for him to realize that foggy-minded players like Simpson could find difficulty in keeping tally of fifty-two cards. Simpson flung down his hand.

'You know too much about the game,' he said. 'You know the backs of the cards as well as the fronts.'

Hornblower gulped. He recognized that this could be a decisive moment if he chose. A second before he had merely been playing cards, and enjoying himself. Now he was faced with an issue of life or death. A torrent of thought streamed through his mind. Despite the comfort of his present surroundings he remembered acutely the hideous misery of the life in the *Justinian* to which he must return. This was an opportunity to end that misery one way or the other. He remembered how he had contemplated killing himself, and into the back of his mind stole the germ of the plan upon which he was going to act. His decision crystallized.

'That is an insulting remark, Mr Simpson,' he said. He looked round and met the eyes of Chalk and Caldwell, who were suddenly grave; Simpson was still merely stupid. 'For that I shall have to ask satisfaction.'

'Satisfaction?' said Chalk hastily. 'Come, come. Mr Simpson had a momentary loss of temper. I am sure he will explain.'

'I have been accused of cheating at cards,' said Hornblower. 'That is a hard thing to explain away.'

He was trying to behave like a grown man; more than that, he was trying to act like a man consumed with indignation, while actually there was no indignation within him over the point in dispute, for he understood too well the muddled state of mind which had led Simpson to say what he did. But the opportunity had presented itself, he had determined to avail himself of it, and now what he had to

do was to play the part convincingly of the man who has
received a mortal insult.

'The wine was in and the wit was out,' said Chalk, still
determined on keeping the peace. 'Mr Simpson was speaking in jest, I am sure. Let's call for another bottle and
drink it in friendship.'

'With pleasure,' said Hornblower, fumbling for the
words which would set the dispute beyond reconciliation.
'If Mr Simpson will beg my pardon at once before you two
gentlemen, and admit that he spoke without justification
and in a manner no gentleman would employ.'

He turned and met Simpson's eye with defiance as he
spoke, metaphorically waving a red rag before the bull,
who charged with gratifying fury.

'Apologize to *you*, you little whippersnapper!' exploded
Simpson, alcohol and outraged dignity speaking simul-
taneously. 'Never this side of Hell.'

'You hear that, gentlemen?' said Hornblower. 'I have
been insulted and Mr Simpson refuses to apologize, while
insulting me further. There is only one way now in which
satisfaction can be given.'

For the next two days, until the West India convoy came
in, Hornblower and Simpson, under Chalk's orders, lived
the curious life of two duellists forced into each other's
society before the affair of honour. Hornblower was careful
—as he would have been in any case—to obey every order
given him, and Simpson gave them with a certain amount
of self-consciousness and awkwardness. It was during those
two days that Hornblower elaborated on his original idea.
Pacing through the dockyards with his patrol of seamen at
his heels he had plenty of time to think the matter over.
viewed coldly—and a boy of seventeen in a mood of black
despair can be objective enough on occasions—it was as

simple as the calculations of the chances in a problem at whist. Nothing could be worse than his life in the *Justinian*, not even (as he had thought already) death itself. Here was an easy death open to him, with the additional attraction that there was a chance of Simpson dying instead. It was at that moment that Hornblower advanced his idea one step further—a new development, startling even to him, bringing him to a halt so that the patrol behind him bumped into him before they could stop.

'Beg your pardon, sir,' said the petty officer.

'No matter,' said Hornblower, deep in his thoughts.

He first brought forward his suggestion in conversation with Preston and Danvers, the two master's mates whom he asked to be his seconds as soon as he returned to the *Justinian*.

'We'll act for you, of course,' said Preston, looking dubiously at the weedy youth when he made his request. 'How do you want to fight him? As the aggrieved party you have the choice of weapons.'

'I've been thinking about it ever since he insulted me,' said Hornblower temporizing. It was not easy to come out with his idea in bald words, after all.

'Have you any skill with the small-sword?' asked Danvers.

'No,' said Hornblower. Truth to tell, he had never even handled one.

'Then it had better be pistols,' said Preston.

'Simpson is probably a good shot,' said Danvers. 'I wouldn't care to stand up before him myself.'

'Easy now,' said Preston hastily. 'Don't dishearten the man.'

'I'm not disheartened,' said Hornblower, 'I was thinking the same thing myself.'

'You're cool enough about it, then,' marvelled Danvers.

Hornblower shrugged.

'Maybe I am. I hardly care. But I've thought that we might make the chances more even.'

'How?'

'We could make them exactly even,' said Hornblower, taking the plunge. 'Have two pistols, one loaded and the other empty. Simpson and I would take our choice without knowing which was which. Then we stand within a yard of each, and at the word we fire.'

'My God!' said Danvers.

'I don't think that would be legal,' said Preston. 'It would mean one of you would be killed for certain.'

'Killing is the object of duelling,' said Hornblower. 'If the conditions aren't unfair I don't think any objection can be raised.'

'But would you carry it out to the end?' marvelled Danvers.

'Mr Danvers——' began Hornblower; but Preston interfered.

'We don't want another duel on our hands,' he said. 'Danvers only meant he wouldn't care to do it himself. We'll discuss it with Cleveland and Hether, and see what they say.'

Within an hour the proposed conditions of the duel were known to everyone in the ship. Perhaps it was to Simpson's disadvantage that he had no real friend in the ship, for Cleveland and Hether, his seconds, were not disposed to take too firm a stand regarding the conditions of the duel, and agreed to the terms with only a show of reluctance. The tyrant of the midshipmen's berth was paying the penalty for his tyranny. There was some cynical amusement shown by some of the officers; some of both officers and men eyed Hornblower and Simpson with the curiosity that the prospect of death excites in some minds, as if the two destined opponents were men condemned to the gallows. At noon Lieutenant Masters sent for Hornblower.

'The captain has ordered me to make inquiry into this duel, Mr Hornblower,' he said. 'I am instructed to use my best endeavours to compose the quarrel.'

'Yes, sir.'

'Why insist on this satisfaction, Mr Hornblower? I understand there were a few hasty words over wine and cards.'

'Mr Simpson accused me of cheating, sir, before witnesses who were not officers of this ship.'

That was the point. The witnesses were not members of the ship's company. If Hornblower had chosen to disregard Simpson's words as the ramblings of a drunken ill-tempered man, they might have passed unnoticed. But as he had taken the stand he did, there could be no hushing it up now, and Hornblower knew it.

'Even so, there can be satisfaction without a duel, Mr Hornblower.'

'If Mr Simpson will make me a full apology before the same gentlemen, I would be satisfied, sir.'

Simpson was no coward. He would die rather than submit to such a formal humiliation.

'I see. Now I understand you are insisting on rather unusual conditions for the duel?'

'There are precedents for it, sir. As the insulted party I can choose any conditions which are not unfair.'

'You sound like a sea lawyer to me, Mr Hornblower.'

The hint was sufficient to tell Hornblower that he had verged upon being too glib, and he resolved in future to bridle his tongue. He stood silent and waited for Masters to resume the conversation.

'You are determined, then, Mr Hornblower, to continue with this murderous business?'

'Yes, sir.'

'The captain has given me further orders to attend the duel in person, because of the strange conditions on which you insist. I must inform you that I shall request the seconds to arrange for that.'

'Yes, sir.'

'Very good, then, Mr Hornblower.'

Masters looked at Hornblower as he dismissed him even more keenly than he had done when Hornblower first came on board. He was looking for signs of weakness or wavering—indeed, he was looking for any signs of human feeling at all—but he could detect none. Hornblower had reached a decision, he had weighed all the pros and cons, and his logical mind told him that having decided in cold blood upon a course of action it would be folly to allow himself to be influenced subsequently by untrustworthy emotions. The conditions of the duel on which he was insisting were mathematically advantageous. If he had once considered with favour escaping from Simpson's persecution by a voluntary death it was surely a gain to take an even chance of escaping from it without dying. Similarly, if Simpson were (as he almost certainly was) a better swordsman and a better pistol shot than him, the even chance was again mathematically advantageous. There was nothing to regret about his recent actions.

All very well; mathematically the conclusions were irrefutable, but Hornblower was surprised to find that mathematics were not everything. Repeatedly during that dreary afternoon and evening Hornblower found himself suddenly gulping with anxiety as the realization came to him afresh that to-morrow morning he would be risking his life on

The Heritage of
Literature Series

SECTION A NO. 70

MR MIDSHIPMAN
HORNBLOWER

THE HERITAGE OF LITERATURE SERIES

General Editor: E. W. PARKER, M.C.

A series that will lead to wider horizons by awakening a love of good books, and by providing a key to the treasures of the world's best thought.

TRAVEL AND ADVENTURE
ESSAYS AND BELLLES LETTRES
DRAMA
FICTION
MYTHS AND FOLK LORE
HISTORY
LIFE AND LETTERS
POETRY

the spin of a coin. One chance out of two and he would be dead, his consciousness at an end, his flesh cold, and the world, almost unbelievably, would be going on without him. The thought sent a shiver through him despite himself. And he had plenty of time for these reflections, for the convention that forbade him from encountering his destined opponent before the moment of the duel kept him necessarily in isolation, as far as isolation could be found on the crowded decks of the *Justinian*. He slung his hammock that night in a depressed mood, feeling unnaturally tired; and he undressed in the clammy, stuffy dampness of the 'tweendecks feeling more than usually cold. He hugged the blankets round himself, yearning to relax in their warmth, but relaxation would not come. Time after time as he began to drift off to sleep he woke again tense and anxious, full of thoughts of the morrow. He turned over wearily a dozen times, hearing the ship's bell ring out each half-hour, feeling a growing contempt at his cowardice. He told himself in the end that it was as well that his fate to-morrow depended upon pure chance, for if he had to rely upon steadiness of hand and eye he would be dead for certain after a night like this.

That conclusion presumably helped him to go to sleep for the last hour or two of the night, for he awoke with a start to find Danvers shaking him.

'Five bells,' said Danvers. 'Dawn in an hour. Rise and shine!'

Hornblower slid out of his hammock and stood in his shirt; the 'tweendecks was nearly dark and Danvers was almost invisible.

'Number One's letting us have the second cutter,' said Danvers. 'Masters and Simpson and that lot are going first in the launch. Here's Preston.'

Another shadowy figure loomed up in the darkness.

'Hellish cold,' said Preston. 'The devil of a morning to turn out. Nelson, where's that tea?'

The mess attendant came with it as Hornblower was hauling on his trousers. It maddened Hornblower that he shivered enough in the cold for the cup to clatter in the saucer as he took it. But the tea was grateful, and Hornblower drank it eagerly.

'Give me another cup,' he said, and was proud of himself that he could think about tea at that moment.

It was still dark as they went down into the cutter.

'Shove off,' said the coxswain, and the boat pushed off from the ship's side. There was a keen cold wind blowing which filled the dipping lug as the cutter headed for the twin lights that marked the jetty.

'I ordered a hackney coach at the George to be waiting for us,' said Danvers. 'Let's hope it is.'

It was there, with the driver sufficiently sober to control his horse moderately well despite his overnight potations. Danvers produced a pocket flask as they settled themselves in with their feet in the straw.

'Take a sip, Hornblower?' he asked, proffering it. 'There's no special need for a steady hand this morning.'

'No, thank you,' said Hornblower. His empty stomach revolted at the idea of pouring spirits into it.

'The others will be there before us,' commented Preston. 'I saw the quarter boat heading back just before we reached the jetty.'

The etiquette of the duel demanded that the two opponents should reach the ground separately; but only one boat would be necessary for the return.

'The sawbones is with them,' said Danvers. 'Though God knows what use he thinks he'll be to-day.'

He sniggered, and with overlate politeness tried to cut his snigger off short.

'How are you feeling, Hornblower?' asked Preston.

'Well enough,' said Hornblower, forbearing to add that he only felt well enough while this kind of conversation was not being carried on.

The hackney coach levelled itself off as it came over the crest of the hill, and stopped beside the common. Another coach stood there waiting, its single candle-lamp burning yellow in the growing dawn.

'There they are,' said Preston; the faint light revealed a shadowy group standing on frosty turf among the gorse bushes.

Hornblower, as they approached, caught a glimpse of Simpson's face as he stood a little detached from the others. It was pale, and Hornblower noticed that at that moment he swallowed nervously, just as he himself was doing. Masters came towards them, shooting his usual keen inquisitive look at Hornblower as they came together.

'This is the moment,' he said, 'for this quarrel to be composed. This country is at war. I hope, Mr Hornblower, that you can be persuaded to save a life for the King's service by not pressing this matter.'

Hornblower looked across at Simpson, while Danvers answered for him.

'Has Mr Simpson offered the proper redress?' asked Danvers.

'Mr Simpson is willing to acknowledge that he wishes the incident had never taken place.'

'That is an unsatisfactory form,' said Danvers. 'It does not include an apology, and you must agree that an apology is necessary, sir.'

'What does your principal say?' persisted Masters.

B

'It is not for any principal to speak in these circumstances,' said Danvers, with a glance at Hornblower, who nodded. All this was as inevitable as the ride in the hangman's cart, and as hideous. There could be no going back now; Hornblower had never thought for one moment that Simpson would apologize, and without an apology the affair must be carried to a bloody conclusion. An even chance that he did not have five minutes longer to live.

'You are determined, then, gentlemen,' said Masters. 'I shall have to state that fact in my report.'

'We are determined,' said Preston.

'Then there is nothing for it but to allow this deplorable affair to proceed. I left the pistols in the charge of Doctor Hepplewhite.'

He turned and led them towards the other group— Simpson with Hether and Cleveland, and Doctor Hepplewhite standing with a pistol held by the muzzle in each hand. He was a bulky man with the red face of a persistent drinker; he was actually grinning a spirituous grin at that moment, rocking a little on his feet.

'Are the young fools set in their folly?' he asked; but everyone very properly ignored him as having no business to ask such a question at such a moment.

'Now,' said Masters. 'Here are the pistols, both primed, as you see, but one loaded and the other unloaded, in accordance with the conditions. I have here a guinea which I propose to spin to decide the allocation of the weapons. Now, gentlemen, shall the spin give your principals one pistol each irrevocably—for instance, if the coin shows heads shall Mr Simpson have this one—or shall the winner of the spin have choice of weapons? It is my design to eliminate all possibility of collusion as far as possible.'

Hether and Cleveland and Danvers and Preston exchanged dubious glances.

'Let the winner of the spin choose,' said Preston at length.

'Very well, gentlemen. Please call, Mr Hornblower.'

'Tails!' said Hornblower as the gold piece spun in the air. Masters caught it and clapped a hand over it.

'Tails it is,' said Masters, lifting his hand and revealing the coin to the grouped seconds. 'Please make your choice.'

Hepplewhite held out the two pistols to him, death in one hand and life in the other. It was a grim moment. There was only pure chance to direct him; it called for a little effort to force his hand out.

'I'll have this one,' he said; as he touched it the weapon seemed icy cold.

'Then now I have done what was required of me,' said Masters. 'The rest is for you gentlemen to carry out.'

'Take this one, Simpson,' said Hepplewhite. 'And be careful how you handle yours, Mr Hornblower. You're a public danger.'

The man was still grinning, gloating over the fact that someone else was in mortal danger while he himself was in none. Simpson took the pistol Hepplewhite offered him and settled it into his hand; once more his eyes met Hornblower's, but there was neither recognition nor expression in them.

'There are no distances to step out,' Danvers was saying. 'One spot's as good as another. It's level enough here.'

'Very good,' said Hether. 'Will you stand here, Mr Simpson?'

Preston beckoned to Hornblower, who walked over. It was not easy to appear brisk and unconcerned. Preston took him by the arm and stood him up in front of Simpson, almost breast to breast—close enough to smell the alcohol on his breath.

'For the last time, gentlemen,' said Masters loudly. 'Cannot you be reconciled?'

There was no answer from anybody, only deep silence, during which it seemed to Hornblower that the frantic beating of his heart must be clearly audible. The silence was broken by an exclamation from Hether.

'We haven't settled who's to give the word!' he said. 'Who's going to?'

'Let's ask Mr Masters to give it,' said Danvers.

Hornblower did not look round. He was looking steadfastly at the grey sky past Simpson's right ear—somehow he could not look him in the face, and he had no idea where Simpson was looking. The end of the world as he knew it was close to him—soon there might be a bullet through his heart.

'I will do it if you are agreed, gentlemen,' he heard Masters say.

The grey sky was featureless; for this last look on the world he might as well have been blindfolded. Masters raised his voice again.

'I will say "one, two, three, fire",' he announced, 'with those intervals. At the last word, gentlemen, you can fire as you will. Are you ready?'

'Yes,' came Simpson's voice, almost in Hornblower's ear, it seemed.

'Yes,' said Hornblower. He could hear the strain in his own voice

'One,' said Masters, and Hornblower felt at that moment the muzzle of Simpson's pistol against his left ribs, and he raised his own.

It was in that second that he decided he could not kill Simpson even if it were in his power, and he went on lifting his pistol, forcing himself to look to see that it was pressed against the point of Simpson's shoulder. A slight wound would suffice.

'Two,' said Masters. 'Three. Fire!'

Hornblower pulled his trigger. There was a click and a spurt of smoke from the lock of his pistol. The priming had gone off but no more—his was the unloaded weapon, and he knew what it was to die. A tenth of a second later there was a click and spurt of smoke from Simpson's pistol against his heart. Stiff and still they both stood, slow to realize what had happened.

'A misfire, by God!' said Danvers.

The seconds crowded round them.

'Give me those pistols!' said Masters, taking them from the weak hands that held them. 'The loaded one might be hanging fire, and we don't want it to go off now.'

'Which was the loaded one?' asked Hether, consumed with curiosity.

'That is something it is better not to know,' answered Masters, changing the two pistols rapidly from hand to hand so as to confuse everyone.

'What about a second shot?' asked Danvers, and Masters looked up straight and inflexibly at him.

'There will be no second shot,' he said. 'Honour is completely satisfied. These two gentlemen have come through this ordeal extremely well. No one can now think little of Mr Simpson if he expresses his regret for the occurrence, and no one can think little of Mr Hornblower if he accepts that statement in reparation.'

Hepplewhite burst into a roar of laughter.

'Your faces!' he boomed, slapping his thigh. 'You ought to see how you look! Solemn as cows!'

'Mr Hepplewhite,' said Masters, 'your behaviour is indecorous. Gentlemen, our coaches are waiting on the road, the cutter is at the jetty. And I think all of us would be the better for some breakfast; including Mr. Hepplewhite.'

That should have been the end of the incident. The excited talk which had gone round the anchored squadron about the unusual duel died away in time, although everyone knew Hornblower's name now, and not as the midshipman who was seasick in Spithead but as the man who was willing to take an even chance in cold blood. But in the *Justinian* herself there was other talk; whispers which were circulated forward and aft.

'Mr Hornblower has requested permission to speak to you, sir,' said Mr Clay, the first lieutenant, one morning while making his report to the captain.

'Oh, send him in when you go out,' said Keene, and sighed.

Ten minutes later a knock on his cabin door ushered in a very angry young man.

'Sir!' began Hornblower.

'I can guess what you're going to say,' said Keene.

'Those pistols in the duel I fought with Simpson were not loaded!'

'Hepplewhite blabbed, I suppose,' said Keene.

'And it was by your orders, I understand, sir.'

'You are quite correct. I gave those orders to Mr Masters.'

'It was an unwarrantable liberty, sir!'

That was what Hornblower meant to say, but he stumbled without dignity over the polysyllables.

'Possibly it was,' said Keene patiently, rearranging, as always, the papers on his desk.

The calmness of the admission disconcerted Hornblower, who could only splutter for the next few moments.

'I saved a life for the King's service,' went on Keene, when the spluttering died away. 'A young life. No one has suffered any harm. On the other hand, both you and Simpson have had your courage amply proved. You both know you can stand fire now, and so does everyone else.'

'You have touched my personal honour, sir,' said Hornblower, bringing out one of his rehearsed speeches, 'for that there can only be one remedy.'

'Restrain yourself, please, Mr Hornblower.' Keene shifted himself in his chair with a wince of pain as he prepared to make a speech. 'I must remind you of one salutary regulation of the Navy, to the effect that no junior officer can challenge his superior to a duel. The reasons for it are obvious—otherwise promotion would be too easy. The mere issuing of a challenge by a junior to a senior is a court-martial offence, Mr Hornblower.'

'Oh!' said Hornblower feebly.

'Now here is some gratuitous advice,' went on Keene. 'You have fought one duel and emerged with honour. That is good. Never fight another—that is better. Some people, oddly enough, acquire a taste for duelling, as a tiger acquires a taste for blood. They are never good officers, and never popular ones either.'

It was then that Hornblower realized that a great part of the keen excitement with which he had entered the captain's cabin was due to anticipation of the giving of the challenge. There could be a morbid desire for danger—and a morbid desire to occupy momentarily the centre of the stage. Keene was waiting for him to speak, and it was hard to say anything.

'I understand, sir,' he said at last.

Keene shifted in his chair again.

'There is another matter I wanted to take up with you, Mr Hornblower. Captain Pellew of the *Indefatigable* has room for another midshipman. Captain Pellew is partial to a game of whist, and has no good fourth on board. He and I have agreed to consider favourably your application for a transfer should you care to make one. I don't have to point out that any ambitious young officer would jump at the chance of serving in a frigate.'

'A frigate!' said Hornblower.

Everybody knew of Pellew's reputation and success. Distinction, promotion, prize money—an officer under Pellew's command could hope for all these. Competition for nomination to the *Indefatigable* must be intense, and this was the chance of a lifetime. Hornblower was on the point of making a glad acceptance, when further considerations restrained him.

'That is very good of you, sir,' he said. 'I do not know how to thank you. But you accepted me as a midshipman here, and of course I must stay with you.'

The drawn, apprehensive face relaxed into a smile.

'Not many men would have said that,' said Keene. 'But I am going to insist on your accepting the offer. I shall not live very much longer to appreciate your loyalty. And this ship is not the place for you—this ship with her useless captain—don't interrupt me—and her worn-out first lieutenant and her old midshipmen. You should be where there may be speedy opportunities of advancement. I have the good of the service in mind, Mr Hornblower, when I suggest you accept Captain Pellew's invitation—and it might be less disturbing for me if you did.'

'Aye aye, sir,' said Hornblower.

CHAPTER TWO

THE CARGO OF RICE

THE wolf was in among the sheep. The tossing grey water of the Bay of Biscay was dotted with white sails as far as the eye could see, and although a strong breeze was blowing every vessel was under perilously heavy canvas. Every ship but one was trying to escape; the exception was His Majesty's frigate *Indefatigable*, Captain Sir Edward Pellew. Farther out in the Atlantic, hundreds of miles away, a great battle was being fought, where the ships of the line were thrashing out the question as to whether England or France should wield the weapon of sea power; here in the Bay the convoy which the French ships were intended to escort was exposed to the attack of a ship of prey at liberty to capture any ship she could overhaul. She had come surging up from leeward, cutting off all chance of escape in that direction, and the clumsy merchant ships were forced to beat to windward; they were all filled with the food which revolutionary France (her economy disordered by the convulsion through which she was passing) was awaiting so anxiously, and their crews were all anxious to escape confinement in an English prison. Ship after ship was overhauled; a shot of two, and the newfangled tricolour came fluttering down from the gaff, and a prize-crew was hurriedly sent on board to conduct the captive to an English port while the frigate dashed after fresh prey.

On the quarterdeck of the *Indefatigable* Pellew fumed over each necessary delay. The convoy, each ship as close to the wind as she would lie, and under all the sail she

35   B*

could carry, was slowly scattering, spreading farther and farther with the passing minutes, and some of these would find safety in mere dispersion if any time was wasted. Pellew did not wait to pick up his boat; at each surrender he merely ordered away an officer and an armed guard, and the moment the prize-crew was on its way he filled his main-topsail again and hurried off after the next victim. The brig they were pursuing at the moment was slow to surrender. The long nine-pounders in the *Indefatigable*'s bows bellowed out more than once; on that heaving sea it was not so easy to aim accurately and the brig continued on her course, hoping for some miracle to save her.

'Very well,' snapped Pellew. 'He has asked for it. Let him have it.'

The gunlayers at the bow chasers changed their point of aim, firing at the ship instead of across her bows.

'Not into the hull, damn it,' shouted Pellew—one shot had struck the brig perilously close to her waterline. 'Cripple her.'

The next shot by luck or by judgment was given better elevation. The slings of the foretopsail yard were shot away, the reefed sail came down, the yard hanging lopsidedly, and the brig came up into the wind for the *Indefatigable* to heave-to close beside her, her broadside ready to fire into her. Under that threat her flag came down.

'What brig's this?' shouted Pellew through his megaphone.

'*Marie Galante* of Bordeaux,' translated the officer beside Pellew as the French captain made reply. 'Twenty-four days out from New Orleans with rice.'

'Rice!' said Pellew. 'That'll sell for a pretty penny when we get her home. Two hundred tons, I should say. Twelve of a crew at most. She'll need a prize-crew of four, a mid-shipman's command.'

He looked round him as though for inspiration before giving his next order.

'Mr Hornblower!'

'Sir!'

'Take four men of the cutter's crew and board that brig. Mr Soames will give you our position. Take her into any English port you can make, and report there for orders.'

'Aye aye, sir.'

Hornblower was at his station at the starboard quarter-deck carronades—which was perhaps how he had caught Pellew's eye—his dirk at his side and a pistol in his belt. It was a moment for fast thinking, for anyone could see Pellew's impatience. With the *Indefatigable* cleared for action, his sea chest would be part of the surgeon's operating table down below, so that there was no chance of getting anything out of it. He would have to leave just as he was. The cutter was even now clawing up to a position on the *Indefatigable*'s quarter, so he ran to the ship's side and hailed her, trying to make his voice sound as big and as manly as he could, and at the word of the lieutenant in command she turned her bows in towards the frigate.

'Here's our latitude and longitude, Mr Hornblower,' said Soames, the master, handing a scrap of paper to him.

'Thank you,' said Hornblower, shoving it into his pocket.

He scrambled awkwardly into the mizzen-chains and looked down into the cutter. Ship and boat were pitching together, almost bows on to the sea, and the distance between them looked appallingly great; the bearded seaman standing in the bows could only just reach up to the chains with his long boat-hook. Hornblower hesitated for a long second; he knew he was ungainly and awkward—book learning was of no use when it came to jumping into a boat—but he had to make the leap, for Pellew was fuming behind him and the eyes of the boat's crew and of the whole ship's company were on him. Better to jump and hurt himself, better to jump and make an exhibition of himself, than to delay the ship. Waiting was certain failure, while he still had a choice if he jumped. Perhaps at a word from Pellew the *Indefatigable*'s helmsman allowed the ship's head to fall off from the sea a little. A somewhat diagonal wave lifted the *Indefatigable*'s stern and then passed on, so that the cutter's bows rose as the ship's stern sank a trifle. Hornblower braced himself and leaped. His feet reached the gunwhale and he tottered there for one indescribable second. A seaman grabbed the breast of his jacket and he fell forward rather than backward. Not even the stout arm of the seaman, fully extended, could hold him up, and he pitched headforemost, legs in the air, upon the hands on the second thwart. He cannoned on to their bodies, knocking the breath out of his own against their muscular shoulders, and finally struggled into an upright position.

'I'm sorry,' he gasped to the men who had broken his fall.

'Never you mind, sir,' said the nearest one, a real tarry sailor, tattooed and pigtailed. 'You're only a featherweight.'

The lieutenant in command was looking at him from the sternsheets.

'Would you go to the brig, please, sir?' he asked, and the lieutenant bawled an order and the cutter swung round as Hornblower made his way aft.

It was a pleasant surprise not to be received with the broad grins of tolerantly concealed amusement. Boarding a small boat from a big frigate in even a moderate sea was no easy matter; probably every man on board had arrived headfirst at some time or other, and it was not in the tradition of the service, as understood in the *Indefatigable*, to laugh at a man who did his best without shirking.

'Are you taking charge of the brig?' asked the lieutenant.

'Yes, sir. The captain told me to take four of your men.'

'They had better be topmen, then,' said the lieutenant, casting his eyes aloft at the rigging of the brig. The fore-topsail yard was hanging precariously, and the jib halliard had slacked off so that the sail was flapping thunderously in the wind. 'Do you know these men, or shall I pick 'em for you?'

'I'd be obliged if you would, sir.'

The lieutenant shouted four names, and four men replied.

'Keep 'em away from drink and they'll be all right,' said the lieutenant. 'Watch the French crew. They'll recapture the ship and have you in a French gaol before you can say "Jack Robinson" if you don't.'

'Aye aye, sir,' said Hornblower.

The cutter surged alongside the brig, white water creaming between the two vessels. The tattooed sailor hastily concluded a bargain with another man on his thwart and pocketed a lump of tobacco—the men were leaving their possessions behind just like Hornblower—and sprang for the mainchains. Another man followed him, and they stood and waited while Hornblower with difficulty made his way forward along the plunging boat. He stood, balancing precariously, on the forward thwart. The mainchains of the brig were far lower than the mizzen-chains of the *Indefatigable*, but this time he had to jump upwards. One of the seamen steadied him with an arm on his shoulder.

'Wait for it, sir,' he said. 'Get ready. Now jump, sir.'

Hornblower hurled himself, all arms and legs, like a leaping frog, at the mainchains. His hands reached the shrouds, but his knee slipped off, and the brig, rolling, lowered him thigh deep into the sea as the shrouds slipped through his hands. But the waiting seamen grabbed his wrists and hauled him on board, and two more seamen followed him. He led the way on to the deck.

The first sight to meet his eyes was a man seated on the hatch cover, his head thrown back, holding to his mouth a bottle, the bottom pointing straight up to the sky. He was one of a large group all sitting round the hatch cover; there were more bottles in evidence; one was passed by one man to another as he looked, and as he approached a roll of the ship brought an empty bottle rolling past his toes to clatter into the scuppers. Another of the group, with white hair blowing in the wind, rose to welcome him, and stood for a moment with waving arms and rolling eyes, bracing himself as though to say something of immense importance and seeking earnestly for the right words to use.

'Goddam English,' was what he finally said, and, having said it, he sat down with a bump on the hatch cover and from a seated position proceeded to lie down and compose himself to sleep with his head on his arms.

'They've made the best of their time, sir, by the Holy,' said the seaman at Hornblower's elbow.

'Wish we were as happy,' said another.

A case still a quarter full of bottles, each elaborately sealed, stood on the deck beside the hatch cover, and the seaman picked out a bottle to look at it curiously. Hornblower did not need to remember the lieutenant's warning; on his shore excursions with press gangs he had already had experience of the British seaman's tendency to drink. His boarding party would be as drunk as the Frenchmen in half an hour if he allowed it. A frightful mental picture of himself drifting in the Bay of Biscay with a disabled ship and a drunken crew rose in his mind and filled him with anxiety.

'Put that down,' he ordered.

The urgency of the situation made his seventeen-year-old voice crack like a fourteen-year-old's, and the seaman hesitated, holding the bottle in his hand.

'Put it down, d'ye hear?' said Hornblower, desperate with worry. This was his first independent command; conditions were absolutely novel, and excitement brought out all the passion of his mercurial temperament, while at the same time the more calculating part of his mind told him that if he were not obeyed now he never would be. His pistol was in his belt, and he put his hand on the butt, and it is conceivable that he would have drawn it and used it (if the priming had not got wet, he said to himself bitterly when he thought about the incident later on), but the seaman with one more glance at him put the bottle back into the case. The incident was closed, and it was time for the next step.

'Take these men forrard,' he said, giving the obvious order. 'Throw 'em into the forecastle.'

'Aye aye, sir.'

Most of the Frenchmen could still walk, but three were dragged by their collars, while the British herded the others before them.

'Come alongee,' said one of the seamen. 'Thisa waya.'

He evidently believed a Frenchman would understand him better if he spoke like that. The Frenchman who had greeted their arrival now awakened, and, suddenly realizing he was being dragged forward, broke away and turned back to Hornblower.

'I officer,' he said, pointing to himself. 'I not go wit' zem.'

'Take him away!' said Hornblower. In his tense condition he could not stop to debate trifles.

He dragged the case of bottles down to the ship's side and pitched them overboard two at a time—obviously it was wine of some special vintage which the Frenchmen had decided to drink before the English could get their hands on it, but that weighed not at all with Hornblower, for a British seaman could get drunk on vintage claret as easily as upon service rum. The task was finished before the last of the Frenchmen disappeared into the forecastle, and Hornblower had time to look about him. The strong breeze blew confusingly round his ears, and the ceaseless thunder of the flapping jib made it hard to think as he looked at the ruin aloft. Every sail was flat aback, the brig was moving jerkily, gathering sternway for a space before her untended rudder threw her round to spill the wind and bring her up again like a jibbing horse. His mathematical mind had already had plenty of experience with a well-handled ship, with the delicate adjustment between after sails and headsails. Here the balance had been disturbed, and Hornblower was at work on the problem of forces acting on plane surfaces when his men came trooping back to him. One thing at least was certain, and that was that the precariously hanging foretopsail yard would tear itself free to do all sorts of unforeseeable damage if it were tossed about much more. The ship must be properly hove to, and Hornblower could guess how to set about it, and he formulated the order in his mind just in time to avoid any appearance of hesitation.

'Brace the after yards to larboard,' he said. 'Man the braces, men.'

They obeyed him, while he himself went gingerly to the wheel; he had served a few tricks as helmsman, learning his professional duties under Pellew's orders, but he did not feel happy about it. The spokes felt foreign to his fingers as he took hold; he spun the wheel experimentally but timidly. But it was easy. With the after yards braced round, the brig rode more comfortably at once, and the spokes told their own story to his sensitive fingers as the ship became a thing of logical construction again. Hornblower's mind completed the solution of the problem of the effect of the rudder at the same time as his senses solved it empirically. The wheel could be safely lashed, he knew, in these conditions, and he slipped the becket over the spoke and stepped away from the wheel, with the *Marie Galante* riding comfortably and taking the seas on her starboard bow.

The seaman took his competence gratifyingly for granted, but Hornblower, looking at the tangle on the foremast, had not the remotest idea of how to deal with the next problem. He was not even sure about what was wrong. But the hands under his orders were seamen of vast experience, who must have dealt with similar emergencies a score of times. The first—indeed the only—thing to do was to delegate his responsibility.

'Who's the oldest seaman among you?' he demanded—his determination not to quaver made him curt.

'Matthews, sir,' said someone at length, indicating with his thumb the pigtailed and tattooed seaman upon whom he had fallen in the cutter.

'Very well, then. I'll rate you petty officer, Matthews. Get to work at once and clear that raffle away forrard. I'll be busy here aft.'

It was a nervous moment for Hornblower, but Matthews put his knuckles to his forehead.

'Aye aye, sir,' he said, quite as a matter of course.

'Get that jib in first, before it flogs itself to pieces,' said Hornblower, greatly emboldened.

'Aye aye, sir.'

'Carry on, then.'

The seaman turned to go forward, and Hornblower walked aft. He took the telescope from his becket on the poop, and swept the horizon. There were a few sails in sight; the nearest ones he could recognize as prizes, which, with all sail set that they could carry, were heading for England as fast as they could go. Far away to windward he could see the *Indefatigable*'s topsails as she clawed after the rest of the convoy—she had already overhauled and captured all the slower and less weatherly vessels, so that each succeeding chase would be longer. Soon he would be alone on this wide sea, three hundred miles from England. Three hundred miles—two days with a fair wind; but how long if the wind turned foul?

He replaced the telescope; the men were already hard at work forward, so he went below and looked round the neat cabins of the officers; two single ones for the captain and mate, presumably, and a double one for the bos'un and the cook or the carpenter. He found a lazarette, identifying it by the miscellaneous stores within it; the door was swinging to and fro with a bunch of keys dangling. The French captain, faced with the loss of all he possessed, had not even troubled to lock the door again after taking out the case of wine. Hornblower locked the door and put the keys in his pocket and felt suddenly lonely—his first experience of the loneliness of the man in command at sea. He went on deck again, and at sight of him Matthews hurried aft and knuckled his forehead.

'Beg pardon, sir, but we'll have to use the jeers to sling that yard again.'

'Very good.'

'We'll need more hands than we have, sir. Can I put some o' they Frenchies to work?'

'If you think you can. If any of them are sober enough.'

'I think I can, sir. Drunk or sober.'

'Very good.'

It was at this moment that Hornblower remembered with bitter self-reproach that the priming of his pistol was probably wet, and he had not scorn enough for himself at having put his trust in a pistol without re-priming after evolutions in a small boat. While Matthews went forward he dashed below again. There was a case of pistols which he remembered having seen in the captain's cabin, with a powder flask and bullet bag hanging beside it. He loaded both weapons and re-primed his own, and came on deck again with three pistols in his belt just as his men appeared from the forecastle herding half a dozen Frenchmen. He posed himself in the poop, straddling with his hands behind his back, trying to adopt an air of magnificent indifference and understanding. With the jeers taking the weight of yard and sail, an hour's hard work resulted in the yard being slung again and the sail reset.

When the work was advancing towards completion, Hornblower came to himself again to remember that in a few minutes he would have to set a course, and he dashed below again to set out the chart and the dividers and parallel rulers. From his pocket he extracted the crumpled scrap of paper with his position on it—he had thrust it in there so carelessly a little while back, at a time when the immediate problem before him was to transfer himself from the *Indefatigable* to the cutter. It made him unhappy to think how cavalierly he had treated that scrap of paper then; he began to feel that life in the Navy, although it seemed to move from one crisis to another, was really one continuous crisis, that even while dealing with one emergency it was necessary to be making plans to deal with the next. He bent over the chart, plotted his position, and laid off his course. It was a queer uncomfortable feeling to think that what had up to this moment been an academic exercise conducted under the reassuring supervision of Mr Soames was now something on which hinged his life and his reputation. He checked his working, decided on his course, and wrote it down on a scrap of paper for fear he should forget it.

So when the foretopsail was re-slung, and the prisoners herded back into the forecastle, and Matthews looked to him for further orders, he was ready.

'We'll square away,' he said. 'Matthews, send a man to the wheel.'

He himself gave a hand at the braces; the wind had moderated and he felt his men could handle the brig under her present sail.

'What course, sir?' asked the man at the wheel, and Hornblower dived into his pocket for his scrap of paper.

'Nor'-east by north,' he said, reading it out.

'Nor'-east by north, sir,' said the helmsman; and the *Marie Galante*, running free, set her course for England.

Night was closing in by now, and all round the circle of the horizon there was not a sail in sight. There must be plenty of ships over the horizon, he knew, but that did not do much to ease his feeling of loneliness as darkness came on. There was so much to do, so much to bear in mind, and all the responsibility lay on his unaccustomed shoulders. The prisoners had to be battened down in the forecastle, a watch had to be set—there was even the trivial matter of hunting up flint and steel to light the binnacle lamp. A hand forward as a look-out, who could also keep an eye on the prisoners below; a hand aft at the wheel. Two hands snatching some sleep—knowing that to get in any sail would be an all-hands job—a hasty meal of water from the scuttle-butt and of biscuit from the cabin stores in the lazarette—a constant eye to be kept on the weather. Hornblower paced the deck in the darkness.

'Why don't you get some sleep, sir?' asked the man at the wheel.

'I will, later on, Hunter,' said Hornblower, trying not to allow his tone to reveal the fact that such a thing had never occurred to him.

He knew it was sensible advice, and he actually tried to follow it, retiring below to fling himself down on the captain's cot; but of course he could not sleep. When he heard the look-out bawling down the companionway to rouse the other two hands to relieve the watch (they were asleep in the next cabin to him) he could not prevent himself from getting up again and coming on deck to see that all was well. With Matthews in charge he felt he should not be anxious, and he drove himself below, but he had hardly fallen on to the cot when a new thought brought him to his feet, his skin cold with anxiety, and a prodigious self-contempt vying with anxiety for first glance in his emotions. He rushed on deck and walked forward to where Matthews was squatting by the knightheads.

'Nothing has been done to see if the brig is taking in any water,' he said—he had hurriedly worked out the wording of that sentence during his walk forward, so as to cast no aspersion on Matthews and yet at the same time, for the sake of discipline, attributing no blame to himself.

'That's so, sir,' said Matthews.

'One of those shots fired by the *Indefatigable* hulled her,' went on Hornblower. 'What damage did it do?'

'I don't rightly know, sir,' said Matthews. 'I was in the cutter at the time.'

'We must look as soon as it's light,' said Hornblower. 'And we'd better sound the well now.'

Those were brave words; during his rapid course in seamanship aboard the *Indefatigable* Hornblower had had a little instruction everywhere, working under the orders of every head of department in rotation. Once he had been with the carpenter when he sounded the well—whether he could find the well in this ship and sound it he did not know.

'Aye aye, sir,' said Matthews, without hesitation, and strolled aft to the pump. 'You'll need a light, sir. I'll get one.'

When he came back with the lantern he shone it on the coiled sounding line hanging beside the pump, so that Hornblower recognized it at once. He lifted it down, inserted the three-foot weighted rod into the aperture of the well, and then remembered in time to take it out again and make sure it was dry. Then he let it drop, paying out the line until he felt the rod strike the ship's bottom with a satisfactory thud. He hauled out the line again, and Matthews held the lantern as Hornblower with some trepidation brought out the timber to examine it.

'Not a drop, sir!' said Matthews. 'Dry as yesterday's pannikin.'

Hornblower was agreeably surprised. Any ship he had ever heard of leaked to a certain extent; even in the well-found *Indefatigable* pumping had been necessary every day. He did not know whether this dryness was a remarkable phenomenon or a very remarkable one. He wanted to be both non-committal and imperturbable.

'H'm,' was the comment he eventually produced. 'Very good, Matthews. Coil that line again.'

The knowledge that the *Marie Galante* was making no water at all might have encouraged him to sleep, if the wind had not chosen to veer steadily and strengthen itself somewhat soon after he retired again. It was Matthews who came down and pounded on his door with the unwelcome news.

'We can't keep the course you set much longer, sir,' concluded Matthews. 'And the wind's coming gusty-like.'

'Very good, I'll be up. Call all hands,' said Hornblower, with a testiness that might have been the result of a sudden awakening if it had not really disguised his inner quaverings.

With such a small crew he dared not run the slightest risk of being taken by surprise by the weather. Nothing could be done in a hurry, as he soon found. He had to take the wheel while his four hands laboured at reefing topsails and snugging the brig down; the task took half the night, and by the time it was finished it was quite plain that with the wind veering northerly the *Marie Galante* could not steer north-east by north any longer. Hornblower gave up the wheel and went below to the chart, but what he saw there only confirmed the pessimistic decision he had already reached by mental calculations. As close to the wind as they could lie on this tack they could not weather Ushant. Shorthanded as he was he did not dare continue in the hope that the wind might back; all his reading and all his instruction had warned him of the terrors of a lee shore. There was nothing for it but to go about; he returned to the deck with a heavy heart.

'All hands wear ship,' he said, trying to bellow the order in the manner of Mr Bolton, the third lieutenant of the *Indefatigable*.

They brought the brig safely round, and she took up her new course, close-hauled on the starboard tack. Now she was heading away from the dangerous shores of France, without a doubt, but she was heading nearly as directly away from the friendly shores of England; gone was any hope of sleep that night for Hornblower.

During the year before he joined the Navy Hornblower had attended classes given by a penniless French émigré in French, music, and dancing. Early enough the wretched émigré had found that Hornblower had no ear for music whatever, which made it almost impossible to teach him to dance, and so he had endeavoured to earn his fee by concentrating on French. A good deal of what he had taught Hornblower had found a permanent resting place in Hornblower's tenacious memory. He had never thought it would be of much use to him, but he discovered the contrary when the French captain at dawn insisted on an interview with him. The Frenchman had a little English, but it was a pleasant surprise to Hornblower to find that they actually could get along better in French, as soon as he could fight down his shyness sufficiently to produce the halting words.

The captain drank thirstily from the scuttlebut; his cheeks were of course unshaven and he wore a bleary look after twelve hours in a crowded forecastle, where he had been battened down three-parts drunk.

'My men are hungry,' said the captain; he did not look hungry himself.

'Mine also,' said Hornblower. 'I also.'

It was natural when one spoke French to gesticulate, to

indicate his men with a wave of the hand and himself with
a tap on the chest.

'I have a cook,' said the captain.

It took some time to arrange the terms of a truce. The
Frenchmen were to be allowed on deck, the cook was to
provide food for everyone on board, and while these ameni-
ties were permitted, until noon, the French would make no
attempt to take the ship.

'Good,' said the captain at length; and when Hornblower
had given the necessary orders permitting the release of
the crew he shouted for the cook and entered into an
urgent discussion regarding dinner. Soon smoke was issuing satisfactorily from the galley chimney.

Then the captain looked up at the grey sky, at the close-
reefed topsails, and glanced into the binnacle at the
compass.

'A foul wind for England,' he remarked.

'Yes,' said Hornblower, shortly. He did not want this
Frenchman to guess at his trepidation and bitterness.

The captain seemed to be feeling the motion of the brig
under his feet with attention.

'She rides a little heavily, does she not?' he said.

'Perhaps,' said Hornblower. He was not familiar with the
Marie Galante, nor with ships at all, and he had no opinion
on the subject, but he was not going to reveal his ignorance.

'Does she leak?' asked the captain.

'There is no water in her,' said Hornblower.

'Ah!' said the captain. 'But you would find none in the
well. We are carrying a cargo of rice, you must remember.'

'Yes,' said Hornblower.

He found it very hard at that moment to remain outwardly unperturbed, as his mind grasped the implications
of what was being said to him. Rice would absorb every

drop of water taken in by the ship, so that no leak would be apparent on sounding the well—and yet every drop of water taken in would deprive her of that much buoyancy, all the same.

'One shot from your cursed frigate struck us in the hull,' said the captain. 'Of course you have investigated the damage?'

'Of course,' said Hornblower, lying bravely.

But as soon as he could he had a private conversation with Matthews on the point, and Matthews instantly looked grave.

'Where did the shot hit her, sir?' he asked.

'Somewhere on the port side, forrard, I should judge.'

He and Matthews craned their necks over the ship's side.

'Can't see nothin', sir,' said Matthews. 'Lower me over the side in a bowline and I'll see what I can find, sir.'

Hornblower was about to agree and then changed his mind.

'I'll go over the side myself,' he said.

He could not analyse the motives which impelled him to say that. Partly he wanted to see things with his own eyes; partly he was influenced by the doctrine that he should never give an order he was not prepared to carry out himself—but mostly it must have been the desire to impose a penance on himself for his negligence.

Matthews and Carson put a bowline round him and lowered him over. He found himself dangling against the ship's side, with the sea bubbling just below him; as the ship pitched the sea came up to meet him, and he was wet to the waist in the first five seconds; and as the ship rolled he was alternately swung away from the side and bumped against it. The men with the line walked steadily aft, giving him the chance the examine the whole side of the brig above water, and there was not a shot-hole to be seen. He said as much to Matthews when they hauled him on deck.

'Then it's below the waterline, sir,' said Matthews, saying just what was in Hornblower's mind. 'You're sure the shot hit her, sir?'

'Yes, I'm sure,' snapped Hornblower.

Lack of sleep and worry and a sense of guilt were all shortening his temper, and he had to speak sharply or break down in tears. But he had already decided on the next move—he had made up his mind about that while they were hauling him up.

'We'll heave her to on the other tack and try again,' he said.

On the other tack the ship would incline over to the other side, and the shot-hole, if there was one, would not be so deeply submerged. Hornblower stood with the water dripping from his clothes as they wore the brig round; the wind was keen and cold, but he was shivering with expectancy rather than cold. The heeling of the brig laid him much more definitely against the side, and they lowered him until his legs were scraping over the marine growths which she carried there between wind and water. They then walked aft with him, dragging him along the side of the ship, and just abaft the foremast he found what he was seeking.

'Avast, there!' he yelled up to the deck, mastering the sick despair that he felt. The motion of the bowline along the ship ceased. 'Lower away! Another two feet!'

Now he was waist-deep in the water, and when the brig swayed the water closed briefly over his head, like a momentary death. Here it was, two feet below the waterline even with the brig hove-to on this tack—a splintered, jagged hole, square rather than round, and a foot across. As the sea boiled round him Hornblower even fancied he could hear it bubbling into the ship, but that might be pure fancy.

He hailed the deck for them to haul him up again, and they stood eagerly listening for what he had to say.

'Two feet below the waterline, sir?' said Matthews. 'She was close-hauled and heeling right over, of course, when we hit her. But her bows must have lifted just as we fired. And of course she's lower in the water now.'

That was the point. Whatever they did now, however much they heeled her, that hole would be under water. And on the other tack it would be far under water, with much additional pressure; yet on the present tack they were headed for France. And the more water they took in, the lower the brig would settle, and the greater would be the pressure forcing water in through the hole. Something must be done to plug the leak, and Hornblower's reading of the manuals of seamanship told him what it was.

'We must fother a sail and get it over that hole,' he announced. 'Call those Frenchmen over.'

To fother a sail was to make something like a vast hairy doormat out of it, by threading innumerable lengths of half-unravelled line through it. When this was done the sail would be lowered below the ship's bottom and placed against the hole. The inward pressure would then force the hairy mass so tightly against the hole that the entrance of water would be made at least much more difficult.

The Frenchmen were not quick to help in the task; it was no longer their ship, and they were heading for an English prison, so that even with their lives at stake they were somewhat apathetic. It took time to get out a new topgallant sail—Hornblower felt that the stouter the canvas the better—and to set a party to work cutting lengths of line, threading them through, and unravelling them. The French captain looked at them squatting on the deck all at work.

'Five years I spent in a prison hulk in Portsmouth during the last war,' he said. 'Five years.'

'Yes,' said Hornblower.

He might have felt sympathy, but he was not only pre-occupied with his own problems but he was numb with cold. He not only had every intention if possible of escorting the French captain to England and to prison again but he also at that very moment intended to go below and appropriate some of his spare clothing.

Down below it seemed to Hornblower as if the noises all about him—the creaks and groans of a wooden ship at sea —were more pronounced than usual. The brig was riding easily enough hove-to, and yet the bulkheads down below were cracking and creaking as if the brig were racking her-self to pieces in a storm. He dismissed the notion as a product of his over-stimulated imagination but by the time he had towelled himself into something like warmth and put on the captain's best suit it recurred to him; the brig was groaning as if in stress.

He came on deck again to see how the working party was progressing. He had hardly been on deck two minutes when one of the Frenchmen, reaching back for another length of line, stopped in his movement to stare at the deck. He picked at a deck seam, looked up and caught Hornblower's eye, and called to him. Hornblower made no pretence of understanding the words; the gestures explained them-selves. The deck seam was opening a little; the pitch was bulging out of it. Hornblower looked at the phenomenon without understanding it—only a foot or two of the seam

was open, and the rest of the deck seemed solid enough.
No! Now that his attention was called to it, and he looked
further, there were one or two other places in the deck
where the pitch had risen in ridges from out of the seams.
It was something beyond his limited experience, even
beyond his extensive reading. But the French captain was
at his side staring at the deck too.

'My God!' he said. 'The rice! The rice!'

The French word '*riz*' that he used was unknown to
Hornblower, but he stamped his foot on the deck and
pointed down through it.

'The cargo!' he said in explanation. 'It—it grows bigger.'

Matthews was with them now, and without knowing a
word of French he understood.

'Didn't I hear this brig was full of rice, sir?' he asked.

'Yes.'

'That's it, then. The water's got into it and it's swelling.'

So it would. Dry rice soaked in water would double or
treble its volume. The cargo was swelling and bursting the
seams of the ship open. Hornblower remembered the unnatural creaks and groans below. It was a black moment;
he looked round at the unfriendly sea for inspiration and
support, and found neither. Several seconds passed before
he was ready to speak, and ready to maintain the dignity
of a naval officer in face of difficulties.

'The sooner we get that sail over that hole the better,
then,' he said. It was too much to be expected that his
voice should sound quite natural. 'Hurry those Frenchmen
up.'

He turned to pace the deck, so as to allow his feelings to
subside and to set his thoughts running in an orderly
fashion again, but the French captain was at his elbow,
voluble as a Job's comforter.

'I said I thought the ship was riding heavily,' he said. 'She is lower in the water.'

'Go to the devil,' said Hornblower, in English—he could not think up the French for that phrase.

Even as he stood he felt a sudden sharp shock beneath his feet, as if someone had hit the deck underneath them with a mallet. The ship was springing apart bit by bit.

'Hurry with that sail!' he yelled, turning back to the working party, and then was angry with himself because the tone of his voice must have betrayed undignified agitation.

At last an area five feet square of the sail was fothered, lines were rove through the grommets, and the working party hurried forward to work the sail under the brig and drag it aft to the hole. Hornblower was taking off his clothes, not out of regard for the captain's property but so as to keep them dry for himself.

'I'll go over and see that it's in place,' he said. 'Matthews, get a bowline ready for me.'

Naked and wet, it seemed to him as if the wind blew clear through him; rubbing against the ship's side as she rolled he lost a good deal of skin, and the waves passing down the ship smacked at him with a boisterous lack of consideration. But he saw the fothered sail placed against the hole, and with intense satisfaction he saw the hairy mass suck into position, dimpling over the hole to form a deep hollow so that he could be sure that the hole was plugged solid. They hauled him up again when he hailed, and awaited his order; he stood naked, stupid with cold and fatigue and lack of sleep, struggling to form his next decision.

'Lay her on the starboard tack,' he said at length.

If the brig were going to sink, it hardly mattered if it were one hundred or two hundred miles from the French coast; if she were to stay afloat he wanted to be well clear of that lee shore and the chance of recapture. The shot-hole with its fothered sail would be deeper under water to increase the risk, but it seemed to be the best chance. The French captain saw them making preparations to wear the brig round, and turned upon Hornblower with voluble protests. With this wind they could make Bordeaux easily on the other tack. Hornblower was risking all their lives, he said. Into Hornblower's numb mind crept, uninvited, the translation of something he had previously wanted to say. He could use it now.

'*Allez au diable,*' he snapped, as he put the Frenchman's stout woollen shirt on over his head.

When his head emerged the Frenchman was still protesting volubly, so violently indeed that a new doubt came into Hornblower's mind. A word to Matthews sent him round the French prisoners to search for weapons. There was nothing to be found except the sailors' knives, but as a matter of precaution Hornblower had them all impounded, and when he had dressed he went to special trouble with his three pistols, drawing the charges from them and reloading and re-priming afresh. Three pistols in his belt looked piratical, as though he were still young enough to be playing imaginative games, but Hornblower felt in his bones that there might be a time when the Frenchmen might try to rise against their captors, and three pistols would not be too many against twelve desperate men who had makeshift weapons ready to hand, belaying pins and the like.

Matthews was awaiting him with a long face.

'Sir,' he said, 'begging your pardon, but I don't like the

looks of it. Straight, I don't. I don't like the feel of her.
She's settlin' down and she's opening up, I'm certain sure.
Beg your pardon, sir, for saying so.'

Down below Hornblower had heard the fabric of the ship
continuing to crack and complain; up here the deck seams
were gaping more widely. There was a very likely explanation; the swelling of the rice must have forced open the
ship's seams below water, so that plugging the shot-hole
would have only eliminated what would be by now only
a minor leak. Water must still be pouring in, the cargo
still swelling, opening up the ship like an overblown flower.
Ships were built to withstand blows from without, and
there was nothing about their construction to resist an outward pressure. Wider and wider would gape the seams,
and faster and faster the sea would again access to the
cargo.

'Look'e there, sir!' said Matthews suddenly.

In the broad light of day a small grey shape was hurrying along the weather scuppers; another one followed it and
another after that. Rats! Something convulsive must be
going on down below to bring them on deck in daytime,
from out of their comfortable nests among the unlimited
food of the cargo. The pressure must be enormous. Hornblower felt another small shock beneath his feet at that
moment, as something further parted beneath them. But
there was one more card to play, one last line of defence
that he could think of.

'I'll jettison the cargo,' said Hornblower. He had never
uttered that word in his life, but he had read it. 'Get the
prisoners and we'll start.'

The battened-down hatch cover was domed upwards
curiously and significantly; as the wedges were knocked out
one plank tore loose at one end with a crash, pointing

C

diagonally upwards, and as the working party lifted off the cover a brown form followed it upwards—a bag of rice, forced out by the underlying pressure until it jammed in the hatchway.

'Tail on to those tackles and sway it up,' said Hornblower.

Bag by bag the rice was hauled up from the hold; sometimes the bags split, allowing a torrent of rice to pour on to the deck, but that did not matter. Another section of the working party swept rice and bags to the lee side and into the ever-hungry sea. After the first three bags the difficulties increased, for the cargo was so tightly jammed below that it called for enormous force to tear each bag out of its position. Two men had to go down the hatchway to pry the bags loose and adjust the slings. There was a momentary hesitation on the part of the two Frenchmen to whom Hornblower pointed—the bags might not all be jammed and the hold of a tossing ship was a dangerous place wherein a roll might bury them alive—but Hornblower had no thought at that moment for other people's human fears. He scowled at the brief check and they hastened to lower themselves down the hatchway. The labour was enormous as it went on hour after hour; the men at the tackles were dripping with sweat and drooping with fatigue, but they had to relieve periodically the men below, for the bags had jammed themselves in tiers, pressed hard against the ship's bottom below and the deck beams above, and when the bags immediately below the hatchway had been swayed up the surrounding ones had to be pried loose, out of each tier. Then when a small clearance had been made in the neighbourhood of the hatchway, and they were getting deeper down into the hold, they made the inevitable discovery. The lower tiers of bags had been wetted, their contents had swelled, and the bags had burst. The lower half of the hold was packed solid with damp rice which could only be got out with shovels and a hoist. The still intact bags of the upper tier, farther away from the hatchway, were still jammed tight, calling for much labour to free them and to manhandle them under the hatchway to be hoisted out.

Hornblower, facing the problem, was distracted by a touch on his elbow when Matthews came up to speak to him.

'It ain't no go, sir,' said Matthews. 'She's lower in the water an' settlin' fast.'

Hornblower walked to the ship's side with him and looked over. There could be no doubt about it. He had been over the side himself and could remember the height of the waterline, and he had for a more exact guide the level of the fothered sail under the ship's bottom. The brig was a full six inches lower in the water—and this after fifty tons of rice at least had been hoisted out and flung over the side. The brig must be leaking like a basket, with water pouring in through the gaping seams to be sucked up immediately by the thirsty rice.

Hornblower's left hand was hurting him, and he looked down to discover that he was gripping the rail with it so tightly as to cause him pain, without knowing he was doing so. He released his grip and looked about him, at the afternoon sun, at the tossing sea. He did not want to give in and admit defeat. The French captain came up to him.

'This is folly,' he said. 'Madness, sir. My men are overcome by fatigue.'

Over by the hatchway, Hornblower saw, Hunter was driving the French seamen to their work with a rope's end, which he was using furiously. There was not much more work to be got out of the Frenchmen; and at that moment the *Marie Galante* rose heavily to a wave and wallowed down the further side. Even his inexperience could detect the sluggishness and ominous deadness of her movements. The brig had not much longer to float, and there was a good deal to do.

'I shall make preparations for abandoning the ship, Matthews,' he said.

He poked his chin upwards as he spoke; he would not allow either a Frenchman or a seaman to guess at his despair.

'Aye aye, sir,' said Matthews.

The *Marie Galante* carried a boat on chocks abaft the mainmast; at Matthews' summons the men abandoned their work on the cargo and hurried to the business of putting food and water in her.

'Beggin' your pardon, sir,' said Hunter aside to Hornblower, 'but you ought to see you have warm clothes, sir. I been in an open boat ten days once, sir.'

'Thank you, Hunter,' said Hornblower.

There was much to think of. Navigating instruments, charts, compass—would he be able to get a good observation with his sextant in a tossing little boat? Common prudence dictated that they should have all the food and water with them that the boat could carry; but—Hornblower eyed the wretched craft dubiously—seventeen men would fill it to overflowing anyway. He would have to leave much to the judgment of the French captain and of Matthews.

The tackles were manned and the boat was swayed up from the chocks and lowered into the water in the tiny lee afforded on the lee quarter. The *Marie Galante* put her nose into a wave, refusing to rise to it; green water came over the starboard bow and poured aft along the deck before a sullen wallow on the part of the brig sent it into the scuppers. There was not much time to spare—a rending crash from below told that the cargo was still swelling and forcing the bulkheads. There was a panic among the Frenchmen, who began to tumble down into the boat with loud cries. The French captain took one look at Hornblower and then followed them; two of the British seamen were already over the side fending off the boat.

'Go along,' said Hornblower to Matthews and Carson, who still lingered. He was the captain; it was his place to leave the ship last.

So waterlogged was the brig now that it was not at all difficult to step down into the boat from the deck; the British seamen were in the sternsheets and made room for him.

'Take the tiller, Matthews,' said Hornblower; he did not feel he was competent to handle that over-loaded boat. 'Shove off, there!'

The boat and the brig parted company; the *Marie Galante*, with her helm lashed, poked her nose into the wind and hung there. She had acquired a sudden list, with the starboard side scuppers nearly under water. Another wave broke over her deck, pouring up to the open hatchway. Now she righted herself, her deck nearly level with the sea, and then she sank, on an even keel, the water closing over her, her masts slowly disappearing. For an instant her sails even gleamed under the green water.

'She's gone,' said Matthews.

Hornblower watched the disappearance of his first command. The *Marie Galante* had been entrusted to him to bring into port, and he had failed, failed on his first independent mission. He looked very hard at the setting sun, hoping no one would notice the tears that were filling his eyes.

CHAPTER THREE

THE PENALTY OF FAILURE

DAYLIGHT crept over the tossing waters of the Bay of Biscay to reveal a small boat riding on its wide expanses. It was a very crowded boat; in the bows huddled the French crew of the sunken brig *Marie Galante*, amidships sat the captain and his mate, and in the sternsheets sat Midshipman Horatio Hornblower and the four English seamen who had once constituted the prize-crew of the brig. Hornblower was seasick, for his delicate stomach, having painfully accustomed itself to the motion of the *Indefatigable*, rebelled at the antics of the small boat as she pitched jerkily to her sea-anchor. He was cold and weary as well as seasick after his second night without sleep—he had been vomiting spasmodically all through the hours of darkness, and in the depression which seasickness brings he had thought gloomily about the loss of the *Marie Galante*. If he had only remembered earlier to plug that shot-hole! Excuses came to his mind only to be discarded. There had been so much to do, and so few men to do it with—the French crew to guard, the damage aloft to repair, the course to set. The absorbent qualities of the cargo of rice which the *Marie Galante* carried had deceived him when he had remembered to sound the well. All this might be true, but the fact remained that he had lost his ship, his first command. In his own eyes there was no excuse for his failure.

The French crew had wakened with the dawn and were chattering like a nest of magpies; Matthews and Carson beside him were moving stiffly to ease their aching joints.

'Breakfast, sir?' said Matthews.

It was like the games Hornblower had played as a lonely little boy, when he had sat in the empty pig-trough and pretended he was cast away in an open boat. Then he had parcelled out the bit of bread or whatever it was which he had obtained from the kitchen into a dozen rations, counting them carefully, each one to last a day. But a small boy's eager appetite had made those days very short, not more than five minutes long; after standing up in the pig-trough and shading his eyes and looking round the horizon for the succour that he could not discover, he would sit down again, tell himself that the life of a castaway was hard, and then decide that another night had passed and that it was time to eat another ration from his dwindling supply. So here under Hornblower's eye the French captain and mate served out a biscuit of hard bread to each person in the boat, and filled the pannikin for each man in turn from the water breakers under the thwarts. But Hornblower when he sat in the pig-trough, despite his vivid imagination, never thought of this hideous seasickness, of the cold and the cramps, nor of how his skinny posterior would ache with its constant pressure against the hard timbers of the sternsheets; nor, in the sublime self-confidence of childhood, had he ever thought how heavy could be the burden of responsibility on the shoulders of a senior naval officer aged seventeen.

He dragged himself back from the memories of that recent childhood to face the present situation. The grey sky, as far as his inexperienced eye could tell, bore no presage of deterioration in the weather. He wetted his finger and held it up, looking in the boat's compass to gauge the direction of the wind.

'Backing westerly a little, sir,' said Matthews, who had been copying his movements.

'That's so,' agreed Hornblower, hurriedly going through in his mind his recent lessons in boxing the compass. His course to weather Ushant was nor'-east by north, he knew, and the boat close-hauled would not lie closer than eight points off the wind—he had lain-to to the sea-anchor all night because the wind had been coming from too far north to enable him to steer for England. But now the wind had backed. Eight points from nor'-east by north was nor'-west by west, and the wind was even more westerly than that. Close-hauled he could weather Ushant and even have a margin for contingencies, to keep him clear of the lee shore, which the seamanship books and his own common sense told him was so dangerous.

'We'll make sail, Matthews,' he said; his hand was still grasping the biscuit which his rebellious stomach refused to accept.

'Aye aye, sir.'

A shout to the Frenchmen crowded in the bows drew their attention; in the circumstances it hardly needed Hornblower's halting French to direct them to carry out the obvious task of getting in the sea-anchor. But it was not too easy, with the boat so crowded and hardly a foot of freeboard. The mast was already stepped, and the lug sail bent ready to hoist. Two Frenchmen, balancing precariously, tailed on to the halliard and the sail rose up the mast.

'Hunter, take the sheet,' said Hornblower. 'Matthews, take the tiller. Keep her close-hauled on the port tack.'

'Close-hauled on the port tack, sir.'

The French captain had watched the proceedings with intense interest from his seat amidships. He had not understood the last, decisive order, but he grasped its meaning quickly enough when the boat came round and steadied on the port tack, heading for England. He stood up, spluttering angry protests.

'The wind is fair for Bordeaux,' he said, gesticulating with clenched fists. 'We could be there by to-morrow. Why do we go north?'

'We go to England,' said Hornblower.

'But—but—it will take us a week! A week even if the wind stays fair. This boat—it is too crowded. We cannot endure a storm. It is madness.'

Hornblower had guessed at the moment the captain stood up what he was going to say, and he hardly bothered to translate the expostulations to himself. He was too tired and too seasick to enter into an argument in a foreign language. He ignored the captain. Not for anything on earth would he turn the boat's head towards France. His naval career had only just begun, and even if it were to be blighted on account of the loss of the *Marie Galante* he had no intention of rotting for years in a French prison.

'Sir!' said the French captain.

The mate who shared the captain's thwart was protesting too, and now they turned to their crew behind them and told them what was going on. An angry movement stirred the crowd.

'Sir!' said the captain again. 'I insist that you head towards Bordeaux.'

He showed signs of advancing upon them; one of the crew behind him began to pull the boat-hook clear, and it would be a dangerous weapon. Hornblower pulled one of

c*

the pistols from his belt and pointed it at the captain, who, with the muzzle four feet from his breast, fell back before the gesture. Without taking his eyes off him, Hornblower took a second pistol with his left hand.

'Take this, Matthews,' he said.

'Aye aye, sir,' said Matthews, obeying; and then, after a respectful pause, 'Beggin' your pardon, sir, but hadn't you better cock your pistol, sir?'

'Yes,' said Hornblower, exasperated at his own forgetfulness.

He drew the hammer back with a click, and the menacing sound made more acute still the French captain's sense of his own danger, with a cocked and loaded pistol pointed at his stomach in a heaving boat. He waved his hands desperately.

'Please,' he said, 'point it some other way, sir.'

He drew farther back, huddling against the men behind him.

'Hey, avast there, you,' shouted Matthews loudly—a French sailor was trying to let go the halliard unobserved.

'Shoot any man who looks dangerous, Matthews,' said Hornblower.

He was so intent on enforcing his will upon these men, so desperately anxious to retain his liberty, that his face was contracted into a beast-like scowl. No one looking at him could doubt his determination for a moment. He would allow no human life to come between him and his decisions. There was still a third pistol in his belt, and the Frenchmen could guess that, if they tried a rush, a quarter of them at least would meet their deaths before they overpowered the Englishmen, and the French captain knew he would be the first to die. His expressive hands, waving out from his sides—he could not take his eyes from the pistol—told his men to make no further resistance. Their murmurings died away, and the captain began to plead.

'Five years I was in an English prison during the last war,' he said. 'Let us reach an agreement. Let us go to France. When we reach the shore—anywhere you choose, sir—we will land and you can continue on your journey. Or we can all land, and I will use all my influence to have you and your men sent back to England under cartel, without exchange or ransom. I swear I will.'

'No,' said Hornblower.

England was far easier to reach from here than from the French Biscay coast; as for the other suggestion, Hornblower knew enough about the new government washed up by the revolution in France to be sure that they would never part with prisoners on the representation of a merchant captain. And trained seamen were scarce in France; it was his duty to keep these dozen from returning.

'No,' he said again, in reply to the captain's fresh protests.

'Shall I clout 'im on the jaw, sir?' asked Hunter, at Hornblower's side.

'No,' said Hornblower again; but the Frenchman saw the gesture and guessed at the meaning of the words, and subsided into sullen silence.

But he was roused again at the sight of Hornblower's pistol on his knee, still pointed at him. A sleepy finger might press that trigger.

'Sir,' he said, 'put that pistol away, I beg of you. It is dangerous.'

Hornblower's eye was cold and unsympathetic.

'Put it away, please. I will do nothing to interfere with your command of this boat. I promise you that.'

'Do you swear it?'

'I swear it.'

'And these others?'

The captain looked round at his crew with voluble explanations, and grudgingly they agreed.

'They swear it too.'

'Very well, then.'

Hornblower started to replace the pistol in his belt, and remembered to put it on half-cock in time to save himself from shooting himself in the stomach. Everyone in the boat relaxed into apathy. The boat was rising and swooping rhythmically now, a far more comfortable motion than when it had jerked to a sea-anchor, and Hornblower's stomach lost some of its resentment. He had been two nights without sleep. His head lowered on his chest, and then he leaned sideways against Hunter, and slept peacefully, while the boat, with the wind nearly abeam, headed steadily for England. What woke him late in the day was when Matthews, cramped and weary, was compelled to surrender the tiller to Carson, and after that they kept watch and watch, a hand at the sheet and a hand at the tiller and the others trying to rest. Hornblower took his turn at the sheet, but he would not trust himself with the tiller, especially when night fell; he knew he had not the knack of keeping the boat on her course by the feel of the wind on his cheek and the tiller in his hand.

It was not until long after breakfast the next day—almost noon in fact—that they sighted the sail. It was a French-man who saw it first, and his excited cry roused them all. There were three square topsails coming up over the horizon on their weather bow, nearing them so rapidly on a converging course that each time the boat rose on a wave a considerably greater area of canvas was visible.

'What do you think she is, Matthews?' asked Hornblower, while the boat buzzed with the Frenchmen's excitement.

'I can't tell, sir, but I don't like the looks of her,' said Matthews doubtfully. 'She ought to have her t'gallants set in this breeze—and her courses too, an' she hasn't. An' I don't like the cut of her jib, sir. She—she might be a Frenchie to me, sir.'

Any ship travelling for peaceful purposes would naturally have all possible sail set. This ship had not. Hence she was engaged in some belligerent design, but there were more chances that she was British than that she was French, even in here in the Bay. Hornblower took a long look at her; a smallish vessel, although ship-rigged. Flush-decked, with a look of speed about her—her hull was visible at intervals now, with a line of gunports.

'She looks French all over to me, sir,' said Hunter. 'Privateer, seemly.'

'Stand by to jibe,' said Hornblower.

They brought the boat round before the wind, heading directly away from the ship. But in war as in the jungle, to fly is to invite pursuit and attack. The ship set courses and topgallants and came tearing down upon them, passed them at half a cable's length and then hove-to, having cut off their escape. The ship's rail was lined with a curious crowd—a large crew for a vessel that size. A hail came across the water to the boat, and the words were French. The English seamen subsided into curses, while the French captain cheerfully stood up and replied, and the French crew brought the boat alongside the ship.

A handsome young man in a plum-coloured coat with a lace stock greeted Hornblower when he stepped on the deck.

'Welcome, sir, to the *Pique*,' he said in French. 'I am Captain Neuville, of this privateer. And you are——?'

'Midshipman Hornblower, of His Britannic Majesty's ship *Indefatigable*,' growled Hornblower.

'You seem to be in evil humour,' said Neuville. 'Please do not be so distressed at the fortunes of war. You will be accommodated in this ship, until we return to port, with every comfort possible at sea. I beg of you to consider yourself quite at home. For instance, those pistols in your belt must discommode you more than a little. Permit me to relieve you of their weight.'

He took the pistols neatly from Hornblower's belt as he spoke, looked Hornblower keenly over, and then went on.

'That dirk that you wear at your side, sir. Would you oblige me by the loan of it? I assure you that I will return it to you when we part company. But while you are on board here I fear that your impetuous youth might lead you into some rash act while you are wearing a weapon which a credulous mind might believe to be lethal. A thousand thanks. And now might I show you the berth that is being prepared for you?'

With a courteous bow he led the way below. Two decks down, presumably at the level of a foot or two below the waterline, was a wide bare 'tweendecks, dimly lighted and scantily ventilated by the hatchways.

'Our slave deck,' explained Neuville carelessly.

'Slave deck?' asked Hornblower.

'Yes. It is here that the slaves were confined during the middle passage.'

Much was clear to Hornblower at once. A slave ship could be readily converted into a privateer. She would already be armed with plenty of guns to defend herself against treacherous attacks while making her purchases in the African rivers; she was faster than the average merchant ship both because of the lack of need of hold space and because with a highly perishable cargo such as slaves speed was a desirable quality, and she was constructed to carry large numbers of men and the great quantities of food and water necessary to keep them supplied while at sea in search of prizes.

'Our market in San Domingo has been closed to us by recent events, of which you must have heard, sir,' went on Neuville, 'and so that the *Pique* could continue to return dividends to me I have converted her into a privateer. Moreover, seeing that the activities of the Committee of Public Safety at present make Paris a more unhealthy spot even than the West Coast of Africa, I decided to take command of my vessel myself. To say nothing of the fact that a certain resolution and hardihood are necessary to make a privateer a profitable investment.'

Neuville's face hardened for a moment into an expression of the grimmest determination, and then softened at once into its previous meaningless politeness.

'This door in this bulkhead,' he continued, 'leads to the quarters I have set aside for captured officers. Here, as you see, is your cot. Please make yourself at home here. Should this ship go into action—as I trust she will frequently do—the hatches above will be battened down. But except on those occasions you will of course be at liberty to move about the ship at your will. Yet I suppose I had better add that any hare-brained attempt on the part of prisoners to interfere with the working or well-being of this ship would be deeply resented by the crew. They serve on shares, you understand, and are risking their lives and their liberty. I would not be surprised if any rash person who endangered their dividends and freedom were dropped over the side into the sea.'

Hornblower forced himself to reply; he would not reveal

that he was almost struck dumb by the calculating callousness of this last speech.

'I understand,' he said.

'Excellent! Now is there anything further you may need, sir?'

Hornblower looked round the bare quarters in which he was to suffer lonely confinement, lit by a dim glimmer of light from a swaying slush lamp.

'Could I have something to read?' he asked.

Neuville thought for a moment.

'I fear there are only professional books,' he said. 'But I can let you have Grandjean's *Principles of Navigation*, and Lebrun's *Handbook on Seamanship* and some similar volumes, if you think you can understand the French in which they are written.'

'I'll try,' said Hornblower.

Probably it was as well that Hornblower was provided with the materials for such strenuous mental exercise. The effort of reading French and of studying his profession at one and the same time kept his mind busy during the dreary days while the *Pique* cruised in search of prizes. Most of the time the Frenchmen ignored him—he had to force himself upon Neuville once to protest against the employment of his four British seamen on the menial work of pumping out the ship, but he had to retire worsted from the argument, if argument it could be called, when Neuville icily refused to discuss the question. Hornblower went back to his quarters with burning cheeks and red ears, and, as ever, when he was mentally disturbed, the thought of his guilt returned to him with new force.

If only he had plugged that shot-hole sooner! A clearer-headed officer, he told himself, would have done so. He had lost his ship, the *Indefatigable*'s precious prize, and there was no health in him. Sometimes he made himself review the situation calmly. Professionally, he might not—probably would not—suffer for his negligence. A midshipman with only four for a prize-crew, put on board a two-hundred-ton brig that had been subjected to considerable firing from a frigate's guns, would not be seriously blamed when she sank under him. But Hornblower knew at the same time that he was at least partly at fault. If it was ignorance—there was no excuse for ignorance. If he had allowed his multiple cares to distract him from the business of plugging the shot-hole immediately, that was incompetence, and there was no excuse for incompetence. When he thought along those lines he was overwhelmed by waves of despair and of self-contempt, and there was no one to comfort him. The day of his birthday, when he looked at himself at the vast age of eighteen, was the worst of all. Eighteen and a discredited prisoner in the hands of a French privateersman! His self-respect was at its lowest ebb.

The *Pique* was seeking her prey in the most frequented waters in the world, the approaches to the Channel, and there could be no more vivid demonstration of the vastness of the ocean than the fact that she cruised day after day without glimpsing a sail. She maintained a triangular course, reaching to the north-west, tacking to the south, running under easy sail north-easterly again, with look-outs at every masthead, with nothing to see but the tossing waste of water. Until the morning when a high-pitched yell from the foretopgallant masterhead attracted the attention of everybody on deck, including Hornblower, standing lonely in the waist. Neuville, by the wheel, bellowed a question to the look-out, and Hornblower, thanks to his recent studies, could translate the answer. There was a sail

visible to windward, and next moment the look-out reported
that it had altered course and was running down towards
them.

That meant a great deal. In wartime any merchant ship
would be suspicious of strangers and would give them as
wide a berth as possible; and especially when she was to
windward and therefore far safer. Only someone prepared to
fight or possessed of a perfectly morbid curiosity would
abandon a windward position. A wild and unreasonable
hope filled Hornblower's breast; a ship of war at sea—
thanks to England's maritime mastery—would be far more
probably English than French. And this was the cruising
ground of the *Indefatigable*, his own ship, stationed there
especially to fulfil the double function of looking out
for French commerce-destroyers and intercepting French
blockade-runners. A hundred miles from here she had put
him and his prize crew on board the *Marie Galante*. It was
a thousand to one, he exaggerated despairingly to himself,
against any ship sighted being the *Indefatigable*. But—hope
reasserted itself—the fact that she was coming down to
investigate reduced the odds to ten to one at most. Less
than ten to one.

He looked over at Neuville, trying to think his thoughts.
The *Pique* was fast and handy, and there was a clear avenue
of escape to leeward. The fact that the stranger had altered
course towards them was a suspicious circumstance, but it
was known that Indiamen, the richest prizes of all, had
sometimes traded on the similarity of their appearance to
that of ships of the line, and by showing a bold front had
scared dangerous enemies away. That would be a tempta-
tion to a man eager to make a prize. At Neuville's orders
all sail was set, ready for instant flight or pursuit and, close-
hauled, the *Pique* stood towards the stranger. It was not

long before Hornblower, on the deck, caught a glimpse of a gleam of white, like a tiny grain of rice, far away on the horizon as the *Pique* lifted on a swell. Here came Matthews, red-faced and excited, running aft to Hornblower's side.

'That's the old *Indefatigable*, sir,' he said. 'I swear it!' He sprang on to the rail, holding on by the shrouds, and stared under his hand.

'Yes! There she is, sir! She's loosing her royals now, sir. We'll be back on board of her in time for grog!'

A French petty officer reached up and dragged Matthews by the seat of his trousers from his perch, and with a blow and a kick drove him forward again, while a moment later Neuville was shouting the orders that wore the ship round to head away directly from the *Indefatigable*. Neuville beckoned Hornblower over to his side.

'Your late ship, I understand, Mr Hornblower?'

'Yes.'

'What is her best point of sailing?'

Hornblower's eyes met Neuville's.

'Do not look so noble,' said Neuville, smiling with thin lips. 'I could undoubtedly induce you to give me the information. I know of ways. But it is unnecessary, fortunately for you. There is no ship on earth—especially none of His Britannic Majesty's clumsy frigates—that can outsail the *Pique* running before the wind. You will soon see that.'

He strolled to the taffrail and looked aft long and earnestly through his glass, but no more earnestly than did Hornblower with his naked eye.

'You see?' said Neuville, proffering the glass.

Hornblower took it, but more to catch a closer glimpse of his ship than to confirm his observations. He was homesick, desperately homesick, at that moment, for the *Indefatigable*. But there could be no denying that she was being left fast behind. Her topgallants were out of sight again now, and only her royals were visible.

'Two hours and we shall have run her mastheads under,' said Neuville, taking back the telescope and shutting it with a snap.

He left Hornblower standing sorrowfully at the taffrail while he turned to berate the helmsman for not steering a steadier course; Hornblower heard the explosive words without listening to them, the wind blowing into his face and ruffling his hair over his ears, and the wake of the ship's passage boiling below him. So might Adam have looked back at Eden; Hornblower remembered the stuffy, dark midshipmen's berth, the smells and the creakings, the bitter cold nights, turning out in response to the call for all hands, the weevilly bread and the wooden beef, and he yearned for them all, with the sick feeling of hopeless long-ing. Liberty was vanishing over the horizon. Yet it was not these personal feelings that drove him below in search of action. They may have quickened his wits, but it was a sense of duty which inspired him.

The slave-deck was deserted, as usual, with all hands at quarters. Beyond the bulkhead stood his cot with the books upon it and the slush lamp swaying above it. There was nothing there to give him any inspiration. There was an-other locked door in the after bulkhead. That opened into some kind of boatswain's store; twice he had seen it un-locked and paint and similar supplies brought out from it. Paint! That gave him an idea; he looked from the door up to the slush lamp and back again, and as he stepped for-ward he took his claspknife out of his pocket. But before very long he recoiled again, sneering at himself. The door was not panelled, but was made of two solid slabs of wood, with the cross-beams on the inside. There was the keyhole of the lock, but it presented no point of attack. It would take him hours and hours to cut through that door with his knife, at a time when minutes were precious.

His heart was beating feverishly—but no more feverishly than his mind was working—as he looked round again. He reached up to the lamp and shook it; nearly full. There was a moment when he stood hesitating, nerving himself, and then he threw himself into action. With a ruthless hand he tore the pages out of Grandjean's *Principes de la Navigation*, crumpling them up in small quantities into little loose balls which he laid at the foot of the door. He threw off his uniform coat and dragged his blue woollen jersey over his head; his long powerful fingers tore it across and plucked eagerly at it to unravel it. After starting some loose threads he would not waste more time on it, and dropped the garment on to the paper and looked round again. The mattress of the cot! It was stuffed with straw, by God! A slash of his knife tore open the ticking, and he scooped the stuff out by the armful; constant pressure had almost solidified it, but he shook it and handled it so that it bulked out far larger in a mass on the deck nearly up to his waist. That would give him the intense blaze he wanted. He stood still, compelling himself to think clearly and logically—it was impetuosity and lack of thought which had occasioned the loss of the *Marie Galante*, and now he had wasted time on his jersey. He worked out the successive steps to take. He made a long spill out of a page of the *Manuel de Matelotage*, and lighted it at the lamp. Then he poured out the grease—the lamp was hot and the grease liquid—over his balls of paper, over the deck, over the base of the door. A touch from his taper lighted one ball, the flame travelled quickly. He was committed now. He piled the straw upon the flames, and in a sudden access of insane strength he tore the cot from its fastenings, smashing it as he did so, and piled the fragments on the straw. Already the flames were racing through the straw. He dropped the lamp upon the pile, grabbed his coat and walked out. He thought of closing the door, but decided against it—the more air the better. He wriggled into his coat and ran up the ladder.

On deck he forced himself to lounge nonchalantly against the rail, putting his shaking hands into his pockets. His excitement made him weak, nor was it lessened as he waited. Every minute before the fire could be discovered was important. A French officer said something to him with a triumphant laugh and pointed aft over the taffrail, presumably speaking about leaving the *Indefatigable* behind. Hornblower smiled bleakly at him; that was the first gesture that occurred to him, and then he thought that a smile was out of place, and he tried to assume a sullen scowl. The wind was blowing briskly, so that the *Pique* could only just carry all plain sail; Hornblower felt it on his cheeks, which were burning. Everyone on deck seemed unnaturally busy and preoccupied; Neuville was watching the helmsman with occasional glances aloft to see that every sail was doing its work; the men were at the guns, two hands and a petty officer heaving the log. God, how much longer would he have?

Look there! The coaming of the after hatchway appeared distorted, wavering in the shimmering air. Hot air must be coming up through it. And was that, or was it not, the ghost of a wreath of smoke? It was! In that moment the alarm was given. A loud cry, a rush of feet, an instant bustle, the loud beating of a drum, high-pitched shouts— '*Au feu! Au feu!*'

The four elements of Aristotle, thought Hornblower

insanely—earth, air, water and fire—were the constant
enemies of the seaman, but the lee shore, the gale, and the
wave were none of them as feared in wooden ships as fire.
Timbers many years old and coated thick with paint burnt
fiercely and readily. Sails and tarry rigging would burn like
fireworks. And within the ship were tons and tons of gunpowder waiting its chance to blast the seamen into fragments. Hornblower watched the fire parties flinging themselves into their work, the pumps being dragged over the
decks, the hoses rigged. Someone came racing aft with a
message for Neuville, presumably to report the site of the
fire. Neuville heard him, and darted a glance at Hornblower against the rail before he hurled orders back at the
messenger. The smoke coming up through the after hatchway was dense now; at Neuville's orders the after guard
flung themselves down the opening through the smoke.
And there was more smoke, and more smoke; smoke caught
up by the following wind and blown forward in wisps—
smoke must be pouring out of the sides of the ship at the
waterline.

Neuville took a stride towards Hornblower, his face
working with rage, but a cry from the helmsman checked
him. The helmsman, unable to take his hands from the
wheel, pointed with his foot to the cabin skylight. There
was a flickering of flame below it. A side pane fell in as they
watched, and a rush of flame came through the opening.
That store of paint, Hornblower calculated—he was calmer
now, with a calm that would astonish him later, when he
came to look back on it—must be immediately under the
cabin, and blazing fiercely. Neuville looked round him, at
the sea and the sky, and put his hands to his head in a
furious gesture. For the first time in his life Hornblower
saw a man literally tearing his hair. But his nerve held. A

shout brought up another portable pump; four men set to work on the handles, and the clank-clank, clank-clank made an accompaniment that blended with the roar of the fire. A thin jet of water was squirted down the gaping skylight. More men formed a bucket chain, drawing water from the sea and passing it from hand to hand to pour in the skylight, but those buckets of water were less effective even than the stream from the pumps. From below came the dull thud of an explosion, and Hornblower caught his breath as he expected the ship to be blown to pieces. But no further explosion followed; either a gun had been set off by the flames or a cask had burst violently in the heat. And then the bucket line suddenly disintegrated; beneath the feet of one of the men a seam had gaped in a broad red smile from which came a rush of flame. Some officer had seized Neuville by the arm and was arguing with him vehemently, and Hornblower could see Neuville yield in despair. Hands were scurrying aloft to get in the foretopsail and forecourse, and other hands went to the main braces. Over went the wheel, and the *Pique* came up into the wind.

The change was dramatic, although at first more apparent than real; with the wind blowing in the opposite direction the roar of the fire did not come so clearly to the ears of those forward of it. But it was an immense gain, all the same; the flames, which had started in the steerage in the farthest after-part of the ship, no longer were blown forward, but were turned back upon timber already half consumed. Yet the after-part of the deck was fully alight; the helmsman was driven from the wheel, and in a flash the flames took hold of the driver and consumed it utterly —one moment the sail was there, and the next there were only charred fragments hanging from the gaff. But, head to wind, the other sails did not catch, and a mizzen-trysail hurriedly set kept the ship bows-on.

It was then that Hornblower, looking forward, saw the *Indefatigable* again. She was tearing down towards them with all sail set; as the *Pique* lifted he could see the white bow wave foaming under her bowsprit. There was no question about surrender, for under the menace of that row of guns no ship of the *Pique*'s force, even if uninjured, could resist. A cable's length to windward the *Indefatigable* rounded-to, and she was hoisting out her boats before even she was fully round. Pellew had seen the smoke, and had deduced the reason for the *Pique*'s heaving to, and had made his preparations as he came up. Longboat and launch had each a pump in their bows where sometimes they carried a carronade; they dropped down to the stern of the *Pique* to cast their jets of water up into the flaming stern without more ado. Two gigs full of men ran straight aft to join in the battle with the flames, but Bolton, the third lieutenant, lingered for a moment as he caught Hornblower's eye.

'Good God, it's you!' he exclaimed. 'What are you doing here?'

Yet he did not stay for an answer. He picked out Neuville as the captain of the *Pique*, strode aft to receive his surrender, cast his eyes aloft to see that all was well there, and then took up the task of combating the fire. The flames were overcome in time, more because they had consumed everything within reach of them than for any other reason; the *Pique* was burnt from the taffrail forward for some feet of her length right to the water's edge, so that she presented a strange spectacle when viewed from the deck of the *Indefatigable*. Nevertheless, she was in no immediate danger; given even moderate good fortune and a little hard work she could be sailed to England to be repaired and sent to sea again.

But it was not her salvage that was important, but rather the fact that she was no longer in French hands, would no longer be available to prey on English commerce. That was the point that Sir Edward Pellew made in conversation with Hornblower, when the latter came on board to report himself. Hornblower had begun, at Pellew's order, by recounting what had happened to him from the time he had been sent as prize master on board the *Marie Galante*. As Hornblower had expected—perhaps as he had even feared —Pellew had passed lightly over the loss of the brig. She had been damaged by gunfire before surrendering, and no one now could establish whether the damage was small or great. Pellew did not give the matter a second thought. Hornblower had tried to save her and had been unsuccessful with his tiny crew—and at that moment the *Indefatigable* could not spare him a larger crew. He did not hold Hornblower culpable. Once again, it was more important that France should be deprived of the *Marie Galante*'s cargo than that England should benefit by it. The situation was exactly parallel to that of the salvaging of the *Pique*. 'It was lucky she caught fire like that,' commented Pellew, looking across to where the *Pique* lay, still hove-to with the boats clustering about her but with only the thinnest trail of smoke drifting from her stern. 'She was running clean away from us, and would have been out of sight in an hour. Have you any idea how it happened, Mr Hornblower?'

Hornblower was naturally expecting that question and was ready for it. Now was the time to answer truthfully and modestly, to receive the praise he deserved, a mention in the *Gazette*, perhaps even appointment as acting-lieutenant. But Pellew did not know the full details of the loss of the brig, and might make a false estimate of them even if he did.

'No, sir,' said Hornblower. 'I think it must have been spontaneous combustion in the paint-locker. I can't account for it otherwise.'

He alone knew of his remissness in plugging that shot-hole, he alone could decide on his punishment, and this was what he had chosen. This alone could re-establish him in his own eyes, and when the words were spoken he felt enormous relief, and not one single twinge of regret.

'It was fortunate, all the same,' mused Pellew.

CHAPTER FOUR

THE MAN WHO FELT QUEER

THIS time the wolf was prowling round outside the sheep-fold. H.M. frigate *Indefatigable* had chased the French corvette *Papillon* into the mouth of the Gironde, and was seeking a way of attacking her where she lay at anchor in the stream under the protection of the batteries at the mouth. Captain Pellew took his ship into shoal water as far as he dared, until in fact the batteries fired warning shots to make him keep his distance, and he stared long and keenly through his glass at the corvette. Then he shut his telescope and turned on his heel to give the order that worked the *Indefatigable* away from the dangerous lee shore—out of sight of land, in fact. His departure might lull the French into a sense of security which, he hoped, would prove unjustified. For he had no intention of leaving them undisturbed. If the corvette could be captured or sunk not only would she be unavailable for raids on British commerce, but also the French would be forced to increase their coastal defences at this point and lessen the effort that could be put out elsewhere. War is a matter of savage blow and counter-blow, and even a forty-gun frigate could strike shrewd blows if shrewdly handled.

Midshipman Hornblower was walking the lee side of the quarterdeck, as became his lowly station as the junior officer of the watch, in the afternoon, when Midshipman Kennedy approached him. Kennedy took off his hat with a flourish and bowed low as his dancing master had once taught him, left foot advanced, hat down by the right knee. Hornblower entered into the spirit of the game, laid his hat against his stomach, and bent himself in the middle three times in quick succession. Thanks to his physical awkwardness he could parody ceremonial solemnity almost without trying.

'Most grave and reverend signor,' said Kennedy, 'I bear the compliments of Captain Sir Ed'ard Pellew, who humbly solicits Your Gravity's attendance at dinner at eight bells in the afternoon watch.'

'My respects to Sir Edward,' replied Hornblower, bowing to his knees at the mention of the name, 'and I shall condescend to make a brief appearance.'

'I am sure the captain will be both relieved and delighted,' said Kennedy. 'I will convey him my felicitations along with your most flattering acceptance.'

Both hats flourished with even greater elaboration than before, but at that moment both young men noticed Mr Bolton, the officer of the watch, looking at them from the windward side, and they hurriedly put their hats on and assumed attitudes more consonant with the dignity of officers holding their warrants from King George.

'What's in the captain's mind?' asked Hornblower.

Kennedy laid one finger alongside his nose.

'If I knew that I should rate a couple of epaulettes,' he said. 'Something's brewing, and I suppose one of these days we shall know what it is. Until then all that we little victims can do is to play unconscious of our doom. Meanwhile, be careful not to let the ship fall overboard.'

There was no sign of anything brewing while dinner was being eaten in the great cabin of the *Indefatigable*. Pellew was a courtly host at the head of the table. Conversation flowed freely and along indifferent channels among the senior officers present—the two lieutenants, Eccles and Chadd, and the sailing master, Soames. Hornblower and the other junior officer—Mallory, a midshipman of over two years' seniority—kept silent, as midshipmen should, thereby being able to devote their undivided attention to the food, so vastly superior to what was served in the midshipmen's berth.

'A glass of wine with you, Mr Hornblower,' said Pellew, raising his glass.

Hornblower tried to bow gracefully in his seat while raising his glass. He sipped cautiously, for he had early found that he had a weak head, and he disliked feeling drunk.

The table was cleared and there was a brief moment of expectancy as the company awaited Pellew's next move.

'Now, Mr Soames,' said Pellew, 'let us have that chart.'

It was a map of the mouth of the Gironde with the soundings; somebody had pencilled in the positions of the shore batteries.

'The *Papillon*,' said Sir Edward (he did not condescend

to pronounce it French-fashion), 'lies just here. Mr Soames took the bearings.'

He indicated a pencilled cross on the chart, far up the channel.

'You gentlemen,' went on Pellew, 'are going in with the boats to fetch her out.'

So that was it. A cutting-out expedition.

'Mr Eccles will be in general command. I will ask him to tell you his plan.'

The grey-haired first lieutenant with the surprisingly young blue eyes looked round at the others.

'I shall have the launch,' he said, 'and Mr Soames the cutter. Mr Chadd and Mr Mallory will command the first and second gigs. And Mr Hornblower will command the jolly boat. Each of the boats except Mr Hornblower's will have a junior officer second in command.'

That would not be necessary for the jolly boat with its crew of seven. The launch and cutter would carry from thirty to forty men each, and the gigs twenty each; it was a large force that was being despatched—nearly half the ship's company.

'She's a ship of war,' explained Eccles, reading their thoughts. 'No merchantman. Ten guns a side, and full of men.'

Nearer two hundred men than a hundred, certainly—plentiful opposition for a hundred and twenty British seamen.

'But we will be attacking her by night and taking her by surprise,' said Eccles, reading their thoughts again.

'Surprise,' put in Pellew, 'is more than half the battle, as you know, gentlemen—please pardon the interruption, Mr Eccles.'

'At the moment,' went on Eccles, 'we are out of sight of

land. We are about to stand in again. We have never hung
about this part of the coast, and the Frogs'll think we've
gone for good. We'll make the land after nightfall, stand
in as far as possible, and then boats will go in. High water
to-morrow morning is at four-fifty; dawn is at five-thirty.
The attack will be delivered at four-thirty so that the
watch below will have had time to get to sleep. The launch
will attack on the starboard quarter, and the cutter on the
larboard quarter. Mr Mallory's gig will attack on the larboard bow, and Mr Chadd's on the starboard bow. Mr
Chadd will be responsible for cutting the corvette's cable
as soon as he has mastered the forecastle, and the other
boats' crews have at least reached the quarterdeck.'

Eccles looked round at the other three commanders of
the large boats, and they nodded understanding. Then he
went on:

'Mr Hornblower with the jolly boat will wait until the
attack has gained a foothold on the deck. He will then
board at the mainchains, either to starboard or larboard
as he sees fit, and he will at once ascend the main rigging,
paying no attention to whatever fighting is going on on
deck. He will see to it that the maintopsail is loosed and he
will sheet it home on receipt of further orders. I myself,
or Mr Soames in the event of my being killed or wounded,
will send two hands to the wheel and will attend to steering the corvette as soon as she is under way. The tide will
take us out, and the *Indefatigable* will be awaiting us just
out of gunshot from the shore batteries.'

'Any comments, gentlemen?' asked Pellew.

That was the moment when Hornblower should have
spoken up—the only moment when he could. Eccles' orders
had set in motion sick feelings of apprehension in his
stomach. Hornblower was no maintopman, and Horn-

blower knew it. He hated heights, and he hated going aloft. He knew he had none of the monkey-like agility and self-confidence of the good seaman. He was unsure of himself aloft in the dark even in the *Indefatigable*, and he was utterly appalled at the thought of going aloft in an entirely strange ship and finding his way among strange rigging. He felt himself quite unfitted for the duty assigned to him, and he should have raised a protest at once on account of his unfitness. But he let the opportunity pass, for he was overcome by the matter-of-fact way in which the other officers accepted the plan. He looked round at the unmoved faces; nobody was paying any attention to him, and he jibbed at making himself conspicuous. He swallowed; he even got as far as opening his mouth, but still no one looked at him, and his protest died stillborn.

'Very well, then, gentlemen,' said Pellew. 'I think you had better go into the details, Mr Eccles.'

Then it was too late. Eccles, with the chart before him, was pointing out the course to be taken through the shoals and mudbanks of the Gironde, and expatiating on the position of the shore batteries and on the influence of the lighthouse of Cordouan upon the distance to which the *Indefatigable* could approach in daylight. Hornblower listened, trying to concentrate despite his apprehensions. Eccles finished his remarks and Pellew closed the meeting.

'Since you all know your duties, gentlemen, I think you should start your preparations. The sun is about to set and you will find you have plenty to do.'

The boats' crews had to be told off; it was necessary to see that the men were armed, and that the boats were provisioned in case of emergency. Every man had to be instructed in the duties expected of him. And Hornblower had to rehearse himself in ascending the main shrouds and laying out along the maintopsail yard. He did it twice, forcing himself to make the difficult climb up the futtock shrouds, which, projecting outwards from the mainmast, made it necessary to climb several feet while hanging back downwards, locking fingers and toes in to the ratlines. He could just manage it, moving slowly and carefully, although clumsily. He stood on the foot-rope and worked his way out to the yard-arm—the foot-rope was attached along the yard so as to hang nearly four feet below it. The principle was to set his feet on the rope with his arms over the yard, then, holding the yard in his armpits, to shuffle sideways along the foot-rope to cast off the gaskets and loose the sail. Twice Hornblower made the whole journey, battling with the disquiet of his stomach at the thought of the hundred-foot drop below him. Finally, gulping with nervousness, he transferred his grip to the brace and forced himself to slide down it to the deck—that would be his best route when the time came to sheet the topsail home. It was a long, perilous descent; Hornblower told himself—as indeed he had said to himself when he had first seen men go aloft—that similar feats in a circus at home would be received with 'ohs' and 'ahs' of appreciation. He was by no means satisfied with himself even when he reached the deck, and at the back of his mind was a vivid mental picture of his missing his hold when the time came for him to repeat the performance in the *Papillon*, and falling headlong to the deck—a second or two of frightful fear while rushing through the air, and then a shattering crash. And the success of the attack hinged on him, as much as on anyone—if the topsail were not promptly set to give the corvette steerage way she would run aground on one of the innumerable shoals in the river mouth, to be ignominiously recaptured, and half the crew of the *Indefatigable* would be dead or prisoners.

D

In the waist the jolly boat's crew was formed up for his inspection. He saw to it that the oars were properly muffled, that each man had pistol and cutlass, and made sure that every pistol was at half-cock so that there was no fear of a premature shot giving warning of the attack. He allocated duties to each man in the loosening of the topsail, laying stress on the possibility that casualties might necessitate unrehearsed changes in the scheme.

'I will mount the rigging first,' said Hornblower.

That had to be the case. He had to lead—it was expected of him. More than that; if he had given any other order it would have excited comment—and contempt.

'Jackson,' went on Hornblower, addressing the coxswain, 'you will quit the boat last and take command if I fall.'

'Aye aye, sir.'

It was usual to use the poetic expression 'fall' for 'die', and it was only after Hornblower had uttered the word that he thought about its horrible real meaning in the present circumstances.

'Is that all understood?' asked Hornblower harshly; it was his mental stress that made his voice grate so.

Everyone nodded except one man.

'Begging your pardon, sir,' said Hales, the young man who pulled stroke oar, 'I'm feeling a bit queer-like.'

Hales was a lightly built young fellow of swarthy countenance. He put his hand to his forehead with a vague gesture as he spoke.

'You're not the only one to feel queer,' snapped Hornblower.

The other men chuckled. The thought of running the gauntlet of the shore batteries, of boarding an armed corvette in the teeth of opposition, might well raise apprehension in the breast of a coward. Most of the men detailed for the expedition must have felt qualms to some extent.

'I don't mean that, sir,' said Hales indignantly. ''Course I don't.'

But Hornblower and the others paid him no attention.

'You just keep your mouth shut,' growled Jackson. There could be nothing but contempt for a man who announced himself sick after being told off on a dangerous duty. Hornblower felt sympathy as well as contempt. He himself had been too much of a coward even to give voice to his apprehensions—too much afraid of what people would say about him.

'Dismiss,' said Hornblower. 'I'll pass the word for all of you when you are wanted.'

There were some hours yet to wait while the *Indefatigable* crept inshore, with the lead going steadily and Pellew himself attending to the course of the frigate. Hornblower, despite his nervousness and his miserable apprehensions, yet found time to appreciate the superb seamanship displayed as Pellew brought the big frigate in through these tricky waters on that dark night. His interest was so caught by the procedure that the little tremblings which had been assailing him ceased to manifest themselves; Hornblower was of the type that would continue to observe and to learn on his deathbed. By the time the *Indefatigable* had reached the point off the mouth of the river where it was desirable to launch the boats, Hornblower had learned a good deal about the practical application of the principles of coastwise navigation and a good deal about the organization of a cutting-out expedition—and by self-analysis he had learned even more about the psychology of a raiding party before a raid.

He had mastered himself to all outside appearance by the time he went down into the jolly boat as she heaved on the inky-black water, and he gave the command to shove off in a quiet, steady voice. Hornblower took the tiller—the feel of that solid bar of wood was reassuring, and it was old habit now to sit in the stern sheets with hand and elbow upon it, and the men began to pull slowly after the dark shapes of the four big boats; there was plenty of time, and the flowing tide would take them up the estuary. That was just as well, for on one side of them lay the batteries of St Dye, and inside the estuary on the other side was the fortress of Blaye, forty big guns trained to sweep the channel, and none of the five boats—certainly not the jolly boat—could withstand a single shot from one of them.

He kept his eyes attentively on the cutter ahead of him. Soames had the dreadful responsibility of taking the boats up the channel, while all he had to do was to follow in her wake—all, except to loose that maintopsail. Hornblower found himself shivering again.

Hales, the man who had said he felt queer, was pulling stroke oar; Hornblower could just see his dark form moving rhythmically back and forward at each slow stroke. After a single glance Hornblower paid him no more attention, and was staring after the cutter when a sudden commotion brought his mind back into the boat. Someone had missed his stroke; someone had thrown all six oars into confusion as a result. There was even a slight clatter.

'Mind what you're doing, blast you, Hales,' whispered Jackson, the coxswain, with desperate urgency.

For answer there was a sudden cry from Hales, loud but fortunately not too loud, and Hales pitched forward against Hornblower's and Jackson's legs, kicking and writhing.

'The bastard's having a fit,' growled Jackson.

The kicking and writhing went on. Across the water through the darkness came a sharp scornful whisper.

'Mr Hornblower,' said the voice—it was Eccles putting a world of exasperation into his *sotto voce* question—'cannot you keep your men quiet?'

Eccles had brought the launch round almost alongside the jolly boat to say this to him, and the desperate need for silence was dramatically demonstrated by the absence of any of the usual blasphemy; Hornblower could picture the cutting reprimand that would be administered to him to-morrow publicly on the quarterdeck. He opened his mouth to make an explanation, but he fortunately realized that raiders in open boats did not make explanations when under the guns of the fortress of Blaye.

'Aye aye, sir,' was all he whispered back, and the launch continued on its mission of shepherding the flotilla in the tracks of the cutter.

'Take his oar, Jackson,' he whispered furiously to the coxswain, and he stooped and with his own hands dragged the writhing figure towards him and out of Jackson's way.

'You might try pouring water on 'im, sir,' suggested Jackson hoarsely, as he moved to the afterthwart. 'There's the baler 'andy.'

Seawater was the seaman's cure for every ill, his panacea; seeing how often sailors had not merely wet jackets but wet bedding as well they should never have a day's illness. But Hornblower let the sick man lie. His struggles were coming to an end, and Hornblower wished to make no noise with the baler. The lives of more than a hundred men depended on silence. Now that they were well into the actual estuary they were within easy reach of cannon shot from the shore —and a single cannon shot would rouse the crew of the *Papillon*, ready to man the bulwarks to beat off the attack, ready to drop cannon balls into the boats alongside, ready to shatter approaching boats with a tempest of grape.

Silently the boats glided up the estuary; Soames in the cutter was setting a slow pace, with only an occasional stroke at the oars to maintain steerage way. Presumably he knew very well what he was doing; the channel he had selected was an obscure one between mudbanks, impracticable for anything except small boats, and he had a twenty-foot pole with him with which to take the soundings —quicker and much more silent than using the lead. Minutes were passing fast, and yet the night was still utterly dark, with no hint of approaching dawn. Strain his eyes as he would Hornblower could not be sure that he could see the flat shores on either side of him. It would call for sharp eyes on the land to detect the little boats being carried up by the tide.

Hales at his feet stirred and then stirred again. His hand, feeling round in the darkness, found Hornblower's ankle and apparently examined it with curiosity. He muttered something, the words dragging out into a moan.

'Shut up!' whispered Hornblower, trying, like the saint of old, to make a tongue of his whole body, that he might express the urgency of the occasion without making a sound audible at any distance. Hales set his elbow on Hornblower's knee and levered himself up into a sitting position, and then levered himself further until he was standing, swaying with bent knees and supporting himself against Hornblower.

'Sit down, damn you!' whispered Hornblower, shaking with fury and anxiety.

'Where's Mary?' asked Hales in a conversational tone.

'Shut up!'

'Mary!' said Hales, lurching against him. 'Mary!'

Each successive word was louder. Hornblower felt instinctively that Hales would soon be speaking in a loud voice, that he might even soon be shouting. Old recollections of conversations with his father stirred at the back of his mind; he remembered that persons emerging from epileptic fits were not responsible for their actions, and might be, and often were, dangerous.

'Mary!' said Hales again.

Victory and the lives of a hundred men depended on silencing Hales, and silencing him instantly. Hornblower thought of the pistol in his belt, and of using the butt, but there was another weapon more conveniently to his hand. He unshipped the tiller, a three-foot bar of solid oak, and he swung it with all the venom and fury of despair. The tiller crashed down on Hales' head, and Hales, an unuttered word cut short in his throat, fell silent in the bottom of the boat. There was no sound from the boat's crew, save for something like a sigh from Jackson, whether approving or disapproving Hornblower neither knew nor cared. He had done his duty, and he was certain of it. He had struck down a helpless idiot; most probably he had killed him, but the surprise upon which the success of the expedition depended had not been imperilled. He reshipped the tiller and resumed the silent task of keeping in the wake of the gigs.

Far away ahead—in the darkness it was impossible to estimate the distance—there was a nucleus of greater darkness, close on the surface of the black water. It might be the corvette. A dozen more strokes, and Hornblower was sure of it. Soames had done a magnificent job of pilotage, leading the boats straight to that objective. The cutter and launch were diverging now from the two gigs. The four boats were separating in readiness to launch their simultaneous converging attack.

'Easy!' whispered Hornblower, and the jolly boat's crew ceased to pull.

Hornblower had his orders. He had to wait until the attack had gained a foothold on the deck. His hand clenched convulsively on the tiller; the excitement of dealing with Hales had driven the thought of having to ascend strange rigging in the darkness clear out of his head, and now it recurred with redoubled urgency. Hornblower was afraid.

Although he could see the corvette, the boats had vanished from his sight, had passed out of his field of vision. The corvette rode to her anchor, her spars just visible against the night sky—that was where he had to climb! She seemed to tower up hugely. Close by the corvette he saw a splash in the dark water—the boats were closing in fast and someone's stroke had been a little careless. At the same moment came a shout from the corvette's deck, and when the shout was repeated it was echoed a hundredfold from the boats rushing alongside. The yelling was lusty and prolonged, of set purpose. A sleeping enemy would be bewildered by the din, and the progress of the shouting would tell each boat's crew of the extent of the success of the others. The British seamen were yelling like madmen. A flash and a bang from the corvette's deck told of the firing of the first shot; soon pistols were popping and muskets banging from several points of the deck.

'Give way!' said Hornblower. He uttered the order as if it had been tore from him by the rack.

The jolly boat moved forward, while Hornblower fought down his feelings and tried to make out what was going on on board. He could see no reason for choosing either side of the corvette in preference to the other, and the larboard side was the nearer, and so he steered the boat to the larboard main-chains. So interested was he in what he was doing that he only remembered in the nick of time to give the order, 'In oars'. He put the tiller over and the boat swirled round and the bowman hooked on. From the deck just above came a noise exactly like a tinker hammering on a cooking-pot—Hornblower noted the curious noise as he stood up in the stern sheets. He felt the cutlass at his side and the pistol in his belt, and then he sprang for the chains. With a mad leap he reached them and hauled himself up. The shrouds came into his hands, his feet found the ratlines beneath them, and he began to climb. As his head cleared the bulwark and he could see the deck the flash of a pistol shot illuminated the scene momentarily, fixing the struggle on the deck in a static moment, like a picture. Before and below him a British seaman was fighting a furious cutlass duel with a French officer, and he realized with vague astonishment that the kettle-mending noise he had heard was the sound of cutlass against cutlass —that clash of steel against steel that poets wrote about. So much for romance.

The realization carried him far up the shrouds. At his elbow he felt the futtock shrouds and he transferred himself to them, hanging back downward with his toes hooked into the ratlines and his hands clinging like death. That only lasted for two or three desperate seconds, and then he hauled himself on to the topmast shrouds and began the final ascent, his lungs bursting with the effort. Here was the topsail yard, and Hornblower flung himself across it and felt with his feet for the foot-rope. Merciful God! There was no foot-rope—his feet searching in the darkness met only unresisting air. A hundred feet above the deck he hung, squirming and kicking like a baby held up at arm's length in his father's hands. There was no foot-rope; it may have been with this very situation in mind that the Frenchmen had removed it. There was no foot-rope, so that he

D*

could not make his way out to the yard-arm. Yet the gaskets must be cast off and the sail loosed—everything depended on that. Hornblower had seen dare-devil seamen run out along the yards standing upright, as though walking a tightrope. That was the only way to reach the yard-arm now.

For a moment he could not breathe as his weak flesh revolted against the thought of walking along that yard above the black abyss. This was fear, the fear that stripped a man of his manhood, turning his bowels to water and his limbs to paper. Yet his furiously active mind continued to work. He had been resolute enough in dealing with Hales. Where he personally was not involved he had been brave enough; he had not hesitated to strike down the wretched epileptic with all the strength of his arm. That was the poor sort of courage he was capable of displaying. In the simple, vulgar matter of physical bravery he was utterly wanting. This was cowardice, the sort of thing that men spoke about behind their hands to other men. He could not bear the thought of that in himself—it was worse (awful though the alternative might be) than the thought of falling through the night to the deck. With a gasp he brought his knee up on to the yard, heaving himself up until he stood upright. He felt the rounded, canvas-covered timber under his feet, and his instincts told him not to dally there for a moment.

'Come on, men!' he yelled, and he dashed out along the yard.

It was twenty feet to the yard-arm, and he covered the distance in a few frantic strides. Utterly reckless by now, he put his hands down on the yard, clasped it, and laid his body across it again, his hands seeking the gaskets. A thump on the yard told him that Oldroyd, who had been detailed to come after him, had followed him out along the yard—he had six feet less to go. There could be no doubt that the other members of the jolly boat's crew were on the yard, and that Clough had led the way to the starboard yard-arm. It was obvious from the rapidity with which the sail came loose. Here was the brace beside him. Without any thought of danger now, for he was delirious with excitement and triumph, he grasped it with both hands and jerked himself off the yard. His waving legs found the rope and twined about it, and he let himself slide down it.

Fool that he was! Would he never learn sense and prudence? Would he never remember that vigilance and precaution must never be relaxed? He had allowed himself to slide so fast that the rope seared his hands, and when he tried to tighten his grip so as to slow down his progress it cause him such agony that he had to relax it again and slide on down with the rope stripping the skin from his hands as though peeling off a glove. His feet reached the deck and he momentarily forgot the pain as he looked round him.

There was the faintest grey light beginning to show now, and there were no sounds of battle. It had been a well-worked surprise—a hundred men flung suddenly on the deck of the corvette had swept away the anchor watch and mastered the vessel in a single rush before the watch below could come up to offer any resistance. Chadd's stentorian voice came pealing from the forecastle.

'Cable's cut, sir!'

Then Eccles bellowed from aft.

'Mr Hornblower!'

'Sir!' yelled Hornblower.

'Man the halliards!'

A rush of men came to help—not only his own boat's crew but every man of initiative and spirit. Halliards, sheets and braces; the sail was trimmed round and was drawing full in the light southerly air, and the *Papillon* swung round to go down with first of the ebb. Dawn was coming up fast, with a trifle of mist on the surface of the water.

Over the starboard quarter came a sullen bellowing roar, and then the misty air was torn by a series of infernal screams, supernaturally loud. The first cannon balls Hornblower ever heard were passing him by.

'Mr Chadd! Set the headsails! Loose the foretops'l. Get aloft, some of you, and set the mizzen tops'l.'

From the port bow came another salvo—Blaye was firing at them from one side, St Dye from the other, now they could guess what had happened on board the *Papillon*. But the corvette was moving fast with wind and tide, and it would be no easy matter to cripple her in the half light. It had been a very near-run thing; a few seconds' delay could have been fatal. Only one shot from the next salvo passed within hearing, and its passage was marked by a loud snap overhead.

'Mr Mallory, get that forestay spliced!'

'Aye aye, sir!'

It was light enough to look round the deck now; he could see Eccles at the break of the poop, directing the handling of the corvette, and Soames beside the wheel conning her down the channel. Two groups of red-coated marines, with bayonets fixed, stood guard over the hatchways. There were four or five men lying on the deck in curiously abandoned attitudes. Dead men; Hornblower could look at them with the callousness of youth. But there was a wounded man, too, crouched groaning over his shattered thigh—Hornblower could not look at him as disinterestedly, and he was glad, maybe only for his own sake, when at that moment a seaman asked for and received permission from Mallory to leave his duties and attend to him.

'Stand by to go about!' shouted Eccles from the poop; the corvette had reached the tip of the middle ground shoal and was about to make the turn that would carry her into the open sea.

The men came running to the braces, and Hornblower tailed on along with them. But the first contact with the harsh rope gave him such pain that he almost cried out. His hands were like raw meat, and fresh-killed at that, for blood was running from them. Now that his attention was called to them they smarted unbearably.

The headsheets came over, and the corvette went handily about.

'There's the old *Indy*!' shouted somebody.

The *Indefatigable* was plainly visible now, lying-to just out of shot from the shore batteries, ready to rendezvous with her prize. Somebody cheered, and the cheering was taking up by everyone, even while the last shots from St Dye, fired at extreme range, pitched sullenly into the water alongside. Hornblower had gingerly extracted his handkerchief from his pocket and was trying to wrap it round his hand.

'Can I help you with that, sir?' asked Jackson.

Jackson shook his head as he looked at the raw surface. 'You was careless, sir. You ought to 'a gone down 'and over 'and,' he said, when Hornblower explained to him how the injury had been caused. 'Very careless, you was, beggin' your pardon for saying so, sir. But you young gennelmen often is. You don't 'ave no thought for your necks, nor your 'ides, sir.'

Hornblower looked up at the maintopsail yard high

above his head, and remembered how he had walked along that slender stick of timber out to the yard-arm in the dark. At the recollection of it, even here with the solid deck under his feet, he shuddered a little.

'Sorry sir. Didn't mean to 'urt you,' said Jackson, tying the knot. 'There's, that's done, as good as I can do it, sir.'

'Thank you, Jackson,' said Hornblower.

'We got to report the jolly boat as lost, sir,' went on Jackson.

'Lost?'

'She ain't towing alongside, sir. You see, we didn't leave no boatkeeper in 'er. Wells, 'e was to be boatkeeper, you remember, sir. But I sent 'im up the rigging a'head o' me, seeing that 'Ales couldn't go. We wasn't too many for the job. So the jolly boat must a' come adrift, sir, when the ship went about.'

'What about Hales, then?' asked Hornblower.

''E was still in the boat, sir.'

Hornblower looked back up the estuary of the Gironde. Somewhere up there the jolly boat was drifting about, and lying in it was Hales, probably dead, possibly alive. In either case the French would find him, surely enough, but a cold wave of regret extinguished the warm feeling of triumph in Hornblower's bosom when he thought about Hales back there. If it had not been for Hales he would never have nerved himself (so at least he thought) to run out to the maintopsail yard-arm; he would at this moment be ruined and branded as coward instead of basking in the satisfaction of having capably done his duty.

Jackson saw the bleak look in his face.

'Don't you take on so, sir,' he said. 'They won't hold the loss of the jolly boat agin you, not the captain and Mr Eccles, they won't.'

'I wasn't thinking about the jolly boat,' said Hornblower. 'I was thinking about Hales.'

'Oh, im?' said Jackson. 'Don't you fret about 'im, sir. 'E would never 'ave made no seaman, not no 'ow.'

CHAPTER FIVE

THE MAN WHO SAW GOD

WINTER had come to the Bay of Biscay. With the passing of the Equinox the gales began to increase in violence, adding infinitely to the labours and dangers of the British Navy watching over the coast of France; easterly gales, bitter cold, which the storm-tossed ships had to endure as best they could, when the spray froze on the rigging and the labouring hulls leaked like baskets; westerly gales, when the ships had to claw their way to safety from a lee shore and make a risky compromise between gaining sufficient sea-room and maintaining a position from which they could pounce on any French vessel venturing out of harbour. The storm-tossed ships, we speak about. But those ships were full of storm-tossed men, who week by week and month by month had to endure the continual cold and the continual wet, the salt provisions, the endless toil, the boredom and misery of life in the blockading fleet. Even in the frigates, the eyes and claws of the blockaders, boredom had to be endured, the boredom of long periods with the hatches battened down, with the deck seams above dripping water on the men below, long nights and short days, broken sleep and yet not enough to do.

Even in the *Indefatigable* there was a feeling of restlessness in the air, and even a mere midshipman like Hornblower could be aware of it as he was looking over the men of his division before the captain's regular weekly inspection.

'What's the matter with your face, Styles?' he asked.

'Boils, sir. Awful bad.'

On Styles' cheeks and lips there were half a dozen dabs of sticking-plaster.

'Have you done anything about them?'

'Surgeon's mate, sir, 'e give me plaister for 'em, an' 'e says they'll soon come right, sir.'

'Very well.'

Now was there, or was there not, something strained about the expressions on the faces of the men on either side of Styles? Did they look like men smiling secretly to themselves? Laughing up their sleeves? Hornblower did not want to be an object of derision; it was bad for discipline—and it was worse for discipline if the men shared some secret unknown to their officers. He glanced sharply along the line again. Styles was standing like a block of wood, with no expression at all on his swarthy face; the black ringlets over his ears were properly combed, and no fault could be found with him. But Hornblower sensed that the recent conversation was a source of amusement to the rest of his division, and he did not like it.

After divisions he tackled Mr Low, the surgeon, in the gun-room.

'Boils?' said Low. 'Of course the men have boils. Salt pork and split peas for nine weeks on end—what d'you expect but boils? Boils—gurry sores—blains—all the plagues of Egypt.'

'On their faces?'

'That's one locality for boils. You'll find out others from your own personal experience.'

'Does your mate attend to them?' persisted Hornblower.

'Of course.'

'What's he like?'

'Muggridge?'

'Is that his name?'

'He's a good surgeon's mate. Get him to compound a black draught for you and you'll see. In fact, I'd prescribe one for you—you seem in a mighty bad temper, young man.'

Mr Low finished his glass of rum and pounded on the table for the steward. Hornblower realized that he was lucky to have found Low sober enough to give him even this much information, and turned away to go aloft so as to brood over the question in the solitude of the mizzen-top. This was his new station in action; when the men were not at their quarters a man might find a little blessed solitude there—something hard to find in the crowded *Indefatigable*. Bundled up in his peajacket, Hornblower sat in the mizzen-top; over his head the mizzen-topmast drew erratic circles against the grey sky; beside him the topmast shrouds sang their high-pitched note in the blustering gale, and below him the life of the ship went on as she rolled and pitched, standing to the northward under close-reefed topsails. At eight bells she would wear to the southward again on her incessant patrol. Until that time Hornblower was free to meditate on the boils on Styles' face and the covert grins on the faces of the other men of the division.

Two hands appeared on the stout wooden barricade surrounding the top, and as Hornblower looked up with annoyance at having his meditations interrupted a head appeared above them. It was Finch, another man in Horn-

blower's division, who also had his station in action here
in the mizzen-top. He was a frail little man with wispy hair
and pale blue eyes and a foolish smile, which lit up his
face when, after betraying some disappointment at finding
the mizzen-top already occupied, he recognized Hornblower.

'Beg pardon, sir,' he said. 'I didn't know as how you was
up here.'

Finch was hanging on uncomfortably, back downwards,
in the act of transferring himself from the futtock shrouds
to the top, and each roll threatened to shake him loose.

'Oh come here if you want to,' said Hornblower, cursing
himself for his soft-heartedness. A taut officer, he felt,
would have told Finch to go back whence he came and not
bother him.

'Thank 'ee, sir. Thank 'ee,' said Finch, bringing his leg
over the barricade and allowing the ship's roll to drop him
into the top.

He crouched down to peer under the foot of the mizzen-
topsail forward to the mainmast head, and then turned
back to smile disarmingly at Hornblower like a child
caught in moderate mischief. Hornblower knew that Finch
was a little weak in the head—the all-embracing press swept
up idiots and landsmen to help man the fleet—although
he was a trained seaman who could hand, reef and steer.
That smile betrayed him.

'It's better up here than down below, sir,' said Finch,
apologetically.

'You're right,' said Hornblower, with a disinterested
intonation which would discourage conversation.

He turned away to ignore Finch, settled his back again
comfortably, and allowed the steady swing of the top to
mesmerize him into dreamy thought that might deal with

his problem. Yet it was not easy, for Finch was as restless almost as a squirrel in a cage, peering forward, changing his position, and so continually breaking in on Hornblower's train of thought, wasting the minutes of his precious half-hour of freedom.

'What the devil's the matter with you, Finch?' he rasped at last, patience quite exhausted.

'The Devil, sir?' said Finch. 'It isn't the Devil. He's not up here, begging your pardon, sir.'

That weak, mysterious grin again, like a mischievous child. A great depth of secrets lay in those strange blue eyes. Finch peered under the topsail again; it was a gesture like a baby's playing peep-bo.

'There!' said Finch. 'I saw him that time, sir. God's come back to the maintop, sir.'

'God?'

'Aye indeed, sir. Sometimes He's in the maintop. More often than not, sir. I saw Him that time, with His beard all a-blowing in the wind. 'Tis only from here that you can see Him, sir.'

What could be said to a man with that sort of delusion? Hornblower racked his brains for an answer, and found none. Finch seemed to have forgotten his presence, and was playing peep-bo again under the foot of the mizzen-topsail.

'There He is!' said Finch to himself. 'There He is again! God's in the maintop, and the Devil's in the cable tier.'

'Very appropriate,' said Hornblower cynically, but to himself. He had no thought of laughing at Finch's delusions.

'The Devil's in the cable tier during the dog watches,' said Finch again to no one at all. 'God stays in the maintop for ever.'

'A curious time-table,' was Hornblower's *sotto voce* comment.

From down on the deck below came the first strokes of eight bells, and at the same moment the pipes of the bosun's mates began to twitter, and the bellow of Waldron the bos'un made itself heard.

'Turn out the watch below! All hands wear ship! All hands! All hands! You, master-at-arms, take the name of the last man up the hatchway. All hands!'

The interval of peace, short as it was, and broken by Finch's disturbing presence, was at an end. Hornblower dived over the barricade and gripped the futtock shrouds; not for him was the easy descent through the lubber's hole, not when the first lieutenant might see him and reprimand him for unseamanlike behaviour. Finch waited for him to quit the top, but even with this lengthy start Hornblower was easily outpaced in the descent to the deck, for Finch, like the skilled seaman he was, ran down the shrouds as lightly as a monkey. Then the thought of Finch's curious illusions was temporarily submerged in the business of laying the ship on her new course.

But later in the day Hornblower's mind reverted inevitably to the odd things Finch had been saying. There could be no doubt that Finch firmly believed he saw what he said he saw. Both his words and his expression made that certain. He had spoken about God's beard—it was a pity that he had not spared a few words to describe the Devil in the cable tier. Horns, cloven hoof, and pitchfork? Hornblower wondered. And why was the Devil only loose in the cable tier during the dog watches? Strange that he should keep to a time-table. Hornblower caught his breath as the sudden thought came to him that perhaps there might be some worldly explanation. The Devil might well be loose in the cable tier in a metaphorical fashion during the dog watches. Devil's work might be going on there. Hornblower had to decide on what was his duty; and he had to decide further on what was expedient. He could report his suspicions to Eccles, the first lieutenant; but after a year of service Hornblower was under no illusions about what might happen to a junior midshipman who worried a first lieutenant with unfounded suspicions. It would be better to see for himself first, as far as that went. But he did not know what he would find—if he should find anything at all —and he did not know how he should deal with it if he found anything. Much worse than that, he did not know if he would be able to deal with it in officer-like fashion. He could make a fool of himself. He might mishandle whatever situation he found, and bring down obloquy and derision upon his head, and he might imperil the discipline of the ship—weaken the slender thread of allegiance that bound officers and men together, the discipline which kept three hundred men at the bidding of their captain suffering untold hardship without demur; which made them ready to face death at the word of command. When eight bells told the end of the afternoon watch and the beginning of the first dog watch it was with trepidation that Hornblower went below to put a candle in a lantern and make his way forward to the cable tier.

It was dark down here, stuffy, odorous; and as the ship heaved and rolled he found himself stumbling over the various obstacles that impeded his progress. Yet forward there was a faint light, a murmur of voices. Hornblower choked down his fear that perhaps mutiny was being planned. He put his hand over the horn window of the lantern, so as to obscure its light, and crept forward. Two lanterns swung from the low deck-beams, and crouching under them were a score or more of men—more than that, even—and the buzz of their talk came loudly but indistinguishably to Hornblower's ears. Then the buzz increased to a roar, and someone in the centre of the circle rose suddenly to as near his full height as the deck-beams allowed. He was shaking himself violently from side to side for no apparent reason; his face was away from Hornblower, who saw with a gasp that his hands were tied behind him. The men roared again, like spectators at a prize-fight, and the man with his hands tied swung round so that Hornblower could see his face. It was Styles, the man who suffered from boils; Hornblower knew him at once. But that was not what made the most impression on Hornblower. Clinging to the man's face, weird in the shifting meagre light, was a grey writhing shape, and it was to shake this off that Styles was flinging himself about so violently. It was a rat; Hornblower's stomach turned over with horror.

With a wild jerk of his head Styles broke the grip of the rat's teeth and flung the creature down, and then instantly plunged down on his knees, with his hands still bound behind him, to pursue it with his own teeth.

'Time!' roared a voice at that moment—the voice of Partridge, bosun's mate. Hornblower had been roused by it often enough to recognize it at once.

'Five dead,' said another voice. 'Pay all bets of evens or better.'

Hornblower plunged forward. Part of the cable had been coiled down to make a rat pit ten feet across in which knelt Styles with dead and living rats about his knees. Partridge squatted beside the ring with a sandglass—used for timing the casting of the log—in front of him.

'Six dead,' protested someone. 'That 'un's dead.'

'No, he ain't.'

"Is back's broken. 'E's a dead 'un.'

"E ain't a dead 'un,' said Partridge.

The man who had protested looked up at that moment and caught sight of Hornblower, and his words died away unspoken; at his silence the others followed his glance and stiffened into rigidity, and Hornblower stepped forward. He was still wondering what he should do; he was still fighting down the nausea excited by the horrible things he had seen. Desperately he mastered his horror, and, thinking fast, took his stand on discipline.

'Who's in charge here?' he demanded.

He ran his eye round the circle. Petty officers and second-class warrant officers, mainly; bosuns' mates, carpenters' mates. Muggridge, the surgeon's mate—his presence explained much. But his own position was not easy. A midshipman of scant service depended for his authority on board largely on the force of his own personality. He was only a warrant officer himself; when all was said and done a midshipman was not nearly as important to the ship's economy—and was far more easily replaced—than, say, Washburn, the cooper's mate, over there, who knew all about the making and storage of the ship's water barrels.

'Who's in charge here?' he demanded again, and once more received no direct reply.

'We ain't on watch,' said a voice in the background.

Hornblower by now had mastered his horror; his indignation still flared within him, but he could appear outwardly calm.

'No, you're not on watch,' he said coldly. 'You're gambling.'

Muggridge took up the defence at that.

'Gambling, Mr Hornblower?' he said. 'That's a very

serious charge. Just a gentlemanly competition. You'll find it hard to sub—substantiate any charges of gambling.'

Muggridge had been drinking, quite obviously, following perhaps the example of the head of his department. There was always brandy to be got in the medical stores. A surge of wrath made Hornblower tremble; the effort necessary to keep himself standing stock still was almost too much for him. But the rise in internal pressure brought him inspiration.

'Mr Muggridge,' he said icily, 'I advise you not to say too much. There are other charges possible, Mr Muggridge. A member of His Maesty's forces can be charged with rendering himself unfit for service, Mr Muggridge. And similarly there might be charges of aiding and abetting which might include *you*. I should consult of the Articles of War if I were you, Mr Muggridge. The punishment for such an offence is flogging round the fleet I believe.'

Hornblower pointed to Styles, with the blood streaming from his bitten face, and gave more force to his argument by the gesture. He had met the men's arguments with a more effective one along the same lines; they had taken up a legalistic defence and he had legalistically beaten it down. He had the upper hand now and could give vent to his moral indignation.

'I could bring charges against every one of you,' he roared. 'You could be court-martialled—disrated—flogged —every man Jack of you. By God, one more look like that from you, Partridge, and I'll do it. You'd all be in irons five minutes after I spoke to Mr Eccles. I'll have no more of these filthy games. Let those rats loose, there you, Oldroyd, and you, Lewis. Styles, get your face plastered up again. You, Partridge, take these men and coil this cable down properly again before Mr Waldron sees it. I'll keep my eye on all of you in future. The next hint I have of misbehaviour and you'll all be at the gratings. I've said it, and by God I mean it!'

Hornblower was surprised both at his own volubility and at his self-possession. He had not known himself capable of carrying off matters with such a high hand. He sought about in his mind for a final salvo with which to make his retirement dignified, and it came to him as he turned away so that he turned back to deliver it.

'After this I want to see you in the dog watches sky-larking on deck, no skulking in the cable tiers like a lot of Frenchmen.'

That was the sort of speech to be expected of a pompous old captain, not a junior midshipman, but it served to give dignity to his retirement. There was a feverish buzz of voices as he left the group. Hornblower went up on deck, under the cheerless grey sky dark with premature night, to walk the deck to keep himself warm while the *Indefatigable* slashed her way to windward in the teeth of a roaring westerly, the spray flying in sheets over her bows, the straining seams leaking and her fabric groaning; the end of a day like all the preceding ones and the predecessor probably of innumerable more.

Yet the days passed, and with them came at last a break in the monotony. In the sombre dawn a hoarse bellow from the look-out turned every eye to windward, to where a dull blotch on the horizon marked the presence of a ship. The watch came running to the braces as the *Indefatigable* was laid as close to the wind as she would lie. Captain Pellew came on deck with a peajacket over his nightshirt, his wigless head comical in a pink nightcap; he trained his glass on the strange sail—a dozen glasses were pointing in that direction. Hornblower, looking through the glass reserved for the junior officer of the watch, saw the grey rectangle split into three, saw, the three grow narrow, and then broaden again to coalesce into a single rectangle again.

'She's gone about,' said Pellew. 'Hands 'bout ship!'

Round came the *Indefatigable* on the other tack; the watch raced aloft to shake out a reef from the topsails while from the deck the officers looked up at the straining canvas to calculate the chances of the gale which howled round their ears splitting the sails or carrying away a spar. The *Indefatigable* lay over until it was hard to keep one's footing on the streaming deck; everyone without immediate duties clung to the weather rail and peered at the other ship.

'Fore- and maintopmasts exactly equal,' said Lieutenant Bolton to Hornblower, his telescope to his eye. 'Topsails white as milady's fingers. She's a Frenchie all right.'

The sails of British ships were darkened with long service in all weathers; when a French ship escaped from harbour to run the blockade her spotless unweathered canvas disclosed her nationality without real need to take into consideration less obvious technical characteristics.

'We're weathering on her,' said Hornblower; his eye was aching with staring through the glass, and his arms even were weary with holding the telescope to his eye, but in the excitement of the chase he could not relax.

'Not as much as I'd like,' growled Bolton.

'Hands to the mainbrace!' roared Pellew at that moment.

It was a matter of the most vital concern to trim the sails so as to lie as close as possible to the wind; a hundred yards gained to windward would count as much as a mile gained in a stern chase. Pellew was looking up at the sails, back at the fleeting wake, across at the French ship, gauging the strength of the wind, estimating the strain on the rigging, doing everything that a lifetime of experience could suggest to close the gap between the two ships. Pellew's next order sent all hands to run out the guns on the weather side; that would in part counteract the heel and give the *Indefatigable* more grip upon the water.

'Now we're walking up to her,' said Bolton with grudging optimism.

'Beat to quarters!' shouted Pellew.

The ship had been expecting that order. The roar of the marine bandsmen's drums echoed through the ship; the pipes twittered as the bosun's mates repeated the order, and the men ran in disciplined fashion to their duties. Hornblower, jumping for the weather mizzen shrouds, saw the eager grins on half a dozen faces—battle and the imminent possibility of death were a welcome change from the eternal monotony of the blockade. Up in the mizzen-top he looked over his men. They were uncovering the locks of their muskets and looking to the priming; satisfied with their readiness for action, Hornblower turned his attention to the swivel gun. He took the tarpaulin from the breech and the tompion from the muzzle, cast off the lashings which secured it, and saw that the swivel moved freely in the socket and the trunnions freely in the crotch. A jerk of the lanyard showed him that the lock was sparkling well and there was no need for a new flint. Finch came climbing into the top with the canvas belt over his shoulder containing the charges for the gun; the bags of musket balls lay handy in a garland fixed to the barricade. Finch rammed home a cartridge down the short muzzle; Hornblower had ready a bag of balls to ram down on to it. Then he took a priming-quill and forced it down the touch-hole, feeling sensitively to make sure the sharp point pierced the thin serge bag of the cartridge. Priming-quill and flintlock were necessary up here in the top, where no slow match or port-fire could be used with the danger of fire so great and where fire would be so difficult to control in the sails and the rigging. Yet musketry and swivel-gun fire from the tops were an important tactical consideration. With the ships laid yard-arm to yard-arm, Hornblower's men could clear the hostile quarterdeck where centred the brains and control of the enemy.

'Stop that, Finch!' said Hornblower irritably; turning, he had caught sight of him peering up at the maintop and at this moment of tension Finch's delusions annoyed him.

'Beg your pardon, sir,' said Finch, resuming his duties.

But a moment later Hornblower heard Finch whispering to himself.

'Mr Bracegirdle's there,' whispered Finch, 'an' Oldroyd's there, an' all those others. But He's there too, so He is.'

'Hands wear ship!' came the shouted order from the deck below.

The old *Indefatigable* was spinning round on her heel, the yards groaning as the braces swung them round. The French ship had made a bold attempt to rake her enemy as she clawed up to her, but Pellew's prompt handling defeated the plan. Now the ships were broadside to broadside, running free before the wind at long cannon shot.

'Just look at 'im!' roared Douglas, one of the musket men in the top. 'Twenty guns a side. Looks brave enough, doesn't he?'

Standing beside Douglas, Hornblower could look down on the Frenchman's deck, her guns run out with the guns' crews clustering round them, officers in white breeches and blue coats walking up and down, the spray flying from her bows as she drove headlong before the wind.

'She'll look braver still when we take her into Plymouth Sound,' said the seaman on the far side of Hornblower.

The *Indefatigable* was slightly the faster ship; an occasional touch of starboard helm was working her in closer to the enemy, into decisive range, without allowing the Frenchman to head-reach upon her. Hornblower was impressed by the silence on both sides; he had always understood that the French were likely to open fire at long range and to squander ineffectively the first carefully loaded broadside.

'When's he goin' to fire?' asked Douglas, echoing Hornblower's thoughts.

'In his own good time,' piped Finch.

The gap of tossing water between the two ships was growing narrower. Hornblower swung the swivel gun round and looked along the sights. He could aim well enough at the Frenchmen's quarterdeck, but it was much too long a range for a bag of musket balls—in any case he dared not open fire until Pellew gave permission.

'Them's the men for us!' said Douglas, pointing to the Frenchman's mizzen-top.

It looked as if there were soldiers up there, judging by the blue uniforms and the crossbelts; the French often eked out their scanty crews of trained seamen by shipping soldiers; in the British Navy the marines were never employed aloft. The French soldiers saw the gesture and shook their fists, and a young officer among them drew his sword and brandished it over his head. With the ships parallel to each other like this the French mizzen-top would be Hornblower's particular objective should he decide on trying to silence the firing there instead of sweeping the quarterdeck. He gazed curiously at the men it was his duty to kill. So interested was he that the bang of a cannon took him by surprise; before he could look down the rest of the Frenchman's broadside had gone off in straggling fashion, and a moment later the *Indefatigable* lurched as all her guns went off together. The wind blew the smoke forward, so that in the mizzen-top they were not troubled by it at all. Hornblower's glance showed him dead men flung about on the *Indefatigable*'s deck, dead men falling on the Frenchman's deck. Still the range was too great—very long musket shot, his eye told him.

'They're shootin' at us, sir,' said Herbert.

'Let 'em,' said Hornblower.

No musket fired from a heaving masthead at that range could possibly score a hit; that was obvious—so obvious that even Hornblower, madly excited as he was, could not help but be aware of it, and his certainty was apparent in his tone. It was interesting to see how the two calm words steadied the men. Down below the guns were roaring away continuously, and the ships were nearing each other fast.

'Open fire now, men!' said Hornblower. 'Finch!'

He stared down the short length of the swivel gun. In the coarse V of the notch on the muzzle he could see the Frenchman's wheel, the two quartermasters standing behind it, the two officers beside it. He jerked the lanyard. A tenth of a second's delay, and then the gun roared out. He was conscious, before the smoke whirled round him, of the firing quill, blown from the touchhole, flying past his temple. Finch was already sponging out the gun. The musket balls must have spread badly; only one of the helmsmen was down and someone else was already running to take his place. At that moment the whole top lurched frightfully; Hornblower felt it but he could not explain it.

There was too much happening at once. The solid timbers under his feet jarred him as he stood—perhaps a shot had hit the mizzen-mast. Finch was ramming in the cartridge; something struck the breech of the gun a heavy blow and left a bright splash of metal there—a musket bullet from the Frenchman's mizzen-top. Hornblower tried to keep his head; he took out another sharpened quill and coaxed it down into the touchhole. It had to be done purposefully and yet gently; a quill broken off in the touchhole was likely to be a maddening nuisance. He felt the point of the quill pierce the cartridge; Finch rammed home the wad on top of the musket balls. A bullet struck the barricade beside him as Hornblower trained the gun down, but he gave it no thought. Surely the top was swaying more even than the heavy sea justified? No matter. He had a clear shot at the enemy's quarterdeck. He tugged at the lanyard. He saw men fall. He actually saw the spokes of the wheel spin round as it was left untended. Then the two ships came together with a shattering crash and his world dissolved into chaos compared with which what had gone before was orderly.

The mast was falling. The top swung round in a dizzy arc so that only his fortunate grip on the swivel saved him from being flung out like a stone from a sling. It wheeled round. With the shrouds on one side shot away and two cannon balls in its heart the mast tottered and rolled. Then the tug of the mizzen-stays inclined it forward, the tug of the other shrouds inclined it to starboard, and the wind in the mizzen-topsail took charge when the back stays parted. The mast crashed forward; the topmast caught against the mainyard and the whole structure hung there before it could dissolve into its constituent parts. The severed butt-end of the mast must be resting on the deck for the moment; mast and topmast were still united at the cap and the trestle-trees into one continuous length, although why the topmast had not snapped at the cap was hard to say. With the lower end of the mast resting precariously on the deck and the topmast resting against the mainyard, Hornblower and Finch still had a chance of life, but the ship's motion, another shot from the Frenchman, or the parting of the over-strained material could all end that chance. The mast could slip outwards, the topmast could break, the butt-end of the mast could slip along the deck—they had to save themselves if they could before any one of these imminent events occurred. The maintopmast and everything above it was involved in the general ruin. It too had fallen and was dangling, sail spars and ropes in one frightful tangle. The mizzen-topsail had torn itself free. Hornblower's eyes met Finch's; Finch and he were clinging to the swivel gun, and there was no one else in the steeply inclined top.

The starboard side mizzen-topmast shrouds still survived; they, as well as the topmast, were resting across the mainyard, strained taut as fiddle strings, the mainyard tightening them just as the bridge tightens the strings of a fiddle. But along those shrouds lay the only way to safety—a sloping path from the peril of the top to the comparative safety of the mainyard.

The mast began to slip, to roll, out towards the end of the yard. Even if the mainyard held, the mizzen-mast would soon fall into the sea alongside. All about them were thunderous noises—spars smashing, ropes parting; the guns were still bellowing and everyone below seemed to be yelling and screaming.

The top lurched again, frightfully. Two of the shrouds parted with the strain, with a noise clearly audible through the other din, and as they parted the mast twisted with a jerk, swinging further round the mizzen-top, the swivel gun, and the two wretched beings who clung to it. Finch's staring blue eyes rolled with the movement of the top. Later, Hornblower knew that the whole period of the fall of the mast was no longer than a few seconds, but at this time it seemed as if he had at least long minutes in which to think. Like Finch's, his eyes stared round him, saw the chance of safety.

'The mainyard!' he screamed.

Finch's face bore its foolish smile. Although instinct or training kept him gripping the swivel gun he seemingly had no fear, no desire to gain the safety of the main-yard.

'Finch, you fool!' yelled Hornblower.

He locked a desperate knee round the swivel so as to free a hand with which to gesticulate, but still Finch made no move.

'Jump, damn you!' raved Hornblower. 'The shrouds—the yard. Jump!'

Finch only smiled.

'Jump and get to the maintop! Oh, Christ——!' Inspiration came in that frightful moment. 'The maintop! God's there, Finch! Go along to God, quick!'

Those words penetrated into Finch's addled brain. He nodded with sublime unworldliness. Then he let go of the swivel and seemed to launch himself into the air like a frog. His body fell across the mizzen-topmast shrouds and he began to scramble along them. The mast rolled again, so that when Hornblower launched himself at the shrouds it was a longer jump. Only his shoulders reached the outer-most shroud. He swung off, clung, nearly lost his grip, but regained it as a counterlurch of the leaning mast came to

E

his assistance. Then he was scrambling along the shrouds, mad with panic. Here was the precious mainyard, and he threw himself across it, grappling its welcome solidity with his body, his feet feeling for the foot-rope. He was safe and steady on the yard just as the outward roll of the *Indefatigable* gave the balancing spars their final impetus, and the mizzen-topmast parted company from the broken mizzen-mast and the whole wreck fell down into the sea alongside. Hornblower shuffled along the yard, whither Finch had preceded him, to be received with rapture in the maintop by Midshipman Bracegirdle. Bracegirdle was not God, but as Hornblower leaned across the breastwork of the maintop he thought to himself that if he had not spoken about God being in the maintop Finch would never have made that leap.

'Thought we'd lost you,' said Bracegirdle, helping him in and thumping him on the back. 'Midshipman Hornblower, our flying angel.'

Finch was in the top, too, smiling his fool's smile and surrounded by the crew of the top. Everything seemed mad and exhilarating. It was a shock to remember that they were in the midst of a battle, and yet the firing had ceased, and even the yelling had almost died away. He staggered to the side of the top—strangely how difficult it was to walk—and looked over. Bracegirdle came with him. Foreshortened by the height he could make out a crowd of figures on the Frenchman's deck. Those check shirts must surely be worn by British sailors. Surely that was Eccles, the *Indefatigable*'s first lieutenant, on the quarterdeck with a speaking trumpet.

'What has happened?' he asked Bracegirdle, bewildered.

'What has happened?' Bracegirdle stared for a moment before he understood. 'We carried her by boarding. Eccles and the boarders were over the ship's side the moment we touched. Why, man, didn't you see?'

'No, I didn't see it,' said Hornblower. He forced himself to joke. 'Other matters demanded my attention at that moment.'

He remembered how the mizzen-top had lurched and swung, and he felt suddenly sick. But he did not want Bracegirdle to see it.

'I must go on deck and report,' he said.

The descent of the main shrouds was a slow, ticklish business, for neither his hands nor his feet seemed to wish to go where he tried to place them. Even when he reached the deck he still felt insecure. Bolton was on the quarter-deck supervising a clearing away of the wreck of the mizzen-mast. He gave a start of surprise as Hornblower approached.

'I thought you were overside with Davy Jones,' he said. He glanced aloft. 'You reached the mainyard in time?'

'Yes, sir.'

'Excellent. I think you're born to be hanged, Hornblower.' Bolton turned away to bellow at the men. "Vast heaving, there! Clynes, get down into the chains with that tackle! Steady, now, or you'll lose it.'

He watched the labours of the men for some moments before the turned back to Hornblower.

'No more trouble with the men for a couple of months,' he said. 'We'll work 'em 'til they drop, refitting. Prize crew will leave us shorthanded, to say nothing of our butcher's bill. It'll be a long time before they want something new. It'll be a long time for you, too, I fancy, Hornblower.'

'Yes, sir,' said Hornblower.

CHAPTER SIX

THE FROGS AND THE LOBSTERS

'They're coming,' said Midshipman Kennedy.

Midshipman Hornblower's unmusical ear caught the raucous sounds of a military band, and soon, with a gleam of scarlet and white and gold, the head of the column came round the corner. The hot sunshine was reflected from the brass instruments; behind them the regimental colour flapped from its staff, borne proudly by an ensign with the colour guard round him. Two mounted officers rode behind the colour, and after them came the long red serpent of the half-battalion, the fixed bayonets flashing in the sun, while all the children of Plymouth, still not sated with military pomp, ran along with them.

The sailors standing ready on the quay looked at the soldiers marching up curiously, with something of pity and something of contempt mingled with their curiosity. The rigid drill, the heavy clothing, the iron discipline, the dull routine of the soldier were in sharp contrast with the far more flexible conditions in which the sailor lived. The sailors watched as the band ended with a flourish, and one of the mounted officers wheeled his horse to face the column. A shouted order turned every man to face the quayside, the movements being made so exactly together that five hundred boot-heels made a single sound. A huge sergeant-major, his sash gleaming on his chest, and the silver mounting of his cane winking in the sun, dressed the already perfect line. A third order brought down every musket-butt to earth.

'Unfix—bayonets!' roared the mounted officer, uttering the first words Hornblower had understood.

Hornblower positively goggled at the ensuing formalities, as the fuglemen strode their three paces forward, all exactly to time like marionettes worked by the same strings, turned their heads to look down the line, and gave the time for detaching the bayonets, for sheathing them, and for returning the muskets to the men's sides. The fuglemen fell back into their places, exactly to time again as far as Hornblower could see, but not exactly enough apparently, as the sergeant-major bellowed his discontent and brought the fuglemen out and sent them back again.

'I'd like to see him laying aloft on a stormy night,' muttered Kennedy. 'D'ye think he could take the maintops'l ear-ring?'

'These lobsters!' said Midshipman Bracegirdle.

The scarlet lines stood rigid, all five companies, the sergeants with their halberds indicating the intervals—from halberd to halberd the line of faces dipped down and then up again, with the men exactly sized off, the tallest men at the flanks and the shortest men in the centre of each company. Not a finger moved, not an eyebrow twitched. Down every back hung rigidly a powdered pigtail.

The mounted officer trotted down the line to where the naval party waited, and Lieutenant Bolton, in command, stepped forward with his hand to his hat rim.

'My men are ready to embark, sir,' said the army officer. 'The baggage will be here immediately.'

'Aye aye, major,' said Bolton—the army title and the navy reply in strange contrast.

'It would be better to address me as "My Lord",' said the major.

'Aye aye, sir—my lord,' replied Bolton, caught quite off his balance.

His Lordship, the Earl of Edrington, major commanding this wing of the 43rd Foot, was a heavily built young man in his early twenties. He was a fine soldierly figure in his well-fitting uniform, and mounted on a magnificent charger, but he seemed a little young for his present responsible command. But the practice of the purchase of commissions was liable to put very young men in high command, and the Army seemed satisfied with the system.

'The French auxiliaries have their orders to report here,' went on Lord Edrington. 'I suppose arrangements have been made for their transport as well?'

'Yes, my lord.'

'Not one of the beggars can speak English, as far as I can make out. Have you got an officer to interpret?'

'Yes, sir. Mr Hornblower!'

'Sir!'

'You will attend to the embarkation of the French troops.'

'Aye aye, sir.'

More military music—Hornblower's tone-deaf ear distinguished it as making a thinner noise than the British infantry band—heralded the arrival of the Frenchmen farther down the quay by a side road, and Hornblower hastened there. This was the Royal, Christian, and Catholic French Army, or a detachment of it at least—a battalion of the force raised by the émigré French nobles to fight against the Revolution. There was the white flag with the golden lilies at the head of the column, and a group of mounted officers to whom Hornblower touched his hat. One of them acknowledged his salute.

'The Marquis of Pouzauges, Brigadier General in the

service of His Most Christian Majesty Louis XVII,' said this individual in French by way of introduction. He wore a glittering white uniform with a blue ribbon across it.

Stumbling over the French words, Hornblower introduced himself as an aspirant of His Britannic Majesty's Marine, deputed to arrange the embarkation of the French troops.

'Very good,' said Pouzauges. 'We are ready.'

Hornblower looked down the French column. The men were standing in all attitudes, gazing about them. They were all well enough dressed, in blue uniforms which Hornblower guessed had been supplied by the British government, but the white crossbelts were already dirty, the metalwork tarnished, the arms dull. Yet doubtless they could fight.

'Those are the transports allotted to your men, sir,' said Hornblower, pointing. 'The *Sophia* will take three hundred, and the *Dumbarton*—that one over there—will take two hundred and fifty. Here at the quay are the lighters to ferry the men out.'

'Give the orders, M. de Moncoutant,' said Pouzauges to one of the officers beside him.

The hired baggage carts had now come creaking up along the column, piled high with the men's kits, and the column broke into chattering swarms as the men hunted up their possessions. It was some time before the men were re-assembled, each with his own kit-bag; and then there arose the question of detailing a fatigue party to deal with the regimental baggage, and the men who were given the task yielded up their bags with obvious reluctance to their comrades, clearly in despair of ever seeing any of the contents again. Hornblower was still giving out information.

'All horses must go to the *Sophia*,' he said. 'She has accommodation for six chargers. The regimental baggage——'

He broke off short, for his eye had been caught by a singular jumble of apparatus lying in one of the carts.

'What is that, if you please?' he asked, curiosity overpowering him.

'That, sir,' said Pouzauges, 'is a guillotine.'

'A guillotine?'

Hornblower had read much lately about this instrument. The Red Revolutionaries had set one up in Paris and kept it hard at work. The King of France, Louis XVI himself, had died under it. He did not expect to find one in the train of a counter-revolutionary army.

'Yes,' said Pouzauges, 'we take it with us to France. It is in my mind to give those anarchists a taste of their own medicine.'

Hornblower did not have to make reply, fortunately, as a bellow from Bolton interrupted the conversation.

'What the hell's all this delay for, Mr Hornblower? D'you want us to miss the tide?'

It was of course typical of life in any service that Hornblower should be reprimanded for the time wasted by the inefficiency of the French arrangements—that was the sort of thing he had already come to expect, and he had already learned that it was better to submit silently to reprimand than to offer excuses. He addressed himself again to the task of getting the French aboard their transports. It was a weary midshipman who at last reported himself to Bolton with his tally sheets and the news that the last Frenchman and horse and pieces of baggage were safely aboard, and he was greeted with the order to get his things together quickly and transfer them and himself to the *Sophia*, where his services as interpreter were still needed.

The convoy dropped quickly down Plymouth Sound, rounded the Eddystone, and headed down-channel, with H.M.S. *Indefatigable* flying her distinguishing pennant, the two gun-brigs which had been ordered to assist in convoying the expedition, and the four transports—a small enough force, it seemed to Hornblower, with which to attempt the overthrow of the French republic. There were only eleven hundred infantry; the half-battalion of the 43rd and the weak battalion of Frenchmen (if they could be called that, seeing that many of them were soldiers of fortune of all nations) and, although Hornblower had enough sense not to try to judge the Frenchmen as they lay in rows in the dark and stinking 'tweendecks in the agonies of seasickness, he was puzzled that anyone could expect results from such a small force. His historical reading had told him of many small raids, in many wars, launched against the shores of France, and although he knew that they had once been described by an opposition statesman as 'breaking windows with guineas' he had been inclined to approve of them in principle, as bringing about a dissipation of the French strength—until now, when he found himself part of such an expedition.

So it was with relief that he heard from Pouzauges that the troops he had seen did not constitute the whole of the force to be employed—were indeed only a minor fraction of it. A little pale with seasickness, but manfully combating it, Pouzauges laid out a map on the cabin table and explained the plan.

'The Christian Army,' explained Pouzauges, 'will land here, at Quiberon. They sailed from Portsmouth—these English names are hard to pronounce—the day before we

E*

left Plymouth. There are five thousand men under the Baron de Charette. They will march on Vannes and Rennes.'

'And what is your regiment to do?' asked Hornblower.

Pouzauges pointed to the map again.

'Here is the town of Muzillac,' he said. 'Twenty leagues from Quiberon. Here the main road from the south crosses the river Marais, where the tide ceases to flow. It is only a little river, as you see, but its banks are marshy, and the road passes it not only by a bridge but by a long causeway. The rebel armies are to the south, and on their northward march must come by Muzillac. We shall be there. We shall destroy the bridge and defend the crossing, delaying the rebels long enough to enable M. de Charette to raise all Brittany. He will soon have twenty thousand men in arms, the rebels will come back to their allegiance, and we shall march on Paris to restore His Most Christian Majesty to the throne.'

So that was the plan. Hornblower was infected with the Frenchmen's enthusiasm. Certainly the road passed within ten miles of the coast, and there, in the broad estuary of the Vilaine, it should be possible to land a small force and seize Muzillac. There should be no difficulty about defending a causeway such as Pouzauges described for a day or two against even a large force. That would afford Charette every chance.

'My friend M. de Moucoutant here,' went on Pouzauges, 'is Lord of Muzillac. The people there will welcome him.'

'Most of them will,' said Moucoutant, his grey eyes narrowing. 'Some will be sorry to see me. But I shall be glad of the encounter.'

Western France, the Vendée and Brittany, had long been

in a turmoil, and the population there, under the leadership of the nobility, had risen in arms more than once against the Paris government. But every rebellion had ended in defeat; the Royalist force now being convoyed to France was composed of the fragments of the defeated armies—a final cast of the dice, and a desperate one. Regarded in that light, the plan did not seem so sound.

It was a grey morning—a morning of grey sky and grey rocks—when the convoy rounded Belle Ile and stood in towards the estuary of the Vilaine river. Far to the northward were to be seen white topsails in Quiberon Bay—Hornblower, from the deck of the *Sophia*, saw signals pass back and forth from the *Indefatigable* as she reported her arrival to the senior officer of the main expedition there. It was a proof of the mobility and ubiquity of naval power that it could take advantage of the configuration of the land so that two blows could be struck almost in sight of each other from the sea yet separated by forty miles of roads on land. Hornblower raked the forbidding shore with his glass, re-read the orders for the captain of the *Sophia*, and stared again at the shore. He could distinguish the narrow mouth of the Marais river and the strip of mud where the troops were to land. The lead was going in the chains as the *Sophia* crept towards her allotted anchorage, and the ship was rolling uneasily; these waters, sheltered though they were, were a Bedlam of conflicting currents that could make a choppy sea even in a calm. Then the anchor cable rumbled out through the hawsehole and the *Sophia* swung to the current, while the crew set to work hoisting out the boats.

'France, dear beautiful France,' said Pouzauges at Hornblower's side.

A hail came over the water from the *Indefatigable*.

'Mr Hornblower!'

'Sir!' yelled Hornblower back through the captain's megaphone.

'You will go on shore with the French troops and stay with them until you receive further orders.'

'Aye aye, sir.'

So that was the way in which he was to set foot on foreign soil for the first time in his life.

Pouzauge's men were now pouring up from below; it was a slow and exasperating business getting them down the ship's side into the waiting boats. Hornblower wondered idly regarding what was happening on shore at this moment—without doubt mounted messengers were galloping north and south with the news of the arrival of the expedition, and soon the French Revolutionary generals would be parading their men and marching them hurriedly towards this place; it was well that the important strategic point that had to be seized was less than ten miles inland. He turned back to his duties; as soon as the men were ashore he would have to see that the baggage and reserve ammunition were landed, as well as the horses, now standing miserably in improvised stalls forward of the mainmast.

The first boats had left the ship's side; Hornblower watched the men stagger up the shore through mud and water, the French on the left and the red-coated British infantry on the right. There were some fishermen's cottages in sight up the beach, and Hornblower saw advance parties go forward to seize them; at least the landing had been effected without a single shot being fired. He came on shore with the ammunition, to find Bolton in charge of the beach.

'Get those ammunition boxes well above high-water

mark,' said Bolton. 'We can't send 'em forward until the Lobsters have found us some carts for 'em. And we'll need horses for those guns too.'

At that moment Bolton's working party was engaged in manhandling two six-pounder guns in field carriages up the beach; they were to be manned by seamen and drawn by horses commandeered by the landing party, for it was in the old tradition that a British expeditionary force should always be thrown on shore dependent for military necessities on the countryside. Pouzauges and his staff were waiting impatiently for their chargers, and mounted them the moment they had been coaxed out of the boats on to the beach.

'Forward for France!' shouted Pouzauges, drawing his sword and raising the hilt to his lips.

Moncoutant and the others clattered forward to head the advancing infantry, while Pouzauges lingered to exchange a few words with Lord Edrington. The British infantry was drawn up in a rigid scarlet line; farther inland occasional red dots marked where the light company had been thrown forward as pickets. Hornblower could not hear the conversation, but he noticed that Bolton was drawn into it, and finally Bolton called him over.

'You must go forward with the Frogs, Hornblower,' he said.

'I'll give you a horse,' added Edrington. 'Take that one—the roan. I've got to have someone I can trust along with them. Keep your eye on them and let me know the moment they get up to any monkey tricks—God knows what they'll do next.'

'Here's the rest of your stores coming ashore,' said Bolton. 'I'll send 'em up as soon as you send some carts back to me. What the hell's *that*?'

'That's a portable guillotine, sir,' said Hornblower. 'Part of the French baggage.'

All three turned and looked at Pouzauges, sitting his horse impatiently during this conversation, which he did not understand. He knew what they were referring to, all the same.

'That's the first thing to be sent to Muzillac,' he said to Hornblower. 'Will you have the goodness to tell these gentlemen so?'

Hornblower translated.

'I'll send the guns and a load of ammunition first,' said Bolton. 'But I'll see he gets it soon. Now off you go.'

Hornblower dubiously approached the roan horse. All he knew about riding he had learned in farmyards, but he got his foot up into the stirrup and climbed in the saddle, grabbing nervously at the reins as the animal started to move off. It seemed as far down to the ground from there as it did from the maintopgallant yard. Pouzauges wheeled his horse about and started up the beach, and the roan followed its example, with Hornblower hanging on desperately, spattered by the mud thrown up by the French horse's heels.

From the fishing hamlet a muddy lane, bordered by green turf banks, led inland, and Pouzauges trotted smartly along it, Hornblower jolting behind him. They covered three or four miles before they overtook the rear of the French infantry, marching rapidly through the mud, and Pouzauges pulled his horse to a walk. When the column climbed a slight undulation they could see the white banner far ahead. Over the banks Hornblower could see rocky fields; out on the left there was a small farmhouse of grey stone. A blue-uniformed soldier was leading away a white horse pulling a cart, while two or three more soldiers were holding back the farmer's frantic wife. So the expeditionary force had secured some of its necessary transport. In another field a soldier was prodding a cow along with his bayonet—Hornblower could not imagine with what motive. Twice he heard distant musket shots to which no one seemed to pay any attention. Then, coming down the road, they encountered two soldiers leading bony horses towards the beach; the jests hurled at them by the marching column had set the men's faces in broad grins. But a little way farther on Hornblower saw a plough standing lonely in a little field, and a grey bundle lying near it. The bundle was a dead man.

Over on their right was the marshy river valley, and it was not long before Hornblower could see, far ahead, the bridge and the causeway which they had been sent to seize. The lane they were following came down a slight incline into the town, passing between a few grey cottages before emerging into the highroad along which there lay the town. There was a grey stone church, there was a building that could easily be identified as an inn and postinghouse with soldiers swarming round it, a slight broadening of the highroad, with an avenue of trees, which Hornblower assumed must be the central square of the town. A few faces peered from upper windows, but otherwise the houses were shut and there were no civilians to be seen except two women hastily shuttering their shops. Pouzauges reined up his horse in the square and began issuing orders. Already the horses were being led out of the posthouse, and groups of men were bustling to and fro on seemingly urgent errands. In obedience to Pouzauges one officer called his men together—he had to expostulate and gesticulate before he succeeded—and started towards the bridge.

Another party started along the highway in the opposite
direction to guard against the possible surprise attack from
there. A crowd of men squatted in the square devouring
the bread that was brought out from one of the shops after
its door had been beaten in, and two or three times civilians
were dragged up to Pouzauges and at his orders were
hurried away again to the town jail. The seizure of the
town of Muzillac was complete.

Pouzauges seemed to think so, too, after an interval, for,
with a glance at Hornblower, he turned his horse and
trotted towards the causeway. The town ended before the
road entered the marshes, and in a bit of waste ground
beside the road the party sent out in this direction had
already lighted a fire, and the men were gathered round it,
toasting on their bayonets chunks of meat cut from a cow
whose half-flayed corpse lay beside the fire. Farther on,
where the causeway became the bridge over the river, a
sentry sat sunning himself, with his musket leaning against
the parapet of the bridge at his back. Everything was peaceful enough. Pouzauges trotted as far as the crown of the
bridge, with Hornblower beside him, and looked over the
country on the farther side. There was no sign of any
enemy, and when they returned there was a mounted red-
coated soldier waiting for them—Lord Edrington.

'I've come to see for myself,' he said. 'The position looks
strong enough in all conscience here. Once you have the
guns posted you should be able to hold this bridge until
you can blow up the arch. But there's a ford, passable at
low water, half a mile lower down. That is where I shall
station myself—if we lose the ford they can turn the whole
position and cut us off from the shore. Tell this gentleman
—what's his name?—what I said.'

Hornblower translated as well as he could, and stood by

as interpreter while the two commanders pointed here and there and settled their respective duties.

'That's settled, then,' said Edrington at length. 'Don't forget, Mr Hornblower, that I must be kept informed of every development.'

He nodded to them and wheeled his horse and trotted off. As he left, a cart approached from the direction of Muzillac, while behind it a loud clanking heralded the arrival of the two six-pounders, each drawn painfully by a couple of horses led by seamen. Sitting upon the front of the cart was Midshipman Bracegirdle, who saluted Hornblower with a broad grin.

'From quarterdeck to dung cart is no more than a step,' he announced, swinging himself down. 'From midshipman to captain of artillery.'

He looked along the causeway and then around him.

'Put the guns over there and they'll sweep the whole length,' suggested Hornblower.

'Exactly,' said Bracegirdle.

Under his orders the guns were wheeled off the road and pointed along the causeway, and the dung cart was unloaded of its contents, a tarpaulin spread on the ground, the gunpowder cartridges laid on it and covered with another tarpaulin. The shot and the bags of grape were piled beside the guns, the seamen working with a will under the stimulus of their novel surroundings.

'Poverty brings strange bedfellows,' said Bracegirdle. 'And wars strange duties. Have you ever blown up a bridge?'

'Never,' said Hornblower.

'Neither have I. Come, and let us do it. May I offer you a place in my carriage?'

Hornblower climbed up into the cart with Bracegirdle,

and two seamen led the plodding horse along the causeway to the bridge. There they halted and looked down at the muddy water—running swiftly with the ebb—craning their heads over the parapet to look at the solid stone construction.

'It is the keystone of the arch which we should blow out,' said Bracegirdle.

That was the proverbial recipe for the destruction of a bridge, but as Hornblower looked from the bridge to Bracegirdle and back again the idea did not seem easy to execute. Gunpowder exploded upwards and had to be held in on all sides—how was that to be done under the arch of the bridge?

'What about the pier?' he asked tentatively.

'We can but look and see,' said Bracegirdle, and turned to the seaman by the cart. 'Hannay, bring a rope.'

They fastened the rope to the parapet and slid down it to a precarious foothold on the slippery ledge round the base of the pier, the river gurgling at their feet.

'That seems to be the solution,' said Bracegirdle, crouching almost double under the arch.

Time slipped by fast as they made their preparations; a working party had to be brought from the guard of the bridge, picks and crowbars had to be found or extemporized, and some of the huge blocks with which the pier was built had to be picked out at the shoulder of the arch. Two kegs of gunpowder, lowered gingerly from above, had to be thrust into the holes so formed, a length of slow match put in at each bung-hole and led to the exterior, while the kegs were tamped into their caves with all the stones and earth that could be crammed into them. It was almost twilight under the arch when the work was finished, and the working party made laboriously to climb the rope up to the bridge and Bracegirdle and Hornblower left to look at each other again.

'I'll fire the fuses,' said Bracegirdle. 'You go next, sir.'

It was not a matter for much argument. Bracegirdle was under orders to destroy the bridge, and Hornblower addressed himself to climbing up the rope while Bracegirdle took his tinderbox from his pocket. Once on the roadway of the bridge Hornblower sent away the cart and waited. It was only two or three minutes before Bracegirdle appeared, frantically climbing the rope and hurling himself over the parapet.

'Run!' was all that was said.

Together they scurried down the bridge and halted breathless to crouch by the abutment of the causeway. Then came a dull explosion, a tremor of the earth under their feet, and a cloud of smoke.

'Let's come and see,' said Bracegirdle.

They retraced their steps towards where the bridge was still shrouded in smoke and dust.

'Only partly——' began Bracegirdle as they neared the scene and the dust cleared away.

And at that moment there was a second explosion which made them stagger as they stood. A lump of the road-bed hit the parapet beside them and burst like a shell, spattering them with fragments. There was a rumble and a clatter as the arch subsided into the river.

'That must have been the second keg going off,' said Bracegirdle, wiping his face. 'We should have remembered the fuses were likely to be of different lengths. Two promising careers might have ended suddenly if we had been any nearer.'

'At any rate, the bridge is gone,' said Hornblower.

'All's well that ends well,' said Bracegirdle.

Seventy pounds of gunpowder had done their work. The bridge was cut clear across, leaving a ragged gap several feet wide, beyond which the roadway reached out towards the gap from the farther pier as a witness to the toughness of the mortar. Beneath their feet as they peered over they could see the riverbed almost choked with lumps of stone.

'We'll need no more than an anchor watch to-night,' said Bracegirdle.

Hornblower looked round to where the roan horse was tethered; he was tempted to return to Muzillac on foot, leading the animal, but shame forbade. He climbed with an effort into the saddle and headed the animal back up the road; ahead of him the sky was beginning to turn red with the approach of sunset.

He entered the main street of the town and rounded the slight bend to the central square, to see something that made him, without his own volition, tug at his reins and halt his horse. The square was full of people, townsfolk and soldiers, and in the centre of the square a tall narrow rectangle reached upwards towards the sky with a glittering blade at its upper end. The blade fell with a reverberating thump, and the little group of men round the base of the rectangle dragged something to one side and added it to the heap already there. The portable guillotine was at work.

Hornblower sat sick and horrified—this was worse than any flogging at the gratings. He was about to urge his horse forward when a strange sound caught his ear. A man was singing, loud and clear, and out from a building at the side of the square emerged a little procession. In front walked a big man with dark curly hair, wearing a white shirt and dark breeches. At either side and behind him walked soldiers. It was this man who was singing; the tune meant nothing to Hornblower, but he could hear the words distinctly—it was one of the verses of the French revolutionary song, echoes of which had penetrated even across the Channel.

'Oh, sacred love of the Fatherland . . .' sang the man in the white shirt; and when the civilians in the square heard what he was singing, there was a rustle among them and they dropped to the knees, their heads bowed and their hands crossed upon their breasts.

The executioners were winding the blade up again, and the man in the white shirt followed its rise with his eyes while he still sang without a tremor in his voice. The blade reached the top, and the singing ceased at last as the executioners fell on the man with the white shirt and led him to the guillotine. Then the blade fell with another echoing crash.

It seemed that this was to be the last execution, for the soldiers began to push the civilians back towards their homes, and Hornblower urged his horse forward through the dissolving crowd. He was nearly thrown from his saddle when the animal plunged sideways, snorting furiously— it had scented the horrid heap that lay beside the guillotine. At the side of the square was a house with a balcony, and Hornblower looked up at it in time to see Pouzauges still standing there, wearing his white uniform and blue ribbon, his staff about him and his hands on the rail. There were sentries at the door, and to one of them Hornblower handed over his horse as he entered; Pouzauges was just descending the stairs.

'Good evening, sir,' said Pouzauges with perfect courtesy. 'I am glad you have found your way to headquarters. I trust it was without trouble? We are about to dine and will enjoy your company. You have your horse, I suppose?

M. de Villers here will give orders for it to be looked after, I am sure.'

It was all hard to believe. It was hard to believe that this polished gentleman had ordered the butchery that had just ended; it was hard to believe that the elegant young men with whom he sat at dinner were staking their lives on the overthrow of a barbarous but lusty young republic. But it was equally hard to believe, when he climbed into a four-poster bed that night, that he, Midshipman Horatio Hornblower, was in imminent deadly peril himself.

Outside in the street women wailed as the headless corpses, the harvest of the executions, were carried away, and he thought he would never sleep, but youth and fatigue had their way, and he slept for most of the night, although he awoke with the feeling that he had just been fighting off a nightmare. Everything was strange to him in the darkness, and it was several moments before he could account for the strangeness. He was in a bed and not—as he had spent the preceding three hundred nights— in a hammock; and the bed was steady as a rock instead of swaying about with the lively motion of a frigate. The stuffiness about him was the stuffiness of bed curtains, and not the stuffiness of the midshipmen's berth with its compound smell of stale humanity and stale bilgewater. He was on shore, in a house, in a bed, and everything about him was dead quiet, unnaturally so to a man accustomed to the noises of a wooden ship at sea.

Of course; he was in a house in the town of Muzillac in Brittany. He was sleeping in the headquarters of Brigadier General the Marquis de Pouzauges, commanding the French troops who constituted part of this expedition, which was itself part of a larger force invading Revolutionary France in the royalist cause. Hornblower felt a quickening of the pulse, a faint sick feeling of insecurity, as he realized afresh that he was now in France, ten miles from the sea and the *Indefatigable* with only a rabble of Frenchmen—half of them mercenaries only nominally Frenchmen at that—around him to preserve him from death or captivity. He regretted his knowledge of French— if he had had none he would not be here, and good fortune might even have put him among the British half-battalion of the 43rd guarding the ford a mile away.

It was partly the thought of the British troops which roused him out of bed. It was his duty to see that liaison was kept up with them, and the situation might have changed while he slept. He drew aside the bed curtains and stepped down to the floor; as his legs took the weight of his body they protested furiously—all the riding he had done yesterday had left every muscle and joint aching so that he could hardly walk. But he hobbled in the darkness over to the window, found the latch of the shutters, and pushed them open. A three-quarter moon was shining down into the empty street of the town, and looking down he could see the three-cornered hat of the sentry posted outside, and the bayonet reflecting the moonlight. Returning from the window, he found his coat and shoes and put them on, belted his cutlass about him, and then he crept downstairs as quietly as he could. In the room off the entrance hall a tallow dip guttered on the table, and beside it a French sergeant slept with his head on his arms, lightly, for he raised his head as Hornblower paused in the doorway. On the floor of the room the rest of the guard off duty were snoring stertorously, huddled together like pigs in a sty, their muskets stacked against the wall.

Hornblower nodded to the sergeant, opened the front door and stepped out into the street. His lungs expanded gratefully as he breathed in the clean night air—morning air, rather, for there to the east the sky was assuming a lighter tinge—and the sentry, catching sight of the British naval officer, came clumsily to attention. In the square there still stood the gaunt harsh framework of the guillotine reaching up to the moonlit sky, and round it the black patch of blood of its victims. Hornblower wondered who they were, who it could have been that the Royalists should seize and kill at such short notice, and he decided that they must have been petty officials of the Revolutionary government—the mayor and the customs officer and so on —if they were not merely men against whom the émigrés had cherished grudges since the days of the Revolution itself. It was a savage, merciless world, and at the moment he was very much alone in it, lonely, depressed, and unhappy.

He was distracted from these thoughts by the sergeant of the guard emerging from the door with a file of men; the sentry in the street was relieved, and the party went on round the house to relieve the others. Then across the street he saw four drummers appear from another house, with a sergeant commanding them. They formed into a line, their drumsticks poised high before their faces, and then, at a word from the sergeant, the eight drumsticks fell together with a crash, and the drummers proceeded to march slowly along the street beating out a jerky exhilarating rhythm. At the first corner they stopped, and the drums rolled long and menacingly, and then they marched on again, beating out the previous rhythm. They were beating to arms, calling the men to their duties from their billets, and Hornblower, tone-deaf but highly sensitive to rhythm, thought it was fine music, real music. He turned back to headquarters with his depression fallen away from him. The sergeant of the guard came marching back with the relieved sentries; the first of the awakened soldiers were beginning to appear sleepily in the streets, and then, with a clatter of hoofs, a mounted messenger came riding up to headquarters, and the day was begun.

A pale young French officer read the note which the messenger brought, and politely handed it to Hornblower to read; he had to puzzle over it for a space—he was not accustomed to hand-written French—but its meaning became clear to him at length. It implied no new development; the main expeditionary force, landed yesterday at Quiberon, would move forward this morning on Vannes and Rennes while the subsidiary force to which Hornblower was attached must maintain its position at Muzillac, guarding its flank. The Marquis de Pouzauges, immaculate in his white uniform and blue ribbon, appeared at that moment, read the note without comment, and turned to Hornblower with a polite invitation to breakfast.

They went back to the big kitchen with its copper cooking pans glittering on the walls, and a silent woman brought them coffee and bread. She might be a patriotic Frenchwoman and an enthusiastic counter-revolutionary, but she showed no signs of it. Her feelings, of course, might easily have been influenced by the fact that this horde of men had taken over her house and were eating her food and sleeping in her rooms without payment. Maybe some of the horses and wagons seized for the use of the army were hers too—and maybe some of the people who had died under the guillotine last night were her friends. But she brought coffee, and the staff, standing about in the big kitchen with their spurs clinking, began to breakfast. Hornblower took his cup and a piece of bread—for four months before this his only bread had been ship's biscuit—and

sipped at the stuff. He was not sure if he liked it; he had
only tasted coffee three or four times before. But the second
time he raised his cup to his lips he did not sip; before
he could do so, the distant boom of a cannon made him
lower his cup and stand stock still. The cannon shot was
repeated, and again, and then it was echoed by a sharper,
nearer note—Midshipman Bracegirdle's six-pounders on
the causeway.

In the kitchen there was instant stir and bustle. Somebody knocked a cup over and sent a river of black liquid
swirling across the table. Somebody else managed to catch
his spurs together so that he stumbled into somebody
else's arms. Everyone seemed to be speaking at once. Hornblower was as excited as the rest of them; he wanted to
rush out and see what was happening, but he thought at
that moment of the disciplined calm which he had seen
in H.M.S. *Indefatigable* as she went into action. He was not
of this breed of Frenchmen, and to prove it he made himself put his cup to his lips again and drink calmly. Already
most of the staff had dashed out of the kitchen shouting
for their horses. It would take time to saddle up; he met
Pouzauges' eyes as the latter strode up and down the
kitchen, and drained his cup—a trifle too hot for comfort,
but he felt it was a good gesture. There was bread to eat,
and he made himself bite and chew and swallow, although
he had no appetite; if he was to be in the field all day, he
could not tell when he would get his next meal, and so he
crammed a half-loaf into his pocket.

The horses were being brought into the yard and
saddled; the excitement had infected them, and they
plunged and sidled about amid the curses of the officers.
Pouzauges leapt up into his saddle and clattered away
with the rest of the staff behind him, leaving behind only

a single soldier holding Hornblower's roan. That was as it had better be—Hornblower knew that he would not keep his for half a minute if the horse took it into his head to plunge or rear. He walked slowly out to the animal, which was calmer now when the groom petted him, and climbed with infinite slowness and precaution into the saddle. With a pull of the bit he checked the brute's exuberance and walked it sedately into the street and towards the bridge in the wake of the galloping staff. It was better to make sure of arriving by keeping his horse down to a walk than to gallop and be thrown. The guns were still booming and he could see the puffs of smoke from Bracegirdle's six-pounders. On his left, the sun was rising in a clear sky.

At the bridge the situation seemed obvious enough. Where the arch had been blown up a few skirmishers on either side were firing at each other across the gap, and at the far end of the causeway, across the Marais, a cloud of smoke revealed the presence of a hostile battery firing slowly and at extreme range. Beside the causeway on this side were Bracegirdle's two six-pounders, almost perfectly covered by a dip in the ground. Bracegirdle, with his cutlass belted round him, was standing between the guns which his party of seamen were working, and he waved his hand light-heartedly at Hornblower when he caught sight of him. A dark column of infantry appeared on the distant causeway. Bang—bang went Bracegirdle's guns. Hornblower's horse plunged at the noise, distracting him, but when he had time to look again, the column had disappeared. Then suddenly the causeway parapet near him flew into splinters; something hit the roadbed beside his horse's feet a tremendous blow and passed on with a roar —that was the closest so far in his life that a cannon shot had missed him. He lost a stirrup during the resultant struggle with his horse, and deemed it wiser, as soon as he regained moderate control, to dismount and lead the animal off the causeway towards the guns. Bracegirdle met him with a grin.

'No chance of their crossing here,' he said. 'At least, not if the Frogs stick to their work, and it looks as if they're willing to. The gap's within grapeshot range, they'll never bridge it. Can't think what they're burning powder for.'

'Testing our strength, I suppose,' said Hornblower, with an air of infinite military wisdom.

He would have been shaking with excitement if he had allowed his body to take charge. He did not know if he were being stiltedly unnatural, but even if he were that was better than to display excitement. There was something strangely pleasant, in a nightmare fashion, in standing here posing as a hardened veteran with cannon balls howling overhead; Bracegirdle seemed happy and smiling and quite master of himself, and Hornblower looked sharply at him, wondering if this were as much a pose as his own. He could not tell.

'Here they come again,' said Bracegirdle. 'Oh, only skirmishers.'

A few scattered men were running out along the causeway to the bridge. At long musket range they fell to the ground and began spasmodic firing; already there were some dead men lying over there and the skirmishers took cover behind the corpses. On this side of the gap the skirmishers, better sheltered, fired back at them.

'They haven't a chance, here at any rate,' said Bracegirdle. 'And look there.'

The main body of the Royalist force, summoned from the town, was marching up along the road. While they watched it, a cannon shot from the other side struck the head of the column and ploughed into it—Hornblower saw dead men flung this way and that, and the column wavered. Pouzauges came riding up and yelled orders, and the column, leaving its dead and wounded on the road, changed direction and took shelter in the marshy fields beside the causeway.

With nearly all the Royalist force assembled, it seemed indeed as if it would be utterly impossible for the Revolutionaries to force a crossing here.

'I'd better report on this to the Lobsters,' said Hornblower.

'There was firing down that way at dawn,' agreed Bracegirdle.

Skirting the wide marsh here ran a narrow path through the lush grass, leading to the ford which the 43rd were guarding. Hornblower led his horse on to the path before he mounted; he felt he would be more sure in that way of persuading the horse to take that direction. It was not long before he saw a dab of scarlet on the river bank— pickets thrown out from the main body to watch against any unlikely attempt to cross the marshes and stream round the British flank. Then he saw the cottage that indicated the site of the ford; in the field beside it was a wide patch of scarlet indicating where the main body was waiting for developments. At this point the marsh narrowed where a ridge of slightly higher ground approached the water; a company of redcoats was drawn up here with Lord Edrington on horseback beside them. Hornblower rode up and made his report, somewhat jerkily as his horse moved restlessly under him.

'No serious attack, you say?' asked Edrington.

'No sign of one when I left, sir.'

'Indeed?' Edrington stared across the river. 'And here it's the same story. No attempt to cross the ford in force. Why should they show their hand and then not attack?'

'I thought they were burning powder unnecessarily, sir,' said Hornblower.

'They're not fools,' snapped Edrington, with another penetrating look across the river. 'At any rate, there's no harm in assuming they are not.'

He turned his horse and cantered back to the main body and gave an order to a captain, who scrambled to his feet to receive it. The captain bellowed an order, and his company stood up and fell into line, rigid and motionless. Two further orders turned them to the right and marched them off in file, every man in step, every musket sloped at the same angle. Edrington watched them go.

'No harm in having a flank guard,' he said.

The sound of a cannon across the water recalled them to the river; on the other side of the marsh a column of troops could be seen marching rapidly along the bank.

'That's the same column coming back, sir,' said the company commander. 'That or another just like it.'

'Marching about and firing random shots,' said Edrington. 'Mr Hornblower, have the émigré troops any flank guard out towards Quiberon?'

'Towards Quiberon, sir?' said Hornblower, taken aback.

'Damn it, can't you hear a plain question? Is there, or is there not?'

'I don't know, sir,' confessed Hornblower miserably.

There were five thousand émigré troops at Quiberon, and it seemed quite unnecessary to keep a guard out in that direction.

'Then present my compliments to the French émigré

general, and suggest he posts a strong detachment up the road, if he has not done so.'

'Aye aye, sir.'

Hornblower turned his horse's head back up the path towards the bridge. The sun was shining strongly now over the deserted fields. He could still hear the occasional thud of a cannon shot, but overhead a lark was singing in the blue sky. Then as he headed up the last low ridge towards Muzillac and the bridge he heard a sudden irregular out-burst of firing; he fancied he heard screams and shouts, and what he saw as he topped the rise made him snatch at his reins and drag his horse to a halt. The fields before him were covered with fugitives in blue uniforms with white crossbelts, all running madly towards him. In among the fugitives were galloping horsemen, whirling sabres that flashed in the sunshine. Farther out to the left a whole column of horsemen were trotting fast across the fields, and farther back the sun glittered on lines of bayonets moving rapidly from the high road towards the sea.

There could be no doubt of what had happened; during those sick seconds when he sat and stared, Hornblower realized the truth; the Revolutionaries had pushed in a force between Quiberon and Muzillac, and, keeping the émigrés occupied by demonstrations from across the river, had rushed down and brought off a complete surprise by this attack from an unexpected quarter. Heaven only knew what had happened at Quiberon—but this was no time to think about that. Hornblower dragged his horse's head round and kicked his heels into the brute's sides, urging him frantically back up the path towards the British. He bounced and rolled in his saddle, clinging on madly, con-sumed with fear lest he lose his seat and be captured by the pursuing French.

At the clatter of hoofs every eye turned towards him when he reached the British post. Edrington was there, standing with his horse's bridle over his arm.

'The French!' yelled Hornblower hoarsely, pointing back. 'They're coming!'

'I expected nothing else,' said Edrington.

He shouted an order before he put his foot in the stirrup to mount. The main body of the 43rd was standing in line by the time he was in the saddle. His adjutant went galloping off to recall the company from the water's edge.

'The French are in force, horse, foot, and guns, I suppose?' asked Edrington.

'Horse and foot at least, sir,' gasped Hornblower, trying to keep his head clear. 'I saw no guns.'

'And the émigrés are running like rabbits?'

'Yes, sir.'

'Here come the first of them.'

Over the nearest ridge a few blue uniforms made their appearance, their wearers still running while stumbling with fatigue.

'I suppose we must cover their retreat, although they're not worth saving,' said Edrington. 'Look there!'

The company he had sent out as a flank guard was in sight on the crest of a slight slope: it was formed into a tiny square, red against the green, and as they watched they saw a mob of horsemen flood up the hill towards it and break into an eddy around it.

'Just as well I had them posted there,' remarked Edrington calmly. 'Ah, here comes Mayne's company.'

The force from the ford came marching up. Harsh orders were shouted. Two companies wheeled round while the sergeant-major with his sabre and his silver-headed cane regulated the pace and the alignment as if the men were on the barrack square.

'I would suggest you stay by me, Mr Hornblower,' said Edrington.

He moved his horse up into the interval between the two columns, and Hornblower followed him dumbly. Another order, and the force began to march steadily across the valley, the sergeants calling the step and the sergeant-major watching the intervals. All round them now were fleeing émigré soldiers, most of them in the last stages of exhaustion—Hornblower noticed more than one of them fall down on the ground gasping and incapable of further movement. And then over the low slope to the right appeared a line of plumes, a line of sabres—a regiment of cavalry trotting rapidly forward. Hornblower saw the sabres lifted, saw the horses break into a gallop, heard the yells of the charging men. The redcoats round him halted; another shouted order, another slow, deliberate movement, and the half-battalion was in a square with the mounted officers in the centre and the colours waving over their heads. The charging horsemen were less than a hundred yards away. Some officer with a deep voice began giving orders, intoning them as if at some solemn ceremony. The first order brought the muskets from the men's shoulders, and the second was answered by a simultaneous click of opening priming pans. The third order brought the muskets to the present along one face of the square.

'Too high!' said the sergeant-major. 'Lower, there, number seven.'

The charging horsemen were only thirty yards away; Hornblower saw the leading men, their cloaks flying from their shoulders, leaning along their horses' necks with their sabres pointed forward at the full stretch of their arms.

F

'Fire!' said the deep voice.

In reply came a single sharp explosion as every musket went off at once. The smoke swirled round the square and disappeared. Where Hornblower had been looking there were now a score of horses and men on the ground, some struggling in agony, some lying still. The cavalry regiment split like a torrent encountering a rock and hurtled harmlessly past the other faces of the square.

'Well enough,' said Edrington.

The deep voice was intoning again; like marionettes all on the same string the company that had fired now reloaded, every man biting out his bullet at the same instant, every man ramming home his charge, every man spitting his bullet into his musket barrel with the same instantaneous inclination of the head. Edrington looked keenly at the cavalry collecting together in a disorderly mob down the valley.

'The 43rd will advance!' he ordered.

With solemn ritual the square opened up again into two columns and continued its interrupted march. The detached company came marching up to join them from out of a ring of dead men and horses. Someone raised a cheer.

'Silence in the ranks!' bellowed the sergeant-major. 'Sergeant, take that man's name.'

But Hornblower noticed how the sergeant-major was eyeing keenly the distance between the columns; it had to be maintained exactly so that a company wheeling back filled it to make the square.

'Here they come again,' said Edrington.

The cavalry were forming for a new charge, but the square was ready for them. Now the horses were blown and the men were less enthusiastic. It was not a solid wall of horses that came down on them, but isolated groups, rushing first at one face and then at another, and pulling up or swerving aside as they reached the line of bayonets. The attacks were too feeble to meet with company volleys; at the word of command sections here and there gave fire to the more determined groups. Hornblower saw one man —an officer, judging by his gold lace—rein up before the bayonets and pull out a pistol. Before he could discharge it, half a dozen muskets went off together; the officer's face became a horrible bloody mask, and he and his horse fell together to the ground. Then all at once the cavalry wheeled off, like starlings over a field, and the march could be resumed.

'No discipline about these Frogs, not on either side,' said Edrington.

The march was headed for the sea, for the blessed shelter of the *Indefatigable*, but it seemed to Hornblower as if the pace was intolerably slow. The men were marching at the parade step, with agonizing deliberation, while all round them and far ahead of them the fugitive émigrés poured in a broad stream towards safety. Looking back, Hornblower saw the fields full of marching columns—hurrying swarms, rather—of Revolutionary infantry in hot pursuit of them.

'Once let men run and you can't do anything else with them,' commented Edrington, following Hornblower's gaze.

Shouts and shots over to the flank caught their attention. Trotting over the fields, leaping wildly at the bumps, came a cart drawn by a lean horse. Someone in a seaman's frock and trousers was holding the reins; other seamen were visible over the sides firing muskets at the horsemen hovering about them. It was Bracegirdle with his dung cart; he might have lost his guns but he had saved his men. The pursuers dropped away as the cart neared the columns; Bracegirdle, standing up in the cart, caught sight of Hornblower on his horse and waved to him excitedly.

'Boadicea and her chariot!' he yelled.

'I'll thank you, sir!' shouted Edrington, with lungs of brass, 'to go on and prepare for our embarkation.'

'Aye aye, sir!'

The lean horse trotted on with the cart lurching after it and the grinning seamen clinging on to the sides. At the flank appeared a swarm of infantry, a mad, gesticulating crowd, half running to cut off the 43rd's retreat. Edrington swept his glance round the fields.

'The 43rd will form line!' he shouted.

Like some ponderous machine, well oiled, the half-battalion fronted towards the swarm; the columns became lines, each man moving into his position like bricks laid on a wall.

'The 43rd will advance!'

The scarlet line swept forward, slowly, inexorably. The swarm hastened to meet it, officers to the front waving their swords and calling on their men to follow.

'Make ready!'

Every musket came down together; the priming pans clicked.

'Present!'

Up came the muskets, and the swarm hesitated before that fearful menace. Individuals tried to get back into the crowd to cover themselves from the volley with the bodies of their comrades.

'Fire!'

A crashing volley; Hornblower, looking over the heads of the British infantry from his point of vantage on horseback, saw the whole face of the swarm go down in swathes. Still the red line moved forward, at each deliberate step a shouted order brought a machine-like response as the men reloaded; five hundred mouths spat in five hundred bullets, five hundred right arms raised five hundred ramrods at once. When the muskets came to the present the red line was at the swathe of dead and wounded, for the swarm had withdrawn before the advance, and shrank back still further at the threat of the volley. The volley was fired; the advance went on. Another volley; another advance. Now the swarm was shredding away. Now men were running from it. Now every man had turned tail and fled from that frightful musketry. The hillside was as black with fugitives as it had been when the émigrés were fleeing.

'Halt!'

The advance ceased; the line became a double column, and the retreat began again.

'Very creditable,' remarked Edrington.

Hornblower's horse was trying jerkily to pick its way over a carpet of dead and wounded, and he was so busy keeping his seat, and his brain was in such a whirl, that he did not immediately realize that they had topped the last rise, so that before them lay the glittering waters of the estuary. The strip of muddy beach was packed solid with émigrés. There were the ships riding at anchor, and there, blessed sight, were the boats swarming towards the shore. It was high time, for already the boldest of the Revolutionary infantry were hovering round the columns, taking long shots into them. Here and there a man fell.

'Close up!' snapped the sergeants, and the files marched on stolidly, leaving the wounded and dead behind them.

The adjutant's horse suddenly snorted and plunged, and

then fell first to its knees, and, kicking, to its side, while
the freckle-faced adjutant freed his feet from the stirrups
and flung himself out of the saddle just in time to escape
being pinned underneath.

'Are you hit, Stanley?' asked Edrington.

'No, my lord. All safe and sound,' said the adjutant,
brushing at his scarlet coat.

'You won't have to foot it far,' said Edrington. 'No need
to throw out skirmishers to drive those fellows off. This
is where we must make our stand.'

He looked about him, at the fishermen's cottages above
the beach, the panic-stricken émigrés at the water's edge,
and the masses of Revolutionary infantry coming up in
pursuit, leaving small enough time for preparation. Some
of the redcoats poured into the cottages, appearing a
moment later at the windows; it was fortunate that the
fishing hamlet guarded one flank of the gap down to the
beach while the other was guarded by a steep and inacces-
sible headland on whose summit a small block of redcoats
established themselves. In the gap betwen the two points
the remaining four companies formed a long line just
sheltered by the crest of the beach.

The boats of the squadron were already loading with
émigrés among the small breakers below. Hornblower
heard the crack of a single pistol-shot; he could guess that
some officer down there was enforcing his orders in the
only possible way to prevent the fear-driven men from
pouring into the boats and swamping them. As if in answer
came the roar of cannon on the other side. A battery of
artillery had unlimbered just out of musket range and was
firing at the British position, while all about it gathered
the massed battalions of the Revolutionary infantry. The
cannon balls howled close overhead.

'Let them fire way,' said Edrington. 'The longer the better.'

The artillery could do little harm to the British in the fold of ground that protected them, and the Revolutionary commander must have realized that, as well as the necessity for wasting no time. Over there the drums began to roll—a noise of indescribable menace—and then the columns surged forward. So close were they already that Hornblower could see the features of the officers in the lead, waving their hats and swords.

'43rd make ready!' said Edrington, and the priming pans clicked as one. 'Seven paces forward—march!'

One—two—three—seven paces, painstakingly taken, took the line to the little crest.

'Present! Fire!'

A volley nothing could withstand. The columns halted, swayed, received another smashing volley, and another, and fell back in ruin.

'Excellent!' said Edrington.

The battery boomed again; a file of two redcoat soldiers was tossed back like dolls, to lie in a horrible bloody mass close beside Hornblower's horse's feet.

'Close up!' said a sergeant, and the men on either side had filled the gap.

'43rd, seven paces back—march!'

The line was below the crest again, as the redcoated marionettes withdrew in steady time. Hornblower could not remember later whether it was twice or three times more that the Revolutionary masses came on again, each time to be dashed back by that disciplined musketry. But the sun was nearly setting in the ocean behind him when he looked back to see the beach almost cleared and Bracegirdle plodding up to them to report.

'I can spare one company now,' said Edrington in reply but not taking his eyes off the French masses. 'After they are on board, have every boat ready and waiting.'

One company filed off; another attack was beaten back— after the preceding failures it was not pressed home with anything like the dash and fire of the earlier ones. Now the battery was turning its attention to the headland on the flank, and sending its balls among the redcoats there, while a battalion of French moved over to the attack at that point.

'That gives us time,' said Edrington. 'Captain Griffin, you can march the men off. Colour party, remain here.'

Down the beach went the centre companies to the wait-ing boats, while the colours still waved to mark their old position, visible over the crest to the French. The company in the cottages came out, formed up, and marched down as well. Edrington trotted across to the foot of the little headland; he watched the French forming for the attack and the infantry wading out to the boats.

'Now, grenadiers!' he yelled suddenly. 'Run for it! Colour party!'

Down the steep seaward face of the headland came the last company, running, sliding, and stumbling. A musket, clumsily handled, went off unexpectedly. The last man came down the slope as the colour party reached the water's edge and began to climb into a boat with its precious burden. A wild yell went up from the French, and their whole mass came rushing towards the evacuated position.

'Now, sir,' said Edrington, turning his horse seawards.

Hornblower fell from his saddle as his horse splashed into the shallows. He let go of the reins and plunged out,

waist deep, shoulder deep, to where the longboat lay on
its oars with its four-pounder gun in its bows and Bracegirdle beside it to haul him in. He looked up in time to
see a curious incident; Edrington had reached the *Indefatigable*'s gig, still holding his horse's reins. With the
French pouring down the beach towards them, he turned
and took a musket from the nearest soldier, pressed the
muzzle to the horse's head, and fired. The horse fell in its
death agony in the shallows; only Hornblower's roan
remained as prize to the Revolutionaries.

'Back water!' said Bracegirdle, and the longboat backed
away from the beach; Hornblower lay in the eyes of the
boat feeling as if he had not the strength to move a limb,
and the beach was covered with shouting, gesticulating
Frenchmen, lit redly by the sunset.

'One moment,' said Bracegirdle, reaching for the lanyard
of the four-pounder, and tugging at it smartly.

The gun roared out in Hornblower's ear, and the charge
cut a swathe of destruction on the beach.

'That was canister,' said Bracegirdle. 'Eighty-four balls.
Easy, port! Give way, starboard!'

The longboat turned away from the beach and towards
the welcoming ships. Hornblower looked back at the
darkening coast of France. This was the end of an incident;
his country's attempt to overturn the Revolution had met
with a bloody repulse. Newspapers in Paris would exult;
the *Gazette* in London would give the incident five cold
lines. Clairvoyant Hornblower could foresee that in a year's
time the world would hardly remember the incident. In
twenty years it would be entirely forgotten. Yet those headless corpses up there in Muzillac; those shattered redcoats;
those Frenchmen caught in the four-pounder's blast of
canister—they were all as dead as if it had been a day in

F*

which history had been changed. And he was just as weary. And in his pocket there was still the bread he had put there that morning and forgotten all about.

CHAPTER SEVEN

THE SPANISH GALLEYS

THE old *Indefatigable* was lying at anchor in the Bay of Cadiz at the time when Spain made peace with France. Hornblower happened to be midshipman on the watch, and it was he who called the attention of Lieutenant Chadd to the approach of the eight-oared pinnace, with the red and yellow of Spain dropping at her stern. Chadd's glass made out the gleam of gold on epaulette and cocked hat, and bellowed the order for sideboys and marine guard to give the traditional honours to a captain in an allied service. Pellew, hurriedly warned, was at the gangway to meet his visitor, and it was at the gangway that the entire interview took place. The Spaniard, making a low bow with his hat across his stomach, offered a sealed envelope to the Englishman.

'Here, Mr Hornblower,' said Pellew, holding the letter unopened, 'speak French to this fellow. Ask him to come below for a glass of wine.'

But the Spaniard, with a further bow, declined the refreshment, and, with another bow, requested that Pellew open the letter immediately. Pellew broke the seal and read the contents, struggling with the French which he could read to a small extent although he could not speak it at all. He handed it to Hornblower.

'This means the Dagoes have made peace, doesn't it?'

Hornblower struggled through twelve lines of compliments addressed by His Excellency the Duke of Belchite (Grandee of the First Class, with eighteen other titles ending with Captain-General of Andalusia) to the Most Gallant Ship-Captain Sir Edward Pellew, Knight of the Bath. The second paragraph was short and contained only a brief intimation of peace. The third paragraph was as long as the first, and repeated its phraseology almost word for word in a ponderous farewell.

'That's all, sir,' said Hornblower.

But the Spanish captain had a verbal message with which to supplement the written one.

'Please tell your captain,' he said, in his lisping Spanish-French, 'that now, as a neutral power, Spain must enforce her rights. You have already been at anchor here for twenty-four hours. Six hours from now'—the Spaniard took a gold watch from his pocket and glanced at it—'if you are within range of the batteries at Puntales there they will be given orders to fire on you.'

Hornblower could only translate the brutal message without any attempt at softening it, and Pellew listened, white with anger despite his tan.

'Tell him——' he began, and then mastered his rage. 'Damme if I'll let him see he has made me angry.'

He put his hat across his stomach and bowed in as faithful an imitation of the Spaniard's courtliness as he could manage, before he turned to Hornblower.

'Tell him I have received his message with pleasure. Tell him I much regret that circumstances are separating him from me, and that I hope I shall always enjoy his personal friendship whatever the relations between our countries. Tell him—oh, you can tell him the sort of thing I want said, can't you, Hornblower? Let's see him over the side with dignity. Sideboys! Bosun's mates! Drummers!'

Hornblower poured out compliments to the best of his ability, and at every phrase the two captains exchanged bows, the Spaniard withdrawing a pace at each bow and Pellew following him up, not to be outdone in courtesy. The drums beat a ruffle, the marines presented arms, the pipes shrilled and twittered until the Spaniard's head had descended to the level of the maindeck, when Pellew stiffened up, clapped his hat on his head, and swung round on his first lieutenant.

'Mr Eccles, I want to be under way within the hour, if you please.'

Then he stamped down below to regain his equanimity in private.

Hands were aloft loosing sail ready to sheet home, while the clank of the capstan told how other men were heaving the cable short, and Hornblower was standing on the portside gangway with Mr Wales the carpenter, looking over at the white houses of one of the most beautiful cities in Europe.

'I've been ashore there twice,' said Wales. 'The wine's good—*vino*, they calls it—if you happens to like that kind o' muck. But don't you ever try that brandy, Mr Hornblower. Poison, it is, rank poison. Hello! We're going to have an escort, I see.'

Two long, sharp prows had emerged from the inner bay, and were pointing towards the *Indefatigable*. Hornblower could not restrain himself from giving a cry of surprise as he followed Wales' gaze. The vessels approaching were galleys; along each side of them the oars were lifting and falling rhythmically, catching the sunlight as they feathered. The effect, as a hundred oars swung like one, was perfectly beautiful. Hornblower remembered a line in a Latin poem which he had translated as a schoolboy, and recalled his surprise when he discovered that to a Roman the 'white wings' of a ship of war were her oars. Now the simile was plain; even a gull in flight, which Hornblower had always looked upon until now as displaying the perfection of motion, was not more beautiful than those galleys. They lay low in the water, immensely long for their beam. Neither the sails nor the lateen yards were set on the low-raking masts. The bows blazed with gilding, while the waters of the bay foamed round them as they headed into the teeth of the gentle breeze with the Spanish red and gold streaming aft from the masthead. Up—forward—down—went the oars with unchanging rhythm, the blades not varying an inch in their distance apart during the whole of the stroke. From the bows of each two long guns looked straight forward in the direction the galleys pointed.

'Twenty-four pounders,' said Wales. 'If they catch you in a calm, they'll knock you to pieces. Lie off on your quarter where you can't bring a gun to bear and rake you till you strike. An' then God help you—better a Turkish prison than a Spanish one.'

In a line-ahead that might have been drawn with a ruler and measured with a chain the galleys passed close along the port side of the *Indefatigable* and went ahead of her. As they passed, the roll of the drum and the call of the pipes summoned the crew of the *Indefatigable* to attention out of compliment to the flag and the commission pendant going by, while the galleys' officers returned the salute.

'It don't seem right, somehow,' muttered Wales under his breath, 'to salute 'em like they was a frigate.'

Level with the *Indefatigable*'s bowsprit the leader backed her starboard side oars, and spun like a top, despite her length and narrow beam, across the frigate's bows. The gentle wind blew straight to the frigate from the galley, and then from her consort as the latter followed; and a foul stench came back on the air and assailed Hornblower's nostrils, and not Hornblower's alone, clearly, for it brought forth cries of disgust from all the men on deck.

'They all stink like that,' explained Wales. 'Four men to the oar an' fifty oars. Two hundred galley slaves, that is. All chained to their benches. When you goes aboard one of them as a slave you're chained to your bench, an' you're never unchained until they drop you overside. Sometimes when the hands aren't busy they'll hose out the bilge, but that doesn't happen often, bein' Dagoes an' not many of 'em.'

Hornblower, as always, sought exact information.

'How many, Mr Wales?'

'Thirty, mebbe. Enough to hand the sails if they're making a passage. Or to man the guns—they strike the yards and sails, like now, before they goes into action, Mr Hornblower,' said Wales, pontifical as usual, and with that slight emphasis on the 'Mister' inevitable when a warrant officer of sixty with no hope of further promotion addressed a warrant officer of eighteen (his nominal equal in rank) who might some day be an admiral. 'So you see how it is. With no more than thirty of a crew an' two hundred slaves they daren't let 'em loose, not ever.'

The galleys had turned again, and were now passing down the *Indefatigable*'s starboard side. The beat of the oars had slowed very noticeably, and Hornblower had ample time to observe the vessels closely, the low fore-castle and high poop with the gangway connecting them along the whole length of the galley; upon that gangway walked a man with a whip. The rowers were invisible below the bulwarks, the oars being worked through holes in the sides, closed, as far as Hornblower could see, with sheets of leather round the oar-looms to keep out the sea. On the poop stood two men at the tiller and a small group of officers, their gold lace flashing in the sunshine. Save for the gold lace and the twenty-four-pounder bow chasers, Hornblower was looking at exactly the same sort of vessel as the ancients used to fight their battles. Polybius and Thucydides wrote about galleys almost identical with these —for that matter it was not much more than two hundred years since the galleys had fought their last great battle at Lepanto against the Turks. But those battles had been fought with hundreds of galleys a side.

'How many do they have in commission now?' asked Hornblower.

'A dozen, mebbe—not that I knows for sure, o' course. Carthagena's their usual station, beyond the Gut.'

Wales, as Hornblower understood, meant by this through the Straits of Gibraltar in the Mediterranean.

'Too frail for the Atlantic,' Hornblower commented.

It was easy to deduce the reasons for the survival of this small number—the innate conservatism of the Spaniards would account for it to a large extent. Then there was the point that condemnation to the galleys was one way of dis-posing of criminals. And when all was said and done a galley might still be useful in a calm—merchant ships be-calmed while trying to pass the Straits of Gibraltar might be snapped up by galleys pushing out from Cadiz or Carthagena. And at the very lowest estimate there might be some employment for galleys to tow vessels in and out of harbour with the wind unfavourable.

'Mr Hornblower!' said Eccles. 'My respects to the captain, and we're ready to get under way.'

Hornblower dived below with his message.

'My compliments to Mr Eccles,' said Pellew, looking up from his desk, 'and I'll be on deck immediately.'

There was just enough of a southerly breeze to enable the *Indefatigable* to weather the point in safety. With her anchor catted she braced round her yards and began to steal forward; in the disciplined stillness which prevailed the sound of the ripple of water under the cutwater was clearly to be heard—a musical note which told nothing, in its innocence, of the savagery and danger of the world of the sea into which she was entering. Creeping along under her topsails the *Indefatigable* made no more than three knots, and the galleys came surging past her again, oars beating their fastest rhythm, as if the galleys were boasting of their independence of the elements. Their gilt flashed in the sun as they overtook to windward, and once again their foul stench offended the nostrils of the men of the *Indefatigable*.

'I'd be obliged if they'd keep to leeward of us,' muttered Pellew, watching them through his glass. 'But I suppose that's not Spanish courtesy. Mr Cutler!'

'Sir!' said the gunner.

'You may commence the salute.'

'Aye aye, sir.'

The forward carronade on the lee side roared out the first of its compliments, and the fort of Puntales began its reply. The sound of the salute rolled round the beautiful bay; nation was speaking to nation in all courtesy.

'The next time we hear those guns they'll be shotted, I

fancy,' said Pellew, gazing across at Puntales and the flag of Spain flying above it.

Indeed, the tide of war was turning against England. Nation after nation had retired from the contest against France, some worsted by arms, and some by the diplomacy of the vigorous young republic. To any thinking mind it was obvious that once the step from war to neutrality had been taken, the next step would be easy, from neutrality to war on the other side. Hornblower could foresee, close at hand, a time when all Europe would be arrayed in hostility to England, when she would be battling for her life against the rejuvenescent power of France and the malignity of the whole world.

'Set sail, please, Mr Eccles,' said Pellew.

Two hundred trained pairs of legs raced aloft; two hundred trained pairs of arms let loose the canvas, and the *Indefatigable* doubled her speed, heeling slightly to the gentle breeze. Now she was meeting the long Atlantic swell. So were the galleys; as the *Indefatigable* overtook them, Hornblower could see the leader put her nose into a long roller so that a cloud of spray broke over her forecastle. That was asking too much for such frail craft. Back went one bank of oars; forward went the other. The galleys rolled hideously for a moment in the trough of sea before they completed their turn and headed back for the safe waters of Cadiz Bay. Someone forward in the *Indefatigable* began to boo, and the cry was instantly taken up through the ship. A storm of boos and whistles and catcalls pursued the galleys, the men momentarily quite out of hand while Pellew spluttered with rage on the quarterdeck and the petty officers strove in vain to take the names of the offenders. It was an ominous farewell to Spain.

Ominous indeed. It was not long before Captain Pellew

gave the news to the ship that Spain had completed her change-over; with the treasure convoy safely in, she had declared war against England; the revolutionary republic had won the alliance of the most decayed monarchy in Europe. British resources were now stretched to the utmost; there was another thousand miles of coast to watch, another fleet to blockade, another horde of privateers to guard against, and far fewer harbours in which to take refuge and from which to draw the fresh water and the meagre stores which enabled the hard-worked crews to remain at sea. It was then that friendship had to be cultivated with the half-savage Barbary States, and the insolence of the Deys and the Sultans had to be tolerated so that North Africa could provide the skinny bullocks and the barley grain to feed the British garrisons in the Mediterranean—all of them beleaguered on land—and the ships which kept open the way to them. Oran, Tetuan, Algiers wallowed in unwontedly honest prosperity with the influx of British gold.

It was a day of glassy calm in the Straits of Gibraltar. The sea was like a silver shield, the sky like a bowl of sapphire, with the mountains of Africa on the one hand, the mountains of Spain on the other as dark serrations on the horizon. It was not a comfortable situation for the *Indefatigable*, but that was not because of the blazing sun which softened the pitch in the deck seams. There is almost always a slight current setting inwards into the Mediterranean from the Atlantic, and the prevailing winds blow in the same direction. In a calm like this it was not unusual for a ship to be carried far through the Straits, past the Rock of Gibraltar, and then to have to beat for days and even weeks to make Gibraltar Bay. So that Pellew was not unnaturally anxious about his convoy of grain ships from

Oran. Gibraltar had to be revictualled—Spain had already marched an army up for the siege—and he dared not risk being carried past his destination. His orders to his reluctant convoy had been enforced by flag and gun signals, for no short-handed merchant ship relished the prospect of the labour Pellew wished to be executed. The *Indefatigable* no less than her convoy had lowered boats, and the helpless ships were now all in tow. That was back-breaking, exhausting labour, the men at the oars tugging and straining, dragging the oar blades through the water, while the towlines tightened and buckled with superhuman perversity and the ships sheered freakishly from side to side. It was less than a mile an hour that the ships made in this fashion, at the cost of the complete exhaustion of the boats' crews, but at least it postponed the time when the Gibraltar current would carry them to leeward, and similarly gave more chance for the longed-for southerly wind—two hours of a southerly wind was all they wished for—to waft them up to the Mole.

Down in the *Indefatigable*'s longboat and cutter the men tugging at their oars were so stupefied with their toil that they did not hear the commotion in the ship. They were just tugging and straining, under the pitiless sky, living through their two hours' spell of misery, but they were roused by the voice of the captain himself, hailing them from the forecastle.

'Mr Bolton! Mr Chadd! Cast off there, if you please. You'd better come and arm your men at once. Here come our friends from Cadiz.'

Back on the quarterdeck, Pellew looked through his glass at the hazy horizon; he could make out from here by now what had first been reported from the masthead.

'They're heading straight for us,' he said.

The two galleys were on their way from Cadiz; presumably a fast horseman from the look-out point at Harifa had brought them the news of this golden opportunity, of the flat calm and the scattered and helpless convoy. This was the moment for galleys to justify their continued existence. They could capture and at least burn, although they could not hope to carry off, the unfortunate merchant ships, while the *Indefatigable* lay helpless hardly out of cannon's range. Pellew looked round at the two merchant ships and the three brigs; one of them was within half a mile of him and might be covered by his gunfire, but the others—a mile and a half, two miles away—had no such protection.

'Pistols and cutlasses, my lads!' he said to the men pouring up from overside. 'Clap on to that stay tackle now. Smartly with that carronade, Mr Cutler!'

The *Indefatigable* had been in too many expeditions where minutes counted to waste any time over these preparations. The boats' crews seized their arms, the six-pounder carronades were lowered into the bows of the cutter and longboat, and soon the boats, crowded with armed men, and provisioned against sudden emergency, were pulling away to meet the galleys.

'What the devil d'you think you're doing, Mr Hornblower?'

Pellew had just caught sight of Hornblower in the act of swinging out of the jolly boat which was his special charge. He wondered what his midshipman thought he could achieve against a war-galley with a twelve-foot boat and a crew of six.

'We can pull to one of the convoy and reinforce the crew, sir,' said Hornblower.

'Oh, very well then, carry on. I'll trust to your good sense, even though that's a broken reed.'

'Good on you, sir!' said Jackson ecstatically, as the jolly boat shoved off from the frigate. 'Good on you! No one else wouldn't never have thought of that.'

Jackson, the coxswain of the jolly boat, obviously thought that Hornblower had no intention of carrying out his suggestion to reinforce the crew of one of the merchant ships.

'Those stinking Dagoes,' said stroke oar, between his teeth.

Hornblower was conscious of the presence in his crew of the same feeling of violent hostility towards the Spanish galleys as he felt within himself. In a fleeting moment of analysis, he attributed it to the circumstances in which they had first made the galleys' acquaintance, as well as to the stench which the galleys trailed after them. He had never known this feeling of personal hatred before; when previously he had fought, it had been as a servant of the King, not out of personal animosity. Yet here he was gripping the tiller under the scorching sky and leaning forward in his eagerness to be at actual grips with his enemy.

The longboat and cutter had a long start on them, and even though they were manned by crews who had already served a spell at the oars they were skimming over the water at such a speed that the jolly boat with all the advantage of the glassy-smooth water only slowly caught up to them. Overside the sea was of the bluest, deepest blue until the oar blades churned it white. Ahead of them the vessels of the convoy lay scattered where the sudden calm had caught them, and just beyond them Hornblower caught sight of the flash of oar-blades as the galleys came sweeping down on their prey. Longboat and cutter were diverging in an endeavour to cover as many vessels as possible, and the gig was still far astern. There would hardly be time to board a ship even if Hornblower should wish to. He put the tiller over to incline his course after the cutter; one of the galleys at that moment abruptly made its appearance in the gap between two of the merchant ships. Hornblower saw the cutter swing round to point her six-pounder carronade at the advancing bows.

'Pull, you men! Pull!' he shrieked, mad with excitement.

He could not imagine what was going to happen, but he wanted to be in the fray. That six-pounder popgun was grossly inaccurate at any range longer than musket shot. It would serve to hurl a mass of grape into a crowd of men, but its ball would have small effect on the strengthened bows of a war galley.

'Pull!' shrieked Hornblower again. He was nearly up to them, wide on the cutter's quarter.

The carronade boomed out. Hornblower thought he saw the splinters fly from the galley's bow, but the shot had no more effect on deterring her than a pea-shooter could stop a charging bull. The galley turned a little, getting exactly into line, and then her oars' beat quickened. She was coming down to ram, like the Greeks at Salamis.

'Pull!' shrieked Hornblower.

Instinctively, he gave the tiller a touch to take the jolly boat out into a flanking position.

'Easy!'

The jolly boat's oars stilled, as their way carried them past the cutter. Hornblower could see Soames standing up in the sternsheets looking at the death which was cleaving the blue waters towards him. Bow to bow the cutter might have stood a chance, but too late the cutter tried to evade the blow altogether. Hornblower saw her turn, presenting her vulnerable side to the galley's stem. That was all he could see, for the next moment the galley herself hid from him the final act of the tragedy. The jolly boat's starboard

side oars only just cleared the galley's starboard oars as she
swept by. Hornblower heard a shriek and a crash, saw the
galley's forward motion almost cease at the collision. He was
mad with the lust of fighting, quite insane, and his mind
was working with the rapidity of insanity.

'Give way, port!' he yelled, and the jolly boat swung
round under the galley's stern. 'Give way all!'

The jolly boat leaped after the galley like a terrier after
a bull.

'Grapple them, damn you, Jackson!'

Jackson shouted an oath in reply, as he leaped forward,
seemingly hurdling the men at the oars without breaking
their stroke. In the bows Jackson seized the boat's grapnel
on its long line and flung it hard and true. It caught somewhere in the elaborate gilt rail on the galley's quarter.
Jackson hauled on the line, the oars tugged madly in the
effort to carry the jolly boat up to the galley's stern. At that
moment Hornblower saw it, the sight which would long
haunt his dreams—up from under the galley's stern came
the shattered forepart of the cutter, still with men clinging
to it who had survived the long passage under the whole
length of the galley which had overrun them. There were
straining faces, empurpled faces, faces already relaxing in
death. But in a moment it was past and gone, and Hornblower felt the jerk transmitted through the line to the
jolly boat as the galley leaped forward.

'I can't hold her!' shouted Jackson.

'Take a turn round the cleat, you fool!'

The galley was towing the jolly boat now, dragging her
along at the end of a twenty-foot line close on her quarter,
just clear of the arc of her rudder. The white water bubbled
all around her, her bows were cocked up with strain. It
was a mad moment, as though they had harpooned a whale.

Someone came running aft on the Spaniard's poop, knife in hand, to cut the line.

'Shoot him, Jackson!' shrieked Hornblower again.

Jackson's pistol cracked, and the Spaniard fell to the deck out of sight—a good shot. Despite his fighting madness, despite the turmoil of rushing water and glaring sun, Hornblower tried to think out his next move. Inclination and common sense alike told him that the best plan was to close with the enemy despite the odds.

'Pull up to them, there!' he shouted—everyone in the boat was shouting and yelling. The men in the bows of the jolly boat faced forward and took the grapnel line and began to haul in on it, but the speed of the boat through the water made any progress difficult, and after a yard or so had been gained the difficulty became insurmountable, for the grapnel was caught in the poop rail ten or eleven feet above water, and the angle of pull became progressively steeper as the jolly boat neared the stern of the galley. The boat's bow cocked higher out of the water than ever.

'Belay!' said Hornblower, and then, his voice rising again, 'Out pistols, lads!'

A row of four or five swarthy faces had appeared at the stern of the galley. Muskets were pointing into the jolly boat, and there was a brief but furious exchange of shots. One man fell groaning into the bottom of the jolly boat, but the row of faces disappeared. Standing up precariously in the swaying sternsheets, Hornblower could still see nothing of the galley's poop deck save for the tops of two heads, belonging, it was clear, to the men at the tiller.

'Reload,' he said to his men, remembering by a miracle to give the order. The ramrods went down the pistol barrels.

'Do that carefully if you ever want to see Pompey again,' said Hornblower.

He was shaking with excitement and mad with the fury of fighting, and it was the automatic, drilled part of him which was giving these level-headed orders. His higher faculties were quite negatived by his lust for blood. He was seeing things through a pink mist—that was how he remembered it when he looked back upon it later. There was a sudden crash of glass. Someone had thrust a musket barrel through the big stern window of the galley's after-cabin. Luckily, having thrust it through, he had to recover himself to take aim. An irregular volley of pistols almost coincided with the report of the musket. Where the Spaniard's bullet went no one knew; but the Spaniard fell back from the window.

'By God! That's our way!' screamed Hornblower, and then, steadying himself, 'Reload.'

As the bullets were being spat into the barrels he stood up. His unused pistols were still in his belt; his cutlass was at his side.

'Come aft, here,' he said to stroke oar; the jolly boat would stand no more weight in the bows than she had already. 'And you, too.'

Hornblower poised himself in the thwarts, eyeing the grapnel line and the cabin window.

'Bring 'em after me one at a time, Jackson,' he said.

Then he braced himself and flung himself at the grapnel line. His feet grazed the water as the line sagged, but using all his clumsy strength his arms carried him upwards. Here was the shattered window at his side; he swung up his feet, kicked out a big remaining piece of the pane, and then shot his feet through and then the rest of himself. He came down on the deck of the cabin with a thud; it was

dark in here compared with the blinding sun outside. As
he got to his feet, he trod on something which gave out
a cry of pain—the wounded Spaniard, evidently—and the
hand with which he drew his cutlass was sticky with blood.
Spanish blood. Rising, he hit his head a thunderous crash
on the deck-beams above, for the little cabin was very low,
hardly more than five feet, and so severe was the blow that
his senses almost left him. But before him was the cabin
door and he reeled out through it, cutlass in hand. Over
his head he heard a stamping of feet, and shots were fired
behind him and above him—a further exchange, he pre-
sumed, between the jolly boat and the galley's stern rail.
The cabin door opened into a low half-deck, and Hornblower reeled along it out into the sunshine again. He was
on the tiny strip of maindeck at the break of the poop.
Before him stretched the narrow gangway between the two
sets of rowers; he could look down at these latter—two seas
of bearded faces, mops of hair and lean sunburned bodies,
swinging rhythmically back and forward to the beat of
the oars.

That was all the impression he could form of them at
the moment. At the far end of the gangway at the break
of the forecastle stood the overseer with his whip; he was
shouting words in rhythmic succession to the slaves—
Spanish numbers, perhaps, to give them the time. There
were three or four men on the forecastle; below them the
half-doors through the forecastle bulkhead were hooked
open, through which Hornblower could see the two big
guns illuminated by the light through the port holes out
of which they were run almost at the water level. The
guns' crews were standing by the guns, but numerically
they were far fewer than two twenty-four pounders would
demand. Hornblower remembered Wales' estimate of no

more than thirty for a galley's crew. The men of one gun
at least had been called aft to defend the poop against the
jolly boat's attack.

A step behind him made him leap with anxiety and he
swung round with his cutlass ready to meet Jackson
stumbling out of the half deck, cutlass in hand.

'Nigh on cracked my nut,' said Jackson.

He was speaking thickly like a drunken man, and his
words were chorused by further shots fired from the poop
at the level of the top of their heads.

'Oldroyd's comin' next,' said Jackson. 'Franklin's dead.'

On either side of them a companion ladder mounted to
the poop deck. It seemed logical, mathematical, that they
should each go up one but Hornblower thought better of it.

'Come along,' he said, and headed for the starboard
ladder, and, with Oldroyd putting in an appearance at that
moment, he yelled to him to follow.

The hand-ropes of the ladder were of twisted red and
yellow cord—he even could notice that as he rushed up
the ladder, pistol in hand and cutlass in the other. After
the first step his eye was above deck-level. There were more
than a dozen men crowded on the tiny poop, but two were
lying dead, and one was groaning with his back to the
rail, and two stood by the tiller. The others were looking
over the rail at the jolly boat. Hornblower was still insane
with fighting madness. He must have leaped up the final
two or three steps with a bound like a stag's, and he was
screaming like a maniac as he flung himself at the
Spaniards. His pistol went off apparently without his willing it, but the face of the man a yard away dissolved into
bloody ruin, and Hornblower dropped the weapon and
snatched the second, his thumb going to the hammer as
he whirled his cutlass down with a crash on the sword which

the next Spaniard raised as a feeble guard. He struck and
struck and struck with a lunatic's strength. Here was Jackson beside him, shouting hoarsely and striking out right
and left.

'Kill 'em! Kill 'em!' shouted Jackson.

Hornblower saw Jackson's cutlass flash down on the head
of the defenceless man at the tiller. Then out of the tail
of his eye he saw another sword threaten him as he battered
with his cutlass at the man before him, but his pistol saved
him as he fired automatically again. Another pistol went
off beside him—Oldroyd's, he supposed—and then the fight
on the poop was over. By what miracle of ineptitude the
Spaniards had allowed the attack to take them by surprise
Hornblower never could discover. Perhaps they were
ignorant of the wounding of the man in the cabin, and
had relied on him to defend that route; perhaps it had
never occurred to them that three men could be so utterly
desperate as to attack a dozen; perhaps they never realized
that three men had made the perilous passage of the grapnel line; perhaps—most probably—in the mad excitement
of it all, they simply lost their heads, for five minutes could
hardly have elapsed altogether from the time the jolly boat
hooked on until the poop was cleared. Two or three
Spaniards ran down the companion to the maindeck, and
forward along the gangway between the rows of slaves.
One was caught against the rail and made a gesture of
surrender, but Jackson's hand was already at his throat.
Jackson was a man of immense physical strength; he bent
the Spaniard back over the rail, farther and farther, and
then caught him by the thigh with his other hand and
heaved him over. He fell with a shriek before Hornblower
could interpose. The poop deck was covered with writhing
men, like the bottom of a boat filled with flapping fish. One

man was getting to his knees when Jackson and Oldroyd seized him. They swung him up to toss him over the rail.

'Stop that!' said Hornblower, and quite callously they dropped him again with a crash on the bloody planks.

Jackson and Oldroyd were like drunken men, unsteady on their feet, glazed of eye and stertorous of breath; Hornblower was just coming out of his insane fit. He stepped forward to the break of the poop, wiping the sweat out of his eyes while trying to wipe away the red mist that tinged his vision. Forward by the forecastle were gathered the rest of the Spaniards, a large group of them; as Hornblower came forward, one of them fired a musket at him but the ball went wide. Down below him the rowers were still swinging rhythmically, forward and back, forward and back, the hairy heads and the naked bodies moving in time to the oars; in time to the voice of the overseer, too, for the latter was still standing on the gangway (the rest of the Spaniards were clustered behind him) calling the time —'Seis, siete, ocho'

'Stop!' bellowed Hornblower.

He walked to the starboard side to be in full view of the starboard side rowers. He held up his hand and bellowed again. A hairy face or two was raised, but the oars still swung.

'Uno, doce, tres,' said the overseer.

Jackson appeared at Hornblower's elbow, and levelled a pistol to shoot the nearest rower.

'Oh, belay that!' said Hornblower testily. He knew he was sick of killings now. 'Find my pistols and reload them.'

He stood at the top of the companion like a man in a dream—in a nightmare. The galley slaves went on swinging and pulling; his dozen enemies were still clustered at

the break of the forecastle thirty yards away; behind him
the wounded Spaniards groaned away their lives. Another
appeal to the rowers was as much ignored as the preceding
ones. Oldroyd must have had the clearest head or have
recovered himself quickest.

'I'll haul down his colours, sir, shall I?' he said.

Hornblower woke from his dream. On a staff above the
taffrail fluttered the yellow and red.

'Yes, haul 'em down at once,' he said.

Now his mind was clear, and now his horizon was no
longer bounded by the narrow limits of the galley. He
looked about him, over the blue, blue sea. There were the
merchant ships; over there lay the *Indefatigable*. Behind
him boiled the white wake of the galley—a curved wake.
Not until that moment did he realize that he was in control
of the tiller, and that for the last three minutes the galley
had been cutting over the blue seas unsteered.

'Take the tiller, Oldroyd,' he ordered.

Was that a galley disappearing into the hazy distance?
It must be, and far in its wake was the longboat. And there,
on the port bow, was the gig, resting on her oars—Hornblower could see little figures standing waving in bow and
stern, and it dawned upon him that this was in acknow-
ledgment of the hauling down of the Spanish colours. Another musket banged off forward, and the rail close at his
hip was struck a tremendous blow which sent gilded
splinters flying in the sunlight. But he had all his wits
about him again, and he ran back over the dying men;
at the after end of the poop he was out of sight of the
gangway and safe from shot. He could still see the gig
on the port bow.

'Starboard your helm, Oldroyd.'

The galley turned slowly—her narrow length made her

unhandy if the rudder were not assisted by the oars—but soon the bow was about to obscure the gig.

'Midships!'

Amazing that there, leaping in the white water that boiled under the galley's stern, was the jolly boat, with one live man and two dead men still aboard.

'Where are the others, Bromley?' yelled Jackson.

Bromley pointed overside. They had been shot from the taffrail at the moment that Hornblower and the others were preparing to attack the poop.

'Why in hell don't you come aboard?'

Bromley took hold of his left arm with his right; the limb was clearly useless. There was no reinforcement to be obtained here, and yet full possession must be taken of the galley. Otherwise it was even conceivable that they would be carried off to Algeciras; even if they were masters of the rudder, the man who controlled the oars dictated the course of the ship if he willed. There was only one course left to try.

Now that his fighting madness had ebbed away, Hornblower was in a sombre mood. He did not care what happened to him; hope and fear had alike deserted him, along with his previous exalted condition. It might be resignation that possessed him now. His mind, still calculating, told him that with only one thing left to do to achieve victory he must attempt it, and the flat, dead condition of his spirits enabled him to carry the attempt through like an automaton, unwavering and emotionless. He walked forward to the poop rail again; the Spaniards were still clustered at the far end of the gangway, with the overseer still giving the time to the oars. They looked up at him as he stood there. With the utmost care and attention he sheathed his cutlass, which he had held in his hand up to that moment. He noticed the blood on his coat and on his hands as he did so. Slowly he settled the sheathed weapon at his side.

'My pistols, Jackson,' he said.

Jackson handed him the pistols and with the same callous care he thrust them into his belt. He turned back to Oldroyd, the Spaniards watching every movement fascinated.

'Stay by the tiller, Oldroyd. Jackson, follow me. Do nothing without my orders.'

With the sun pouring down on his face, he strode down the companion ladder, walked to the gangway, and approached the Spaniards along it. On either side of him the hairy heads and naked bodies of the galley slaves still swung with the oars. He neared the Spaniards; swords and muskets and pistols were handled nervously, but every eye was on his face. Behind him Jackson coughed. Two yards only from the group, Hornblower halted and swept them with his glance. Then, with a gesture, he indicated the whole of the group except the overseer; and then pointed to the forecastle.

'Get forrard, all of you,' he said.

They stood staring at him, although they must have understood the gesture.

'Get forrard,' said Hornblower with a wave of his hand and a tap of his foot on the gangway.

There was only one man who seemed likely to demur actively, and Hornblower had it in mind to snatch a pistol from his belt and shoot him on the spot. But the pistol might misfire, the shot might arouse the Spaniards out of their fascinated dream. He stared the man down.

'Get forrard, I say.'

They began to move, they began to shamble off. Horn-

blower watched them go. Now his emotions were returning
to him, and his heart was thumping madly in his chest so
that it was hard to control himself. Yet he must not be
precipitate. He had to wait until the others were well
clear before he could address himself to the overseer.

'Stop those men,' he said.

He glared into the overseer's eyes while pointing to the
oarsmen; the overseer's lips moved, but he made no sound.

'Stop them,' said Hornblower, and this time he put his
hand to the butt of the pistol.

That sufficed. The overseer raised his voice in a high-
pitched order, and the oars instantly ceased. Strange what
sudden stillness possessed the ship with the cessation of the
grinding of the oars in the tholes. Now it was easy to
hear the bubbling of water round the galley as her way
carried her forward. Hornblower turned back to hail
Oldroyd.

'Oldroyd! Where away's the gig?'

'Close on the starboard bow, sir!'

'How close?'

'Two cable's lengths, sir. She's pulling for us now.'

'Steer for her while you've steerage way.'

'Aye, aye, sir.'

How long would it take the gig under oars to cover a
quarter of a mile? Hornblower feared anticlimax, feared
a sudden revulsion of feeling among the Spaniards at
this late moment. Mere waiting might occasion it, and
he must not stand merely idle. He could still hear the
motion of the galley through the water, and he turned to
Jackson.

'This ship carries her way well, Jackson, doesn't she?' he
said, and he made himself laugh as he spoke, as if everything in the world was a matter of sublime certainty.

G

'Aye, sir, I suppose she does, sir,' said the startled Jackson; he was fidgeting nervously with his pistols.

'And look at the man there,' went on Hornblower, pointing to a galley slave. 'Did you ever see such a beard in your life?'

'N-no, sir.'

'Speak to me, you fool. Talk naturally.'

'I—I dunno what to say, sir.'

'You've no sense, damn you, Jackson. See the welt on that fellow's shoulder? He must have caught it from the overseer's whip not so long ago.'

'Mebbe you're right, sir.'

Hornblower was repressing his impatience and was about to make another speech when he heard a rasping thump alongside and a moment later the gig's crew was pouring over the bulwarks. The relief was inexpressible. Hornblower was about to relax completely when he remembered appearance. He stiffened himself up.

'Glad to see you aboard, sir,' he said, as Lieutenant Chadd swung his legs over and dropped to the maindeck at the break of the forecastle.

'Glad to see *you*,' said Chadd, looking about him curiously.

'These men forrard are prisoners, sir,' said Hornblower. 'It might be well to secure them. I think that is all that remains to be done.'

Now he could not relax; it seemed to him as if he must remain strained and tense for ever. Strained and yet stupid, even when he heard the cheers of the hands in the *Indefatigable* as the galley came alongside her. Stupid and dull, making a stumbling report to Captain Pellew, forcing himself to remember to commend the bravery of Jackson and Oldroyd in the highest terms.

'The Admiral will be pleased,' said Pellew, looking at Hornblower keenly.

'I'm glad, sir,' Hornblower heard himself say.

'Now that we've lost poor Soames,' went on Pellew, 'we shall need another watch-keeping officer. I have it in mind to give you an order as acting-lieutenant.'

'Thank you, sir,' said Hornblower, still stupid.

Soames had been a grey-haired officer of vast experience. He had sailed the seven seas, he had fought in a score of actions. But, faced with a new situation, he had not had the quickness of thought to keep his boat from under the ram of the galley. Soames was dead, and Acting-Lieutenant Hornblower would take his place. Fighting madness, sheer insanity, had won him this promise of promotion. Hornblower had never realized the black depths of lunacy into which he could sink. Like Soames, like all the rest of the crew of the *Indefatigable*, he had allowed himself to be carried away by his blind hatred for the galleys, and only good fortune had allowed him to live through it. That was something worth remembering.

CHAPTER EIGHT

THE EXAMINATION FOR LIEUTENANT

H. M. S. *Indefatigable* was gliding into Gibraltar Bay, with Acting-Lieutenant Horatio Hornblower stiff and self-conscious on the quarterdeck beside Captain Pellew. He kept his telescope trained over towards Algeciras; it was a strange situation, this, that major naval bases of two hostile powers should be no more than six miles apart, and while approaching the harbour it was as well to keep close watch on Algeciras, for there was always the possibility that a squadron of Spaniards might push out suddenly to pounce on an unwary frigate coming in.

'Eight ships—nine ships with their yards crossed, sir,' reported Hornblower.

'Thank you,' answered Pellew. 'Hands 'bout ship.'

The *Indefatigable* tacked and headed in towards the Mole. Gibraltar harbour was, as usual, crowded with shipping, for the whole naval effort of England in the Mediterranean was perforce based here. Pellew clewed up his topsails and put his helm over. Then the cable roared out and the *Indefatigable* swung at anchor.

'Call away my gig,' ordered Pellew.

Pellew favoured dark blue and white as the colour scheme for his boat and its crew—dark blue shirts and white trousers for the men, with white hats with blue ribbons. The boat was of dark blue picked out with white, the oars had white looms and blue blades. The general effect was very smart indeed as the drive of the oars sent the gig skimming over the water to carry Pellew to pay his respects to the port admiral. It was not long after his return that a messenger came scurrying up to Hornblower.

'Captain's compliments, sir, and he'd like to see you in his cabin.'

'Examine your conscience well,' grinned Midshipman Bracegirdle. 'What crimes have you committed?'

'I wish I knew,' said Hornblower, quite genuinely.

It is always a nervous moment going in to see the captain in reply to his summons. Hornblower swallowed as he approached the cabin door, and he had to brace himself a little to knock and enter. But there was nothing to be alarmed about; Pellew looked up with a smile from his desk.

'Ah, Mr Hornblower, I hope you will consider this good news. There will be an examination for lieutenant to-morrow, in the *Santa Barbara* there. You are ready to take it, I hope?'

Hornblower was about to say, 'I suppose so, sir,' but checked himself.

'Yes, sir,' he said—Pellew hated slipshod answers.

'Very well, then. You report there at three p.m. with your certificates and journals.'

'Aye aye, sir.'

That was a very brief conversation for such an important subject. Hornblower had Pellew's order as acting-lieutenant for two months now. To-morrow he would take his examination. If he should pass, the admiral would confirm the order next day, and Hornblower would be a lieutenant with two months' seniority already. But if he should fail! That would mean he had been found unfit for lieutenant's rank. He would revert to midshipman, the two months' seniority would be lost, and it would be six months at least before he could try again. Eight months' seniority was a matter of enormous importance. It would affect all his subsequent career.

'Tell Mr Bolton you have my permission to leave the ship to-morrow, and you may use one of the ship's boats.'

'Thank you, sir.'

'Good luck, Hornblower.'

During the next twenty-four hours Hornblower had not merely to try to read all through Norie's *Epitome of Navigation* again, and Clarke's *Complete Handbook of Seamanship*, but he had to see that his number one uniform was spick and span. It cost his spirit ration to prevail on the

warrant cook to allow the gun-room attendant to heat
a flat-iron in the galley and iron out his neck handkerchief.
Bracegirdle lent him a clean shirt, but there was a feverish
moment when it was discovered that the gun-room supply
of shoe blacking had dried to a chip. Two midshipmen had
to work it soft with lard, and the resultant compound, when
applied to Hornblower's buckled shoes, was stubbornly
resistant to taking a polish; only much labour with the
gun-room's moulting shoebrush and then with a soft cloth
brought those shoes up to a condition of brightness worthy
of an examination for lieutenant. And as for the cocked
hat—the life of a cocked hat in the midshipman's berth is
hard, and some of the dents could not be entirely eliminated.

'Take it off as soon as you can and keep it under your
arm,' advised Bracegirdle. 'Maybe they won't see you come
up the ship's side.'

Everybody turned out to see Hornblower leave the ship,
with his sword and his white breeches and his buckled
shoes, his bundle of journals under his arm and his certificates of sobriety and good conduct in his pocket. The
winter afternoon was already far advanced as he was rowed
over to the *Santa Barbara* and went up the ship's side to
report himself to the officer of the watch.

The *Santa Barbara* was a prison hulk, one of the prizes
captured in Rodney's action off Cadiz in 1780 and kept
rotting at her moorings, mastless, ever since, a storeship in
time of peace and a prison in time of war. Red-coated
soldiers, muskets loaded and bayonets fixed, guarded the
gangways; on forecastle and quarterdeck were carronades,
trained inboard and depressed to sweep the waist, wherein
a few prisoners took the air, ragged and unhappy. As Hornblower came up the side he caught a whiff of the stench

within, where two thousand prisoners were confined. Horn-blower reported himself to the officer of the watch as come on board, and for what purpose.

'Whoever would have guessed it?' said the officer of the watch—an elderly lieutenant with white hair hanging down to his shoulders—running his eye over Hornblower's immaculate uniform and the portfolio under his arm. 'Fifteen of your kind have already come on board, and—Holy Gemini, see there!'

Quite a flotilla of small craft was closing in on the *Santa Barbara*. Each boat held at least one cocked-hatted and white-breeched midshipman, and some held four or five.

'Every courtesy young gentleman in Mediterranean Fleet is ambitious for an epaulet,' said the lieutenant. 'Just wait until the examining board sees how many there are of you! I wouldn't be in your shoes, young shaver, for something. Go aft, there, and wait in the portside cabin.'

It was already uncomfortably full; when Hornblower entered, fifteen pairs of eyes measured him up. There were officers of all ages from eighteen to forty, all in their number one's, all nervous—one or two of them had Norie's *Epitome* open on their laps and were anxiously reading passages about which they were doubtful. One little group was passing a bottle from hand to hand, presumably in an effort to keep up their courage. But no sooner had Hornblower entered than a stream of newcomers followed him. The cabin began to fill, and soon it was tightly packed. Half the forty men present found seats on the deck, and the others were forced to stand.

'Forty years back,' said a loud voice somewhere, 'my grandad marched with Clive to revenge the Black Hole of Calcutta. If he could but have witnessed the fate of his posterity!'

'Have a drink,' said another voice, 'and to hell with care.'

'Forty of us,' commented a tall, thin, clerkly officer, counting heads. 'How many of us will pass, do you think? Five?'

'To hell with care,' repeated the bibulous voice in the corner, and lifted itself in song. ' "Begone, dull care; I prithee be gone from me——" '

'Cheese it, you fool!' rasped another voice. 'Hark to that!'

The air was filled with the long-drawn twittering of the pipes of the bos'n's mates, and someone on deck was shouting an order.

'A captain coming on board,' remarked someone.

An officer had his eye at the crack of the door. 'It's Dreadnought Foster,' he reported.

'He's a tail twister if ever there was one,' said a fat young officer, seated comfortably with his back to the bulkhead.

Again the pipes twittered.

'Harvey, of the dockyard,' reported the look-out.

The third captain followed immediately. 'It's Black Charlie Hammond,' said the look-out. 'Looking as if he'd lost a guinea and found sixpence.'

'Black Charlie?' exclaimed someone, scrambling to his feet in haste and pushing to the door. 'Let's see! So it is! Then here is one young gentleman who will not stay for an answer. I know too well what that answer would be. "Six months more at sea, sir, and damn your eyes for your impertinence in presenting yourself for examination in your present state of ignorance." Black Charlie won't ever forget that I lost his pet poodle overside from the cutter in Port-o'-Spain when he was first of the *Pegasus*. Good-bye, gentlemen. Give my regards to the examining board.'

With that he was gone, and they saw him explaining himself to the officer of the watch and hailing a shore boat to take him back to his ship. 'One fewer of us, at least,' said the clerkly officer. 'What is it, my man?'

'The board's compliments, sir,' said the marine messenger, 'an' will the first young gentleman please to come along?'

There was a momentary hesitation; no one was anxious to be the first victim.

'The one nearest the door,' said an elderly master's mate. 'Will you volunteer, sir?'

'I'll be the Daniel,' said the erstwhile look-out desperately. 'Remember me in your prayers.'

He pulled his coat smooth, twitched at his neckcloth, and was gone, the remainder waiting in gloomy silence, relieved only by the glug-glug of the bottle as the bibulous midshipman took another swig. A full ten minutes passed before the candidate for promotion returned, making a brave effort to smile.

'Six months more at sea?' asked someone.

'No,' was the unexpected answer. 'Three! . . . I was told to send the next man. It had better be you.'

'But what did they ask you?'

'They began by asking me to define a rhumb line. . . . But don't keep them waiting, I advise you.' Some thirty officers had their text-books open on the instant, to re-read about rhumb lines.

'You were there ten minutes,' said the clerkly officer, looking at his watch. 'Forty of us, ten minutes each—why, it'll be midnight before they reach the last of us. They'll never do it.'

'They'll be hungry,' said someone.

'Hungry for our blood,' said another.

'Perhaps they'll try us in batches,' suggested a third, 'like the French tribunals.'

Listening to them, Hornblower was reminded of French aristocrats jesting at the foot of the scaffold. Candidates departed and candidates returned, some gloomy, some smiling. The cabin was already far less crowded; Hornblower was able to secure sufficient deck space to seat himself, and he stretched out his legs with a nonchalant sigh of relief, and he no sooner emitted the sigh than he realized that it was a stage effect which he had put on for his own benefit. He was as nervous as he could be. The winter night was falling, and some good Samaritan on board sent in a couple of purser's dips to give a feeble illumination to the darkening cabin.

'They are passing one in three,' said the clerkly officer, making ready for his turn. 'May I be the third.'

Hornblower got to his feet again when he left; it would be his turn next. He stepped out under the half-deck into the dark night and breathed the chill fresh air. A gentle breeze was blowing from the southward, cooled, presumably, by the snow-clad Atlas Mountains of Africa across the strait. There was neither moon nor stars. Here came the clerkly officer back again.

'Hurry,' he said. 'They're impatient.'

Hornblower made his way past the sentry to the after cabin; it was brightly lit, so that he blinked as he entered, and stumbled over some obstruction. And it was only then that he remembered that he had not straightened his neckcloth and seen to it that his sword hung correctly at his side. He went on blinking in his nervousness at the three grim faces across the table.

'Well, sir?' said a stern voice. 'Report yourself. We have no time to waste.'

'H-Hornblower, sir. H-Horatio H-Hornblower. M-Midshipman—I mean Acting-Lieutenant, H.M.S. *Indefatigable*.'

'Your certificates, please,' said the right-hand face.

Hornblower handed them over, and as he waited for them to be examined, the left-hand face suddenly spoke. 'You are close-hauled on the port tack, Mr Hornblower, beating up-channel with a nor-easterly wind blowing hard, with Dover bearing north two miles. Is that clear?'

'Yes, sir.'

'Now the wind veers four points and takes you flat aback. What do you do, sir? What do you do?'

Hornblower's mind, if it was thinking about anything at all at that moment, was thinking about rhumb lines; this question took him as much aback as the situation it envisaged. His mouth opened and shut, but there was no word he could say.

'By now you're dismasted,' said the middle face—a swarthy face; Hornblower was making the deduction that it must belong to Black Charlie Hammond. He could think about that even if he could not force his mind to think at all about his examination.

'Dismasted,' said the left-hand face, with a smile like Nero enjoying a Christian's death agony. 'With Dover cliffs under your lee. You are in serious trouble, Mr—ah—Hornblower.'

Serious indeed. Hornblower's mouth opened and shut again. His dull mind heard, without paying special attention to it, the thud of a cannon shot somewhere not too far off. The board passed no remark on it either, but a moment later there came a series of further cannon shots which brought the three captains to their feet. Unceremoniously they rushed out of the cabin, sweeping out of the way the sentry at the door. Hornblower followed them; they arrived in the waist just in time to see a rocket soar up into the night sky and burst in a shower of red stars.

It was the general alarm; over the water of the anchorage they could hear the drums rolling as all the ships present beat to quarters. On the portside gangway the remainder of the candidates were clustered, speaking excitedly.

'See there!' said a voice.

Across half a mile of dark water a yellow light grew until the ship there was wrapped in flame. She had every sail set and was heading straight into the crowded anchorage.

'Fire ships!'

'Officer of the watch! Call my gig!' bellowed Foster.

A line of fire ships was running before the wind, straight at the crowd of anchored ships. The *Santa Barbara* was full of the wildest bustle as the seamen and marines came pouring on deck, and as captains and candidates shouted for boats to take them back to their ships. A line of orange flame lit up the water, followed at once by the roar of a broadside; some ship was firing her guns in the endeavour to sink a fire ship. Let one of those blazing hulls make contact with one of the anchored ships, even for a few seconds, and the fire would be transmitted to the dry, painted timber, to the tarred cordage, to the inflammable sails, so that nothing would put it out. To men in highly combustible ships filled with explosives fire was the deadliest and most dreaded peril of the sea.

'You shore boat, there!' bellowed Hammond suddenly. 'You shore boat! Come alongside! Come alongside, blast you!'

His eye had been quick to sight the pair-oar rowing up.

'Come alongside or I'll fire into you!' supplemented Foster. 'Sentry, there, make ready to give them a shot!'

At the threat the wherry turned and glided towards the mizzen chains.

'Here you are, gentlemen,' said Hammond.

The three captains rushed to the mizzen chains and flung themselves down into the boat. Hornblower was at their heels. He knew there was small enough chance of a junior officer getting a boat to take him back to his ship, to which it was his bounden duty to go as soon as possible. After the captains had reached their destinations he could use this boat to reach the *Indefatigable*. He threw himself off into stern-sheets as she pushed off, knocking the breath out of Captain Harvey, his sword scabbard clattering on the gunwale. But the three captains accepted his uninvited presence there without comment.

'Pull for the *Dreadnought*,' said Foster.

'Dammit, I'm the senior!' said Hammond. 'Pull for *Calypso*.'

'*Calypso* it is,' said Harvey. He had his hand on the tiller, heading the boat across the dark water.

'Pull! Oh, pull!' said Foster, in agony. There can be no mental tortures like that of a captain whose ship is in peril and he not on board.

'There's one of them,' said Harvey.

Just ahead, a small brig was bearing down on them under topsails; they could see the glow of the fire, and as they watched the fire suddenly burst into roaring fury, wrapping the whole vessel in flames in a moment, like a set-piece in a fireworks display. Flames spouted out of the holes in her sides and roared up through her hatchways. The very water around her glowed vivid red. They saw her halt in her career and begin to swing slowly around.

'She's across *Santa Barbara*'s cable,' said Foster.

'She's nearly clear,' added Hammond. 'God help, 'em on board there. She'll be alongside her in a minute.'

Hornblower thought of two thousand Spanish and French prisoners battened down below decks in the hulk.

'With a man at her wheel she could be steered clear,' said Foster. 'We ought to do it!'

Then things happened rapidly. Harvey put the tiller over. 'Pull away!' he roared at the boatmen.

The latter displayed an easily understood reluctance to row up to that fiery hull.

'Pull!' said Harvey.

He whipped out his sword from its scabbard, and the blade reflected the red fire as he thrust it menacingly at the stroke oar's throat. With a kind of sob, stroke tugged at his oar and the boat leaped forward.

'Lay us under her counter,' said Foster. 'I'll jump for it.'

At last Hornblower found his tongue. 'Let me go, sir. I'll handle her.'

'Come with me, if you like,' replied Foster. 'It may need two of us.'

His nickname of Dreadnought Foster may have had its origin in the name of his ship, but it was appropriate enough in all circumstances. Harvey swung the boat under the fire ship's stern; she was before the wind again now, and just gathering way, just heading down upon the *Santa Barbara*.

For a moment Hornblower was the nearest man in the boat to the brig and there was no time to be lost. He stood up on the thwart and jumped; his hands gripped something, and with a kick and a struggle he dragged his ungainly body up on to the deck. With the brig before the wind, the flames were blown forward; right aft here it was merely frightfully hot, but Hornblower's ears were filled with the roar of the flames and the crackling and banging of the burning wood. He stepped forward to the wheel and seized the spokes, the wheel was lashed with a loop of line, and as he cast this off and took hold of the wheel again he could feel the rudder below him bite into the water. He flung his weight on the spoke and spun the wheel over. The brig was about to collide with the *Santa Barbara*, starboard bow to starboard bow, and the flames lit an anxious, gesticulating crowd on the *Santa Barbara*'s forecastle.

'Hard over!' roared Foster's voice in Hornblower's ear.

'Hard over it is!' said Hornblower, and the brig answered her wheel at that moment, and her bow turned away, avoiding the collision.

An immense fountain of flame poured out from the hatchway abaft the mainmast, setting mast and rigging ablaze, and at the same time a flaw of wind blew a wave of flame aft. Some instinct made Hornblower, while holding the wheel with one hand, snatch out his neckcloth with the other and bury his face in it. The flame whirled round him and was gone again. But the distractions had been dangerous; the brig had continued to turn under full helm, and now her stern was swinging in to bump against the *Santa Barbara*'s bow. Hornblower desperately spun the wheel over the other way. The flames had driven Foster aft to the taffrail, but now he returned.

'Hard-a-lee!'

The brig was already responding. Her starboard quarter bumped the *Santa Barbara* in the waist, and then bumped clear.

At a distance of only two or three yards the fire ship passed on down the *Santa Barbara*'s side; an anxious group ran along her gangways, keeping up with her as she did so. On the quarterdeck another group stood by with a spar to boom the fire ship off; Hornblower saw them out of the tail of his eye as they went by. Now they were clear.

'There's the *Dauntless* on the port bow,' said Foster. 'Keep her clear.'

'Aye, aye, sir.'

The din of the fire was tremendous; it could hardly be believed that on this little area of deck it was still possible to breathe and live. Hornblower felt the appalling heat on his hands and face. Both masts were immense pyramids of flame.

'Starboard a point,' said Foster. 'We'll lay her aground on the shoal by the Neutral Ground.'

'Starboard a point,' responded Hornblower.

He was being borne along on a wave of the highest exaltation; the roar of the fire was intoxicating, and he knew not a moment's fear. Then the whole deck only a yard or two forward of the wheel opened up in flame. Fire spouted out of the gaping seams and the heat was utterly unbearable, and the fire moved rapidly aft as the seams gaped progressively backward.

Hornblower felt for the loopline to lash the wheel, but before he could do so the wheel spun idly under his hand, presumably as the tiller ropes below him were burned away, and at the same time the deck under his feet heaved and warped in the fire. He staggered back to the taffrail. Foster was there.

'Tiller ropes burned away, sir,' reported Hornblower.

Flames roared up beside them. His coat sleeve was smouldering.

'Jump!' said Foster.

Hornblower felt Foster shoving him—everything was insane. He heaved himself over, gasped with fright as he hung in the air, and then felt the breath knocked out of his body as he hit the water. The water closed over him, and he knew panic as he struggled back to the surface. It was cold—the Mediterranean in December is cold. For the moment the air in his clothes supported him, despite the weight of the sword at his side, but he could see nothing in the darkness, with his eyes still dazzled by the roaring flames. Somebody splashed beside him.

'They were following us in the boat to take us off,' said Foster's voice. 'Can you swim?'

'Yes, sir. Not very well.'

'That might describe me,' said Foster; and then he lifted his voice to hail, 'Ahoy! Ahoy! Hammond! Harvey! Ahoy!'

He tried to raise himself as well as his voice, fell back with a splash, and splashed and splashed again, the water flowing into his mouth cutting short something he tried to say. Hornblower, beating the water with increased feebleness, could still spare a thought—such were vagaries of his wayward mind—for the interesting fact that even captains of much seniority were only mortal men after all. He tried to unbuckle his sword belt, failed, and sank deep with the effort, only just succeeding in struggling back to the surface. He gasped for breath, but in another attempt he managed to draw his sword half out of its scabbard, and as he struggled it slid out the rest of the way by its own weight; yet he was not conscious of any noticeable relief.

It was then that he heard the splashing and grinding of oars and loud voices, and he saw the dark shape of the approaching boat, and he uttered a spluttering cry. In a second or two the boat was up to them, and he was clutching the gunwale in panic.

They were lifting Foster in over the stern, and Hornblower knew he must keep still and make no effort to climb in, but it called for all his resolution to make himself hang quietly on to the side of the boat and wait his turn. He was interested in this overmastering fear, while he despised himself for it. It called for a conscious and serious

effort of will-power to make his hands alternately release
their death-like grip on the gunwale, so that the men in the
boat could pass him round to the stern. Then they dragged
him in and he fell face downward in the bottom of the
boat, on the verge of fainting. Then somebody spoke in the
boat, and Hornblower felt a cold shiver pass over his skin,
and his feeble muscles tensed themselves, for the words
spoken were Spanish—at any rate an unknown tongue, and
Spanish presumably.

Somebody else answered in the same language. Hornblower tried to struggle up, and a restraining hand was laid
on his shoulder. He rolled over, and with his eyes now
accustomed to the darkness he could see the three swarthy
faces with the long black moustaches. These men were not
Gibraltarians. On the instant he could guess who they were
—the crew of one of the fire ships who had steered their
craft in past the Mole, set fire to it, and made their escape
in the boat. Foster was sitting doubled up, in the bottom
of the boat, and now he lifted his face from his knees and
stare round him.

'Who are these fellows?' he asked feebly—his struggle in
the water had left him as weak as Hornblower.

'Spanish fire ship's crew, I fancy, sir,' said Hornblower.
'We're prisoners.'

'Are we indeed?'

The knowledge galvanized him into activity just as it had
Hornblower. He tried to get to his feet, and the Spaniard
at the tiller thrust him down with a hand on his shoulder.
Foster tried to put his hand away, and raised his voice in a
feeble cry, but the man at the tiller was standing no nonsense. He brought out, in a lightning gesture, a knife from
his belt. The light from the fire ship, burning itself harmlessly out on the shoal in the distance, ran redly along the

blade, and Foster ceased to struggle. Men might call him Dreadnought Foster, but he could recognize the need for discretion.

'How are we heading?' he asked Hornblower, sufficiently quietly not to irritate their captors.

'North, sir. Maybe they're going to land on the Neutral Ground and make for the Line.'

'That's their best chance,' agreed Foster.

He turned his neck uncomfortably to look back up the harbour.

'Two other ships burning themselves out up there,' he said. 'There were three fire ships came in, I fancy.'

'I saw three, sir.'

'Then there's no damage done. But a bold endeavour. Whoever would have credited the Dons with making such an attempt?'

'They have learned about fire ships from us, perhaps, sir,' suggested Hornblower.

'We may have "nursed the pinion that impelled the steel", you think?'

'It is possible, sir.'

Foster was a cool enough customer, quoting poetry and discussing the naval situation while being carried off into captivity by a Spaniard who guarded him with a drawn knife. Cool might be a too accurate adjective; Hornblower was shivering in his wet clothes as the chill night air blew over him, and he felt weak and feeble after all the excitement and exertions of the day.

'Boat ahoy!' came a hail across the water; there was a dark nucleus in the night over there. The Spaniard in the stern-sheets instantly dragged the tiller over, heading the boat directly away from it, while the two at the oars redoubled their exertions.

'Guard boat——' said Foster, but cut his explanation short at a further threat from the knife.

Of course there would be a boat rowing guard at this northern end of the anchorage; they might have thought of it.

'Boat ahoy!' came the hail again. 'Lay on your oars or I'll fire into you!'

The Spaniard made no reply, and a second later came the flash and report of a musket shot. They heard nothing of the bullet, but the shot would put the fleet—towards which they were heading again—on the alert. But the Spaniards were going to play the game out to the end. They rowed doggedly on.

'Boat ahoy!'

This was another hail, from a boat right ahead of them. The Spaniards at the oars ceased their efforts in dismay, but a roar from the steersman set them instantly to work again. Hornblower could see the new boat almost directly ahead of them, and heard another hail from it as it rested on its oars. The Spaniard at the tiller shouted an order, and the stroke oar backed water and the boat turned sharply; another order, and both rowers tugged ahead again and the boat surged forward to ram. Should they succeed in overturning the intercepting boat they might make their escape even now, while the pursuing boat stopped to pick up their friends.

Everything happened at once, with everyone shouting at the full pitch of his lungs, seemingly. There was the crash of the collision, both boats heeling wildly as the bow of the Spanish boat rode up over the British boat but failed to overturn it. Someone fired a pistol, and the next moment the pursuing guard boat came dashing alongside, its crew leaping madly aboard them. Somebody flung himself on top of Hornblower, crushing the breath out of him and threatening to keep it out permanently with a hand on his throat. Hornblower heard Foster bellowing in protest, and a moment later his assailant released him, so that he could hear the midshipman of the guard boat apologizing for this rough treatment of a post-captain of the Royal Navy. Someone unmasked the guard boat's lantern, and by its light Foster revealed himself, bedraggled and battered. The light shone on their sullen prisoners.

'Boats ahoy!' came another hail, and yet another boat emerged from the darkness and pulled towards them.

'Cap'n Hammond, I believe!' hailed Foster, with an ominous rasp in his voice.

'Thank God!' they heard Hammond say, and the boat pulled into the faint circle of light.

'But no thanks to you,' said Foster bitterly.

'After your fire ship cleared the *Santa Barbara* a puff of wind took you on faster than we could keep up with you,' explained Harvey.

'We followed as fast as we could get those rock scorpions to row,' added Hammond.

'And yet it called for Spaniards to save us from drowning,' sneered Foster. The memory of his struggle in the water rankled, apparently. 'I thought I could rely on two brother captains.'

'What are you implying, sir?' snapped Hammond.

'I make no implications, but others may read implications into a simple statement of fact.'

'I consider that an offensive remark, sir,' said Harvey, 'addressed to me equally with Captain Hammond.'

'I congratulate you on your perspicacity, sir,' replied Foster.

'I understand,' said Harvey. 'This is not a discussion we

can pursue with these men present. I shall send a friend to wait on you.'

'He will be welcome.'

'Then I wish you a very good night, sir.'

'And I, too, sir,' said Hammond. 'Give way there.'

The boat pulled out of the circle of light, leaving an audience open-mouthed at this strange freak of human behaviour, that a man saved first from death and then from captivity should wantonly thrust himself into peril again. Foster looked after the boat for some seconds before speaking; perhaps he was already regretting his rather hysterical outburst.

'I shall have much to do before morning,' he said, more to himself than to anyone near him, and then addressed himself to the midshipman of the guard boat, 'You, sir, will take charge of these prisoners and convey me to my ship.'

'Aye aye, sir.'

'Is there anyone here who can speak their lingo? I would have it explained to them that I shall send them back to Cartagena under cartel, free without exchange. They saved our lives, and that is the least we can do in return.' The final explanatory sentence was addressed to Hornblower.

'I think that is just, sir.'

'And you, my fire-breathing friend. May I offer you my thanks? You did well. Should I live beyond to-morrow, I shall see that authority is informed of your actions.'

'Thank you, sir.' A question trembled on Hornblower's lips. It called for a little resolution to thrust it out, 'And my examination, sir? My certificate?'

Foster shook his head. 'That particular examining board will never reassemble, I fancy. You must wait your opportunity to go before another one.'

'Aye aye, sir,' said Hornblower, with despondency apparent in his tone.

'Now lookee here, Mr Hornblower,' said Foster, turning upon him. 'To the best of my recollection, you were flat aback, about to lose your spars and with Dover cliffs under your lee. In one minute you would have failed—it was the warning gun that saved you. Is not that so?'

'I suppose it is, sir.'

'Then be thankful for small mercies. And even more thankful for big ones.'

CHAPTER NINE

NOAH'S ARK

ACTING-LIEUTENANT HORNBLOWER sat in the stern-sheets of the longboat beside Mr Tapling of the diplomatic service, with his feet among bags of gold. About him rose the steep shores of the Gulf of Oran, and ahead of him lay the city, white in the sunshine, like a mass of blocks of marble dumped by a careless hand upon the hillsides where they rose from the water. The oar blades, as the boat's crew pulled away rhythmically over the gentle swell, were biting into the clearest emerald green, and it was only a moment since they had left behind the bluest the Mediterranean could show.

'A pretty sight from here,' said Tapling, gazing at the town they were approaching, 'but closer inspection will show that the eye is deceived. And as for the nose! The stinks of the true believers have to be smelt to be believed. Lay her alongside the jetty there, Mr Hornblower, beyond those xebecs.'

'Aye, aye, sir,' said the coxswain, when Hornblower gave the order.

'There's a sentry on the waterfront battery here,' commented Tapling, looking about him keenly, 'not more than half asleep, either. And notice the two guns in the two castles. Thirty-two pounders, without a doubt. Stone shot piled in readiness. A stone shot flying into fragments on impact effects damage out of proportion to its size. And the walls seem sound enough. To seize Oran by a *coup de main* would not be easy, I am afraid. If His Nibs the Bey should choose to cut our throats and keep our gold it would be long before we were avenged, Mr Hornblower.'

'I don't think I should find any satisfaction in being avenged in any case, sir,' said Hornblower.

'There's some truth in that. But doubtless His Nibs will spare us this time. The goose lays golden eggs—a boatload of gold every month must make a dazzling prospect for a pirate Bey in these days of convoys.'

'Way 'nough,' called the coxswain. 'Oars!'

The longboat came gliding alongside the jetty and hooked on neatly. A few seated figures in the shade turned eyes at least, and in some cases even their heads as well, to look at the British boat's crew. A number of swarthy Moors appeared on the decks of the xebecs and gazed down at them, and one or two shouted remarks to them.

'No doubt they are describing the ancestry of the infidels,' said Tapling. 'Sticks and stones may break my bones, but names can never hurt me, especially when I do not understand them. Where's our man?'

He shaded his eyes to look along the waterfront.

'No one in sight, sir, that looks like a Christian,' said Hornblower.

'Our man's no Christian,' said Tapling. 'White, but no Christian. White by courtesy at that—French-Arab-Levantine mixture. His Britannic Majesty's Consul at Oran *pro tem.*, and a Mussulman from expediency. Though there are very serious disadvantages from being a true believer. Who would want four wives at any time, especially when he pays for the doubtful privilege by abstaining from wine?'

Tapling stepped up on to the jetty and Hornblower followed him. The gentle swell that rolled up the Gulf broke soothingly below them, and the blinding heat of the noonday sun was reflected up into their faces from the stone blocks on which they stood. Far down the Gulf lay the two anchored ships—the storeship and H.M.S. *Indefatigable*—lovely on the blue and silver surface.

'And yet I would rather see Drury Lane on a Saturday night,' said Tapling.

He turned back to look at the city wall, which guarded the place from seaborne attack. A narrow gate, flanked by bastions, opened on to the waterfront. Sentries in red caftans were visible on the summit. In the deep shadow of the gate something was moving, but it was hard with eyes dazzled by the sun to see what it was. Then it emerged from the shadow as a little group coming towards them—a half-naked Negro leading a donkey, and on the back of the donkey, seated sideways far back towards the root of the tail, a vast figure in a blue robe.

'Shall we meet His Britannic Majesty's Consul halfway?' asked Tapling. ' No. Let him come to us.'

The Negro halted the donkey, and the man on the donkey's back slid to the ground and came towards them—

a mountainous man, waddling straddle-legged in his robe, his huge clay-coloured face topped by a white turban. A scanty black moustache and beard sprouted from his lip and chin.

'Your servant, Mr Duras,' said Tapling. 'And may I present Acting-Lieutenant Horatio Hornblower, of the frigate *Indefatigable*?'

Mr Duras nodded his perspiring head.

'Have you brought the money?' he asked, in guttural French; it took Hornblower a moment or two to adjust his mind to the language and his ear to Duras' intonation.

'Seven thousand golden guineas,' replied Tapling, in reasonably good French.

'Good,' said Duras, with a trace of relief. 'Is it in the boat?'

'It is in the boat, and it stays in the boat at present,' answered Tapling. 'Do you remember the conditions agreed upon? Four hundred fat cattle, fifteen hundred fanegas of barley grain. When I see those in the lighters, and the lighters alongside the ships down the bay, then I hand over the money. Have you the stores ready?'

'Soon.'

'As I expected. How long?'

'Soon—very soon.'

Tapling made a grimace of resignation.

'Then we shall return to the ships. To-morrow, perhaps, or the day after, we shall come back with the gold.'

Alarm appeared on Duras' sweating face.

'No, do not do that,' he said, hastily. 'You do not know His Highness the Bey. He is changeable. If he knows the gold is here he will give orders for the cattle to be brought. Take the gold away, and he will not stir. And—and—he will be angry with me.'

'*Ira principis mors est,*' said Tapling, and in response to Duras' blank look obliged by a translation. 'The wrath of the prince means death. Is not that so?'

'Yes,' said Duras, and he in turn said something in an unknown language, and stabbed at the air with his fingers in a peculiar gesture; and then translated, 'May it not happen.'

'Certainly we hope it may not happen,' agreed Tapling with disarming cordiality. 'The bowstring, the hook, even the bastinado are all unpleasant. It might be better if you went to the Bey and prevailed upon him to give the necessary orders for the grain and the cattle. Or we shall leave at nightfall.'

Tapling glanced up at the sun to lay stress on the time limit.

'I shall go,' said Duras, spreading his hands in a deprecatory gesture. 'I shall go. But I beg of you, do not depart. Perhaps His Highness is busy in his harem. Then no one may disturb him. But I shall try. The grain is here already —it lies in the Kasbah there. It is only the cattle that have to be brought in. Please be patient. I implore you. His Highness is not accustomed to commerce, as you know, sir. Still less is he accustomed to commerce after the fashion of the Franks.'

Duras wiped his streaming face with a corner of his robe.

'Pardon me,' he said, 'I do not feel well. But I shall go to His Highness. I shall go. Please wait for me.'

'Until sunset,' said Tapling implacably.

Duras called to his Negro attendant, who had been crouching huddled up under the donkey's belly to take advantage of the shade it cast. With an effort Duras hoisted his ponderous weight on to the donkey's hindquarters. He wiped his face again and looked at them with a trace of bewilderment.

'Wait for me,' were the last words he said as the donkey was led away back into the city gate.

'He is afraid of the Bey,' said Tapling, watching him go. 'I would rather face twenty Beys than Admiral Sir John Jervis in a tantrum. What will he do when he hears about this further delay, with the Fleet on short rations already? He'll have my guts for a necktie.'

'One cannot expect punctuality of these people,' said Hornblower with the easy philosophy of the man who does not bear the responsibility. But he thought of the British Navy, without friends, without allies, maintaining desperately the blockade of a hostile Europe, in face of superior numbers, storms, disease, and now famine.

'Look at that!' said Tapling pointing suddenly.

It was a big grey rat which had made its appearance in the dry storm gutter that crossed the waterfront here. Regardless of the bright sunshine it sat up and looked round at the world; even when Tapling stamped his foot it showed no great signs of alarm. When he stamped a second time it slowly turned to hide itself again in the drain, missed its footing so that it lay writhing for a moment at the mouth of the drain, and then regained its feet and disappeared into the darkness.

'An old rat, I suppose,' said Tapling meditatively. 'Senile, possibly. Even blind, it may be.'

Hornblower cared nothing about rats, senile or otherwise. He took a step or two back in the direction of the longboat and the civilian officer conformed to his movements.

'Rig that mains'l so that it gives us some shade, Maxwell,' said Hornblower. 'We're here for the rest of the day.'

'A great comfort,' said Tapling, seating himself on a stone bollard beside the boat, 'to be here in a heathen port. No need to worry in case any men run off. No need to worry about liquor. Only about bullocks and barley. And how to get a spark on this tinder.'

He blew through the pipe that he took from his pocket, preparatory to filling it. The boat was shaded by the main-sail now, and the hands sat in the bows yarning in low tones, while the others made themselves as comfortable as possible in the stern-sheets; the boat rolled peacefully in the tiny swell, the rhythmic sound as the fendoffs creaked between her gunwale and the jetty having a soothing effect while city and port dozed in the blazing afternoon heat. Yet it was not easy for a young man of Hornblower's active temperament to endure prolonged inaction. He climbed up on the jetty to stretch his legs, and paced up and down; a Moor in a white gown and turban came staggering in the sunshine along the waterfront. His gait was unsteady, and he walked with his legs well apart to provide a firmer base for his swaying body.

'What was it you said, sir, about liquor being abhorred by the Moslems?' said Hornblower to Tapling down in the stern-sheets.

'Not necessarily abhorred,' replied Tapling, guardedly. 'But anathematized, illegal, unlawful, and hard to obtain.'

'Someone here has contrived to obtain some, sir,' said Hornblower.

'Let me see,' said Tapling, scrambling up; the hands, bored with waiting and interested as ever in liquor, landed from the bows to stare as well.

'That looks like a man who has taken drink,' agreed Tapling.

'Three sheets in the wind, sir,' said Maxwell, as the Moor staggered.

'And taken all aback,' supplemented Tapling, as the Moor swerved wildly to one side in a semicircle.

At the end of the semicircle he fell with a crash on his face; his brown legs emerged from the robe a couple of times and were drawn in again, and he lay passive, his head on his arms, his turban fallen on the ground to reveal his shaven skull with a tassel of hair on the crown.

'Totally dismasted,' said Hornblower.

'And hard aground,' said Tapling.

But the Moor now lay oblivious of everything.

'And here's Duras,' said Hornblower.

Out through the gate came the massive figure on the little donkey; another donkey bearing another portly figure followed, each donkey being led by a Negro slave, and after them came a dozen swarthy individuals whose muskets, and whose pretence at uniform, indicated that they were soldiers.

'The Treasurer of His Highness,' said Duras, by way of introduction when he and the other had dismounted. 'Come to fetch the gold.'

The portly Moor looked loftily upon them; Duras was still streaming with sweat in the hot sun.

'The gold is there,' said Tapling, pointing. 'In the stern-sheets of the longboat. You will have a closer view of it when we have a closer view of the stores we are to buy.'

Duras translated this speech into Arabic. There was a rapid interchange of sentences, before the Treasurer apparently yielded. He turned and waved his arms back to the gate in what was evidently a prearranged signal. A dreary procession immediately emerged—a long line of men, all of them almost naked, white, black, and mulatto, each man staggering along under the burden of a sack of grain. Overseers with sticks walked with them.

'The money,' said Duras, as a result of something said by the Treasurer.

A word from Tapling set the hands to work lifting the heavy bags of gold on to the quay.

'With the corn on the jetty I will put the gold there too,' said Tapling to Hornblower. 'Keep your eye on it while I look at some of those sacks.'

Tapling walked over to the slave gang. Here and there he opened a sack, looked into it, and inspected handfuls of the golden barley grain; other sacks he felt from the outside.

'No hope of looking over every sack in a hundred ton of barley,' he remarked, strolling back again to Hornblower. 'Much of it is sand, I expect. But that is the way of the heathen. The price is adjusted accordingly. Very well, Effendi.'

At a sign from Duras, and under the urgings of the overseers, the slaves burst into activity, trotting up to the quayside and dropping their sacks into the lighter which lay there. The first dozen men were organized into a working party to distribute the cargo evenly into the bottom of the lighter, while the others trotted off, their bodies gleaming with sweat, to fetch fresh loads. At the same time a couple of swarthy herdsmen came out through the gate driving a small herd of cattle.

'Scrubby little creatures,' said Tapling, looking them over critically, 'but that was allowed for in the price, too.'

'The gold,' said Duras.

In reply, Tapling opened one of the bags at his feet, filled his hand with golden guineas, and let them cascade through his fingers into the bag again.

'Five hundred guineas there,' he said. 'Fourteen bags, as you see. They will be yours when the lighters are loaded and unmoored.'

Duras wiped his face with a weary gesture. His knees seemed to be weak, and he leaned upon the patient donkey that stood behind him.

The cattle were being driven down a gangway into another lighter, and a second herd had now appeared and was waiting.

'Things move faster than you feared,' said Hornblower.

'See how they drive the poor wretches,' replied Tapling sententiously. 'See! Things move fast when you have no concern for human flesh and blood.'

A coloured slave had fallen to the ground under his burden. He lay there disregarding the blows rained on him by the sticks of the overseers. There was a small movement of his legs. Someone dragged him out of the way at last and the sacks continued to be carried to the lighter. The other lighter was filling fast with cattle, packed into a tight, bellowing mass in which no movement was possible.

'His Nibs is actually keeping his word,' marvelled Tapling. 'I'd 'a settled for the half, if I had been asked beforehand.'

One of the herdsmen on the quay had sat down with his face in his hands; now he fell over limply on his side.

'Sir——' began Hornblower to Tapling, and the two men looked at each other with the same awful thought occurring to them at the same moment.

Duras began to say something; with one hand on the withers of the donkey and the other gesticulating in the air it seemed that he was making something of a speech, but there was no sense in the words he was roaring out in a hoarse voice. His face was swollen beyond its customary fatness and his expression was widely distorted, while his cheeks were so suffused with blood as to look dark under his tan. Duras quitted his hold of the donkey and began to reel about in half circles, under the eyes of Moors and Englishmen. His voice died away to a whisper, his legs gave way under him, and he fell to his hands and knees and then to his face.

'That's the plague!' said Tapling. 'The Black Death! I saw it in Smyrna in '96.'

He and the other Englishmen had shrunk back on the one side, the soldiers and the Treasurer on the other, leaving the palpitating body lying in the clear space between them.

'The plague, by St Peter!' squealed one of the young sailors. He would have headed a rush to the longboat.

'Stand still, there!' roared Hornblower, scared of the plague but with the habits of discipline so deeply engrained in him by now that he checked the panic automatically.

'I was a fool not to have thought of it before,' said Tapling. 'That dying rat—that fellow over there who we thought was drunk. I should have known!'

The soldier who appeared to be the sergeant in command of the Treasurer's escort was in explosive conversation with the chief of the overseers of the slaves, both of them staring and pointing at the dying Duras; the Treasurer himself was clutching his robe about him and looking down at the wretched man at his feet in fascinated horror.

'Well, sir,' said Hornblower to Tapling, 'what do we do?'

Hornblower was of the temperament that demands immediate action in face of a crisis.

'Do?' replied Tapling with a bitter smile. 'We stay here and rot.'

'Stay *here*?'

H

'The fleet will never have us back. Not until we have served three weeks of quarantine. Three weeks after the last case has occurred. Here in Oran.'

'Nonsense!' said Hornblower, with all the respect due to his senior startled out of him. 'No one would order that.'

'Would they not? Have you ever seen an epidemic in a fleet?'

Hornblower had not, but he had heard enough about them—fleets where nine out of ten had died of putrid fevers. Crowded ships with twenty-two inches of hammock space per man were ideal breeding places for epidemics. He realized that no captain, no admiral, would run that risk for the sake of a longboat's crew of twenty men.

The two xebecs against the jetty had suddenly cast off, and were working their way out of the harbour under sweeps.

'The plague can only have struck to-day,' mused Hornblower, the habit of deduction strong in him despite his sick fear.

The cattle herders were abandoning their work, giving a wide berth to that one of their number who was lying on the quay. Up at the town gate it appeared that the guard was employed in driving people back into the town—apparently the rumour of plague had spread sufficiently therein to cause a panic, while the guard had just received orders not to allow the population to stream out into the surrounding country. There would be frightful things happening in the town soon. The Treasurer was climbing on his donkey; the crowd of grain-carrying slaves was melting away as the overseers fled.

'I must report this to the ship,' said Hornblower; Tapling, as a civilian diplomatic officer, held no authority over him. The whole responsibility was Hornblower's. The longboat and the longboat's crew were Hornblower's command, entrusted to him by Captain Pellew whose authority derived from the King.

Amazing how the panic was spreading. The Treasurer was gone; Duras' Negro slave had ridden off on his late master's donkey; the soldiers had hastened off in a single group. The waterfront was deserted now except for the dead and dying; along the waterfront, presumably, at the foot of the wall, lay the way to the open country which all desired to seek. The Englishmen were standing alone, with the bags of gold at their feet.

'Plague spreads through the air,' said Tapling. 'Even the rats die of it. We have been here for hours. We were near enough to—that'—he nodded at the dying Duras—'to speak to him, to catch his breath. Which of us will be the first?'

'We'll see when the time comes,' said Hornblower. It was his contrary nature to be sanguine in the face of depression; besides, he did not want the men to hear what Tapling was saying.

'And there's the fleet!' said Tapling bitterly. 'This lot'— he nodded at the deserted lighters, one almost full of cattle, the other almost full of grain sacks—'this lot would be a Godsend. The men are on two-thirds rations.'

'Damn it, we can do something about it,' said Hornblower. 'Maxwell, put the gold back in the boat, and get that awning in.'

The officer of the watch in H.M.S. *Indefatigable* saw the ship's longboat returning from the town. A slight breeze had swung the frigate and the *Caroline* (the transport brig) to their anchors, and the longboat, instead of running alongside, came up under the *Indefatigable*'s stern to leeward.

'Mr Christie!' hailed Hornblower, standing up in the bows of the longboat.

The officer of the watch came aft to the taffrail.

'What is it?' he demanded, puzzled.

'I must speak to the Captain.'

'Then come on board and speak to him. What the devil——?'

'Please ask the Captain if I may speak to him.'

Pellew appeared at the after-cabin window; he could hardly have helped hearing the bellowed conversation.

'Yes, Mr Hornblower?'

Hornblower told him the news.

'Keep to loo'ard, Mr Hornblower.'

'Yes, sir. But the stores——'

'What about them?'

Hornblower outlined the situation and made his request.

'It's not very regular,' mused Pellew. 'Besides——'

He did not want to shout aloud his thoughts that perhaps everyone in the longboat would soon be dead of plague.

'We'll be all right, sir. It's a week's rations for the squadron.'

That was the point, the vital matter. Pellew had to balance the possible loss of a transport brig against the possible gain of supplies, immeasurably more important, which would enable the squadron to maintain its watch over the outlet to the Mediterranean. Looked at in that light Hornblower's suggestion had added force.

'Oh, very well, Mr Hornblower. By the time you bring the stores out I'll have the crew transferred. I appoint you to the command of the *Caroline*.'

'Thank you, sir.'

'Mr Tapling will continue as passenger with you.'

'Very good, sir.'

So when the crew of the longboat, toiling and sweating at the sweeps, brought the two lighters down the bay, they found the *Caroline* swinging deserted at her anchors, while a dozen curious telescopes from the *Indefatigable* watched the proceedings. Hornblower went up the brig's side with half a dozen hands.

'She's like a blooming Noah's Ark, sir,' said Maxwell.

The comparison was apt; the *Caroline* was flush-decked, and the whole available deck area was divided by partitions into stalls for the cattle, while to enable the ship to be worked light gangways had been laid over the stalls into a practically continuous upper deck.

'An' all the animiles, sir,' said another seaman.

'But Noah's animals walked in two by two,' said Hornblower. 'We're not so lucky. And we've got to get the grain on board first. Get those hatches unbattened.'

In ordinary conditions a working party of two or three hundred men from the *Indefatigable* would have made short work of getting in the cargo from the lighters, but now it had to be done by the longboat's complement of eighteen. Luckily Pellew had had the forethought and kindness to have the ballast struck out of the holds, or they would have had to do that weary job first.

'Tail on to those tackles, men,' said Hornblower.

Pellew saw the first bundle of grain sacks rise slowly into the air from the lighter, and swung over and down the *Caroline*'s hatchway.

'He'll be all right,' he decided. 'Man the capstan and get under way, if you please, Mr Bolton.'

Hornblower, directing the work on the tackles, heard Pellew's voice come to him through the speaking trumpet.

'Good luck, Mr Hornblower. Report in three weeks at Gibraltar.'

'Very good, sir. Thank you, sir.'

Hornblower turned back to find a seaman at his elbow knuckling his forehead.

'Beg pardon, sir. But can you hear those cattle bellerin', sir? 'Tis mortal hot, an' 'tis water they want, sir.'

'Hell,' said Hornblower.

He would never get the cattle on board before nightfall. He left a small party at work transferring cargo, and with the rest of the men he began to extemporize a method of watering the unfortunate cattle in the lighter. Half *Caroline*'s hold space was filled with water barrels and fodder, but it was an awkward business getting water down to the lighter with pump and hose, and the poor brutes down there surged about uncontrollably at the prospect of water. Hornblower saw the lighter heel and almost capsize; one of his men—luckily one who could swim—went hastily overboard from the lighter to avoid being crushed to death.

'Hell,' said Hornblower again, and that was by no means the last time.

Without any skilled advice he was having to learn the business of managing livestock at sea; each moment brought its lessons. A naval officer on active service indeed found himself engaged on strange duties. It was well after dark before Hornblower called a halt to the labours of his men, and it was before dawn that he roused them up to work again. It was still early in the morning that the last of the grain sacks was stowed away and Hornblower had to face the operation of swaying up the cattle from the lighter. After their night down there, with little water and less food, they were in no mood to be trifled with, but it was easier at first while they were crowded together. A bellyband was slipped round the nearest, the tackle hooked on, and the animal was swayed up, lowered to the deck through an opening in the gangways, and herded into one of the stalls with ease. The seamen, shouting and waving their shirts, thought it was great fun, but they were not sure when the next one, released from its bellyband, went on the rampage and chased them about the deck, threatening death with its horns, until it wandered into its stall where the bar could be promptly dropped to shut it in. Hornblower, looking at the sun rising rapidly in the east, did not think it fun at all.

And the emptier the lighter became, the more room the cattle had to rush about in it; to capture each one so as to put a bellyband on it was a desperate adventure. Nor were those half-wild bullocks soothed by the sight of their companions being successively hauled bellowing into the air over their heads. Before the day was half done Hornblower's men were as weary as if they had fought a battle, and there was not one of them who would not gladly have quitted this novel employment in exchange for some normal seaman's duty like going aloft to reef topsails on a stormy night. As soon as Hornblower had the notion of dividing the interior of the lighter up into sections with barricades of stout spars the work became easier, but it took time, and before it was done the cattle had already suffered a couple of casualties—weaker members of the herd crushed underfoot in the course of the wild rushes about the lighter.

And there was a distraction when a boat came out from the shore, with swarthy Moors at the oars and the Treasurer in the stern. Hornblower left Tapling to negotiate— apparently the Bey at least had not been so frightened of the plague as to forget to ask for his money. All Horn-

blower insisted upon was that the boat should keep well to
leeward, and the money was floated off to it headed up in
an empty rum-puncheon. Night found not more than half
the cattle in the stalls on board, with Hornblower worrying
about feeding and watering them, and snatching at hints
diplomatically won from those members of his crew who
had had bucolic experience. But the earliest dawn saw him
driving his men to work again, and deriving a momentary
satisfaction from the sight of Tapling having to leap for
his life to the gangway out of reach of a maddened bullock
which was charging about the deck and refusing to enter
a stall. And by the time the last animal was safely packed
in Hornblower was faced with another problem—that of
dealing with what one of the men elegantly termed 'mucking out'. Fodder—water—mucking out; that deck-load of
cattle seemed to promise enough work in itself to keep his
eighteen men busy, without any thought of the needs of
handling the ship.

But there were advantages about the men being kept
busy, as Hornblower grimly decided; there had not been a
single mention of plague since the work began. The
anchorage where the *Caroline* lay was exposed to north-
easterly winds, and it was necessary that he should take her
out to sea before such a wind should blow. He mustered
his men to divide them into watches; he was the only
navigator, so that he had to appoint the coxswain and the
under-coxswain, Jordan, as officers of the watch. Someone
volunteered as cook, and Hornblower, running his eye over
his assembled company, appointed Tapling as cook's mate.
Tapling opened his mouth to protest, but there was that in
Hornblower's expression which cut the protest short. There
was no bos'n, no carpenter—no surgeon either, as Hornblower pointed out to himself gloomily. But on the other

hand if the need for a doctor should arise it would, he hoped, be mercifully brief.

'Port watch, loose the jibs and main tops'l,' ordered Hornblower. 'Starboard watch, man the capstan.'

So began the voyage of H.M. transport brig *Caroline* which became legendary (thanks to the highly coloured accounts retailed by the crew during innumerable dogwatches in later commissions) throughout the King's navy. The *Caroline* spent her three weeks of quarantine in homeless wanderings about the western Mediterranean. It was necessary that she should keep close up to the Straits, for fear lest the westerlies and the prevailing inward set of the current should take her out of reach of Gibraltar when the time came, so she beat about between the coasts of Spain and Africa, trailing behind her a growing farmyard stench. The *Caroline* was a worn-out ship; with any sort of sea running she leaked like a sieve; and there were always hands at work on the pumps, either pumping her out or pumping sea water on to her deck to clean it or pumping up fresh water for the cattle.

Her top hamper made her almost unmanageable in a fresh breeze; her deck seams leaked, of course, when she worked, allowing a constant drip of unspeakable filth down below. The one consolation was in the supply of fresh meat—a commodity some of Hornblower's men had not tasted for three months. Hornblower recklessly sacrificed a bullock a day, for in that Mediterranean climate meat could not be kept sweet. So his men feasted on steaks and fresh tongues; there were plenty of men on board who had never in their whole lives before eaten a beef steak.

But fresh water was the trouble—it was a greater anxiety to Hornblower than even it was to the average ship's captain, for the cattle were always thirsty; twice Hornblower had to land a raiding party at dawn on the coast of Spain, seize a fishing village, and fill his water casks in the local stream.

It was a dangerous adventure, and the second landing revealed the danger, for while the *Caroline* was trying to claw off the land again a Spanish guarda-costa lugger came gliding round the point with all sail set. Maxwell saw her first, but Hornblower saw her before he could report her presence.

'Very well, Maxwell,' said Hornblower, trying to sound composed.

He turned his glass upon her. She was no more than three miles off, a trifle to windward, and the *Caroline* was embayed, cut off by the land from all chance of escape. The lugger could go three feet to her two, while the *Caroline*'s clumsy superstructure prevented her from lying nearer than eight points to the wind. As Hornblower gazed, the accumulated irritation of the past seventeen days boiled over. He was furious with fate for having thrust this ridiculous mission on him. He hated the *Caroline* and her clumsiness and her stinks and her cargo. He raged against the destiny which had caught him in this hopeless position.

'Hell!' said Hornblower, actually stamping his feet on the upper gangway in his anger. 'Hell *and* damnation!'

He was dancing with rage, he observed with some curiosity. But with his fighting madness at the boil there was no chance of his yielding without a struggle, and his mental convulsions resulted in his producing a scheme for action. How many men of a crew did a Spanish guarda-costa carry? Twenty? That would be an outside figure—those luggers were only intended to act against petty smugglers. And with surprise on his side there was still a chance, despite the four eight-pounders that the lugger carried.

'Pistols and cutlasses, men,' he said. 'Jordan, choose two men and show yourselves up here. But the rest of you keep under cover. Hide yourselves. Yes, Mr Tapling, you may serve with us. See that you are armed.'

No one would expect resistance from a laden cattle transport; the Spaniard would expect to find on board a crew of a dozen at most, and not a disciplined force of twenty. The problem lay in luring the lugger within reach.

'Full and by,' called Hornblower down to the helmsman below. 'Be ready to jump, men. Maxwell, if a man shows himself before my order shoot him with your own hand. You hear me? That's an order, and you disobey me at your peril.'

'Aye aye, sir,' said Maxwell.

The lugger was romping up towards them; even in that light air there was a white wave under her sharp bows. Hornblower glanced up to make sure that the *Caroline* was displaying no colours. That made his plan legal under the laws of war. The report of a gun and a puff of smoke came from the lugger as she fired across the *Caroline*'s bows.

'I'm going to heave-to, Jordan,' said Hornblower. 'Main tops'l braces. Helm-a-lee.'

The *Caroline* came to the wind and lay there wallowing, a surrendered and helpless ship apparently, if ever there was one.

'Not a sound, men,' said Hornblower.

The cattle bellowed mournfully. Here came the lugger, her crew plainly visible now. Hornblower could see an officer clinging to the main shrouds ready to board, but no one else seemed to have a care in the world. Everyone seemed to be looking up at the clumsy superstructure and laughing at the farmyard noises issuing from it.

'Wait, men, wait,' said Hornblower.

The lugger was coming alongside when Hornblower suddenly realized, with a hot flood of blood under his skin, that he himself was unarmed. He had told his men to take pistols and cutlasses; he had advised Tapling to arm himself, and yet he had clean forgotten about his own need for weapons. But it was too late now to try to remedy that. Someone in the lugger hailed in Spanish, and Hornblower spread his hands in a show of incomprehension. Now they were alongside.

'Come on, men!' shouted Hornblower.

He ran across the superstructure and with a gulp he flung himself across the gap at the officer in the shrouds. He gulped again as he went through the air; he fell with all his weight on the unfortunate man, clasped him round the shoulders, and fell with him to the deck. There were shouts and yells behind him as the *Caroline* spewed her crew into the lugger. A rush of feet, a clatter and a clash. Hornblower got to his feet empty-handed. Maxwell was just striking down a man with his cutlass. Tapling was heading a rush forward into the bows, waving a cutlass and yelling like a madman. Then it was all over; the astonished Spaniards were unable to lift a hand in their own defence.

So it came about that on the twenty-second day of her quarantine the *Caroline* came into Gibraltar Bay with a captured guarda-costa lugger under her lee. A thick barnyard stench trailed with her, too, but at least, when Hornblower went on board the *Indefatigable* to make his report, he had a suitable reply ready for Mr Midshipman Bracegirdle.

'Hullo, Noah, how are Shem and Ham?' asked Mr Brace-girdle.

'Shem and Ham have taken a prize,' said Hornblower. 'I regret that Mr Bracegirdle can't say the same.'

But the Chief Commissary of the squadron, when Hornblower reported to him, had a comment to which even Hornblower was unable to make a reply.

'Do you mean to tell me, Mr Hornblower,' said the Chief Commissary, 'that you allowed your men to eat fresh beef? A bullock a day for your eighteen men? There must have been plenty of ship's provisions on board. That was wanton extravagance, Mr Hornblower, I'm surprised at you.'

CHAPTER TEN

THE DUCHESS AND THE DEVIL

ACTING-LIEUTENANT HORNBLOWER was bringing the sloop Le Rêve, prize of H.M.S. Indefatigable, to anchor in Gibraltar Bay. He was nervous; if anyone had asked him if he thought that all the telescopes in the Mediterranean Fleet were trained upon him he would have laughed at the fantastic suggestion, but he felt as if they were. Nobody ever gauged more cautiously the strength of the gentle following breeze, or estimated more anxiously the distances between the big anchored ships of the line, or calculated more carefully the space Le Rêve would need to swing at her anchor. Jackson, his petty officer, was standing forward awaiting the order to take in the jib, and he acted quickly at Hornblower's hail.

'Helm-a-lee,' said Hornblower next, and *Le Rêve* rounded into the wind. 'Brail up!'

Le Rêve crept forward, her momentum diminishing as the wind took her way off her.

'Let go!'

The cable growled a protest as the anchor took it out through the hawsehole—that welcome splash of the anchor, telling of the journey's end. Hornblower watched carefully while *Le Rêve* took up on her cable, and then relaxed a little. He had brought the prize safely in. The commodore —Captain Sir Edward Pellew of H.M.S. *Indefatigable*— had clearly not yet returned, so that it was Hornblower's duty to report to the port admiral.

'Get the boat hoisted out,' he ordered, and then, remembering his humanitarian duty, 'and you can let the prisoners up on deck.'

They had been battened down below for the last forty-eight hours, because the fear of a recapture was the nightmare of every prize-master. But here in the Bay with the Mediterranean fleet all round that danger was at an end. Two hands at the oars of the gig sent her skimming over the water, and in ten minutes Hornblower was reporting his arrival to the admiral.

'You say she shows a fair turn of speed?' said the latter, looking over at the prize.

'Yes, sir. And she's handy enough,' said Hornblower.

'I'll purchase her into the service. Never enough despatch vessels,' mused the Admiral.

Even with that hint, it was a pleasant surprise to Hornblower when he received heavily sealed official orders and, opening them, read that 'you are hereby requested and required' to take H.M. sloop *Le Rêve* under his command and to proceed 'with the utmost expedition' to Plymouth

as soon as the despatches destined for England should be
put in his charge. It was an independent command; it was
a chance of seeing England again (it was three years since
Hornblower had last set foot on the English shore) and it
was a high professional compliment. But there was another
letter, delivered at the same moment, which Hornblower
read with less elation.

'Their Excellencies, Major-General Sir Hew and Lady
Dalrymple, request the pleasure of Acting-Lieutenant
Horatio Hornblower's company at dinner to-day, at three
o'clock, at Government House.'

It might be a pleasure to dine with the Governor of
Gibraltar and his lady, but it was only a mixed pleasure at
best for an acting-lieutenant with a single sea chest, faced
with the need to dress himself suitably for such a function.
Yet it was hardly possible for a young man to walk up to
Government House from the landing slip without a thrill
of excitement, especially as his friend Mr Midshipman
Bracegirdle, who came from a wealthy family and had a
handsome allowance, had lent him a pair of the finest white
stockings of China silk—Bracegirdle's calves were plump,
and Hornblower's were skinny, but that difficulty had
been artistically circumvented. Two small pads of oakum,
some strips of sticking plaster from the surgeon's
stores, and Hornblower now had a couple of legs of
which no one need be ashamed. He could put his left
leg forward to make his bow without any fear of wrinkles
in his stockings, and sublimely conscious, as Bracegirdle said, of a leg of which any gentleman would be
proud.

At Government House the usual polished and languid
aide-de-camp took charge of Hornblower and led him forward. He made his bow to Sir Hew, a red-faced and fussy

old gentleman, and to Lady Dalrymple, a red-faced and fussy old lady.

'Mr Hornblower,' said the latter, 'I must present you—Your Grace, this is Mr Hornblower, the new captain of *Le Rêve*. Her Grace the Duchess of Wharfedale.'

A duchess, no less! Hornblower poked forward his padded leg, pointed his toe, laid his hand on his heart and bowed with all the depth the tightness of his breeches allowed—he had still been growing when he bought them on joining the *Indefatigable*. Bold blue eyes, and a once beautiful middle-aged face.

'So this 'ere's the feller in question?' said the duchess. 'Matilda, my dear, are you going to hentrust me to a hinfant in harms?'

The startling vulgarity of the accent took Hornblower's breath away. He had been ready for almost anything except that a superbly dressed duchess should speak in the accent of Seven Dials. He raised his eyes to stare, while forgetting to straighten himself up, standing with his chin poked forward and his hand still on his heart.

'You look like a gander on a green,' said the duchess. 'I hexpects you to 'iss hany moment.'

She stuck her own chin out and swung from side to side with her hands on her knees in a perfect imitation of a belligerent goose, apparently with so close a resemblance to Hornblower as well as to excite a roar of laughter from the other guests. Hornblower stood in blushing confusion.

'Don't be 'ard on the young feller,' said the duchess, coming to his defence and patting him on the shoulder. "E's on'y young, an' thet's nothink to be ashamed of. Something to be prard of, for thet matter, to be trusted with a ship at thet hage.'

It was lucky that the announcement of dinner came to save Hornblower from the further confusion into which this kindly remark had thrown him. Hornblower naturally found himself with the riff-raff, the ragtag and bobtail of the middle of the table along with the other junior officers —Sir Hew sat at one end with the duchess, while Lady Dalrymple sat with a commodore at the other. Moreover, there were not nearly as many women as men; that was only to be expected, as Gibraltar was, technically at least, a beleaguered fortress. So Hornblower had no woman on either side of him; at his right sat the young aide-de-camp who had first taken him in charge.

'Your Health, Your Grace,' said the Commodore, looking down the length of the table and raising his glass.

'Thank'ee,' replied the duchess. 'Just in time to save my life. I was wonderin' 'oo'd come to my rescue.'

She raised her brimming glass to her lips and when she put it down again it was empty.

'A jolly boon companion you are going to have,' said the aide-de-camp to Hornblower.

'How is she going to be my companion?' asked Hornblower, quite bewildered.

The aide-de-camp looked at him pityingly.

'So you have not been informed?' he asked. 'As always, the man most concerned is the last to know. When you sail with your despatches to-morrow you will have the honour of bearing Her Grace with you to England.'

'God bless my soul,' said Hornblower.

'Let's hope He does,' said the aide-de-camp piously, nosing his wine. 'Poor stuff this sweet Malaga is. Old Hare bought a job lot in '95, and every governor since then seems to think it's his duty to use it up.'

'But who *is* she?' asked Hornblower.

'Her Grace the Duchess of Wharfedale,' replied the aide-de-camp. 'Did you not hear Lady Dalrymple's introduction?'

'But she doesn't talk like a duchess,' protested Hornblower.

'No. The old duke was in his dotage when he married her. She was an innkeeper's widow, so her friends say. You can imagine, if you like, what her enemies say.'

'But what is she doing here?' went on Hornblower.

'She is on her way back to England. She was at Florence when the French marched in, I understand. She reached Leghorn, and bribed a coaster to bring her here. She asked Sir Hew to find her a passage, and Sir Hew asked the Admiral—Sir Hew would ask anyone for anything on behalf of a duchess, even one said by her friends to be an innkeeper's widow.'

'I see,' said Hornblower.

There was a burst of merriment from the head of the table, and the duchess was prodding the governor's scarlet-coated ribs with the handle of her knife, as if to make sure he saw the joke.

'Maybe you will not lack for mirth on your homeward voyage,' said the aide-de-camp.

Just then a smoking sirloin of beef was put down in front of Hornblower, and all his other worries vanished before the necessity of carving it and remembering his manners. He took the carving knife and fork gingerly in his hands and glanced round at the company.

'May I help you to some of this beef, Your Grace? Madam? Sir? Well done or underdone, sir? A little of the brown fat?'

In the hot room the sweat ran down his face as he wrestled with the joint; he was fortunate that most of the guests desired helpings from the other removes so that he had little carving to do. He put a couple of haggled slices on his own plate as the simplest way of concealing the worst results of his own handiwork.

'Beef from Tetuan,' sniffed the aide-de-camp. 'Tough and stringy.'

That was all very well for a governor's aide-de-camp—he could not guess how delicious was this food to a young naval officer fresh from beating about at sea in an over-crowded frigate. Even the thought of having to act as host to a duchess could not entirely spoil Hornblower's appetite. And the final dishes, the meringues and macaroons, the custards and the fruits, were ecstasy for a young man whose last pudding had been currant duff last Sunday.

'Those sweet things spoil a man's palate,' said the aide-de-camp—much Hornblower cared.

They were drinking formal toasts now. Hornblower stood for the King and the royal family, and raised his glass for the duchess.

'And now for the enemy,' said Sir Hew, 'may their treasure galleons try to cross the Atlantic.'

'A supplement to that, Sir Hew,' said the commodore at the other end, 'may the Dons make up their minds to leave Cadiz.'

There was a growl almost like wild animals from round the table. Most of the naval officers present were from Jervis' Mediterranean squadron which had beaten about in the Atlantic for the past several months hoping to catch the Spaniards should they come out. Jervis had to detach his ships to Gibraltar two at a time to replenish their stores, and these officers were from the two ships of the line present at the moment in Gibraltar.

'Johnny Jervis would say amen to that,' said Sir Hew. 'A

bumper to the Dons then, gentlemen, and may they come out from Cadiz.'

The ladies left them then, gathered together by Lady Dalrymple, and as soon as it was decently possible Hornblower made his excuses and slipped away, determined not to be heavy with wine the night before he sailed in independent command.

Maybe the prospect of the coming on board of the duchess was a useful counter-irritant, and saved Hornblower from worrying too much about his first command. He was up before dawn—before even the brief Mediterranean twilight had begun—to see that his precious ship was in condition to face the sea, and the enemies who swarmed upon the sea. He had four popgun four-pounders to deal with those enemies, which meant that he was safe from no one; his was the weakest vessel at sea, for the smallest trading brig carried a more powerful armament. So that like all weak creatures his only safety lay in flight—Hornblower looked aloft in the half-light, where the sails would be set on which so much might depend. He went over the watch bill with his two watch-keeping officers, Midshipman Hunter and Master's Mate Winyatt, to make sure that every man of his crew of eleven knew his duty. Then all that remained was to put on his smartest seagoing uniform, try to eat breakfast, and wait for the duchess.

She came early, fortunately; Their Excellencies had had to rise at a most unpleasant hour to see her off. Mr Hunter reported the approach of the governor's launch with suppressed excitement.

'Thank you, Mr Hunter,' said Hornblower coldly—that was what the service demanded, even though not so many weeks before they had been playing follow-my-leader through the *Indefatigable*'s rigging together.

The launch swirled alongside, and two neatly dressed seamen hooked on the ladder. *Le Rêve* had such a small freeboard that boarding her presented no problem even for ladies. The governor stepped on board to the twittering of the only two pipes *Le Rêve* could muster, and Lady Dalrymple followed him. Then came the duchess, and the duchess's companion; the latter was a younger woman, as beautiful as the duchess must once have been. A couple of aides-de-camp followed, and by that time the minute deck of *Le Rêve* was positively crowded, so that there was no room left to bring up the duchess's baggage.

'Let us show you your quarters, Your Grace,' said the governor.

Lady Dalrymple squawked her sympathy at sight of the minute cabin, which the two cots almost filled, and everyone's head, inevitably, bumped against the deck-beam above.

'We shall live through it,' said the duchess stoically, 'an' that's more than many a man makin' a little trip to Tyburn could say.'

One of the aides-de-camp produced a last-minute packet of despatches and demanded Hornblower's signature on the receipt; the last farewells were said, and Sir Hew and Lady Dalrymple went down the side again to the twittering of the pipes.

'Man the windlass!' bellowed Hornblower, the moment the launch's crew bent to their oars.

A few seconds' lusty work brought *Le Rêve* up to her anchor.

'Anchor's aweigh, sir,' reported Winyatt.

'Jib halliards!' shouted Hornblower. 'Mains'l halliards!'

Le Rêve came round before the wind as her sails were set and her rudder took a grip on the water. Everyone was so

busy catting the anchor and setting sail that it was Hornblower himself who dipped his colours in salute as *Le Rêve*
crept out beyond the mole before the gentle south-easter,
and dipped her nose to the first of the big Atlantic rollers
coming in through the Gut. Through the skylight beside
him he heard a clatter and a wail, as something fell in the
cabin with that first roll, but he could spare no attention
for the woman below. He had the glass to his eye now,
training it first on Algeciras and then upon Tarifa—some
well-manned privateer or ship of war might easily dash out
to snap up such a defenceless prey as *Le Rêve*. He could
not relax while the forenoon watch wore on. They rounded
Cape Marroqui and he set a course for St Vincent, and
then the mountains of Southern Spain began to sink below
the horizon. Cape Trafalgar was just visible on the starboard bow when at last he shut the telescope and began
to wonder about dinner; it was pleasant to be captain of
his own ship and to be able to order dinner when he chose.
His aching legs told him he had been on his feet too long
—eleven continuous hours; if the future brought him many
independent commands he would wear himself out by this
sort of behaviour.

Down below he relaxed gratefully on the locker, and sent
the cook to knock at the duchess's cabin door to ask with
his compliments if all was well; he heard the duchess's
sharp voice saying that they needed nothing, not even
dinner. Hornblower philosophically shrugged his shoulders
and ate his dinner with a young man's appetite. He went
on deck again as night closed in upon them; Winyatt had
the watch.

'It's coming up thick, sir,' he said.

So it was. The sun was invisible on the horizon, engulfed
in watery mist. It was the price he had to pay for a fair

wind, he knew; in the winter months in these latitudes there was always likely to be fog where the cool land breeze reached the Atlantic.

'It'll be thicker still by morning,' he said gloomily, and revised his night orders, setting a course due west instead of west by north as he originally intended. He wanted to make certain of keeping clear of Cape St Vincent in the event of fog.

That was one of those minute trifles which may affect a man's whole after-life—Hornblower had plenty of time later to reflect on what might have happened had he not ordered that alteration of course. During the night he was often on deck, peering through the increasing mist, but at the time when the crisis came he was down below snatching a little sleep. What woke him was a seaman shaking his shoulder violently.

'Please, sir. Please, sir. Mr Hunter sent me. Please, sir, won't you come on deck, he says, sir.'

'I'll come,' said Hornblower, blinking himself awake and rolling out of his cot.

The faintest beginnings of dawn were imparting some slight luminosity to the mist which was close about them. *Le Rêve* was lurching over an ugly sea with barely enough wind behind her to give her steerage way. Hunter was standing with his back to the wheel in an attitude of tense anxiety.

'Listen!' he said, as Hornblower appeared.

He half-whispered the word, and in his excitement he omitted the 'sir' which was due to his captain—and in his excitement Hornblower did not notice the omission. Hornblower listened. He heard the shipboard noises he could expect—the clattering of the blocks as *Le Rêve* lurched, the sound of the sea at her bows. Then he heard other shipboard noises. There were other blocks clattering; the sea was breaking beneath other bows.

'There's a ship close alongside,' said Hornblower.

'Yes, sir,' said Hunter. 'And after I sent below for you I heard an order given. And it was in Spanish—some foreign tongue, anyway.'

The tenseness of fear was all about the little ship like the fog.

'Call all hands. Quietly,' said Hornblower.

But as he gave the order he wondered if it would be any use. He could send his men to their stations, he could man and load his four-pounders, but if that ship out there in the fog was of any force greater than a merchant ship he was in deadly peril. Then he tried to comfort himself— perhaps the ship was some fat Spanish galleon bulging with treasure, and were he to board her boldly she would become his prize and make him rich for life.

'A 'appy Valentine's day to you,' said a voice beside him, and he nearly jumped out of his skin with surprise. He had actually forgotten the presence of the duchess on board.

'Stop that row!' he whispered furiously at her, and she pulled up abruptly in astonishment. She was bundled up in a cloak and hood against the damp air, and no further detail could be seen of her in the darkness and fog.

'May I hask——' she began.

'Shut up!' whispered Hornblower.

A harsh voice could be heard through the fog, other voices repeating the order, whistles being blown, much noise and bustle.

'That's Spanish, sir, isn't it?' whispered Hunter.

'Spanish for certain. Calling the watch. Listen!'

The two double-strokes of a ship's bell came to them across the water. Four bells in the morning watch. And instantly from all round them a dozen other bells could be heard, as if echoing the first.

'We're in the middle of a fleet, by God!' whispered Hunter.

'Big ships, too, sir,' supplemented Winyatt, who had joined them with the calling of all hands. 'I could hear half a dozen different pipes when they called the watch.'

'The Dons are out, then' said Hunter.

And the course I set has taken us into the midst of them, thought Hornblower bitterly. The coincidence was maddening, heart-breaking. But he forbore to waste breath over it. He even suppressed the frantic gibe that rose to his lips at the memory of Sir Hew's toast about the Spaniards coming out from Cadiz.

'They're setting more sail,' was what he said. 'Dagos snug down at night, just like some fat Indiaman. They only set their t'gallants at daybreak.'

All round them through the fog could be heard the whine of sheaves in blocks, the stamp-and-go of the men at the halliards, the sound of ropes thrown on decks, the chatter of a myriad voices.

'They make enough noise about it, blast 'em,' said Hunter.

The tension under which he laboured was apparent as he stood straining to peer through the mist.

'Please God they're on a different course to us,' said Winyatt, more sensibly. 'Then we'll soon be through 'em.'

'Not likely,' said Hornblower.

Le Rêve was running almost directly before what little wind there was; if the Spaniards were beating against it or had it on their beam they would be crossing her course at a considerable angle, so that the volume of sound from the nearest ship would have diminished or increased considerably in this time, and there was no indication of that whatever. It was far more likely that *Le Rêve* had over-hauled the Spanish fleet under its nightly short canvas and had sailed forward into the middle of it. It was a problem what to do next in that case, to shorten sail, or to heave-to, and let the Spaniards get ahead of them again, or to clap on sail to pass through. But the passage of the minutes brought clear proof that fleet and sloop were on practically the same course, as otherwise they could hardly fail to pass some ship close. As long as the mist held they were safest as they were.

But that was hardly to be expected with the coming of day.

'Can't we alter course, sir?' asked Winyatt.

'Wait,' said Hornblower.

In the faint growing light he had seen shreds of denser mist blowing past them—a clear indication that they could not hope for continuous fog. At that moment they ran out of a fog bank into a clear patch of water.

'There she is, by God!' said Hunter.

Both officers and seamen began to move about in sudden panic.

'Stand still, damn you!' rasped Hornblower, his nervous tension releasing itself in the fierce monosyllables.

Less than a cable's length away a three-decked ship of the line was standing along parallel to them on their star-board side. Ahead and on the port side could be seen the outlines, still shadowy, of other battleships. Nothing could save them if they drew attention to themselves; all that could be done was to keep going as if they had as much right there as the ships of the line. It was possible that in the happy-go-lucky Spanish navy the officer of the watch over there did not know that no sloop like *Le Rêve* was attached to the fleet—or even possibly by a miracle there *might* be one. *Le Rêve* was French built and French rigged, after all. Side by side *Le Rêve* and the battleship sailed the lumpy sea. They were within pointblank range of fifty big guns, when one well-aimed shot would sink them. Hunter was uttering filthy curses under his breath, but discipline had asserted itself; a telescope over there on the Spaniard's deck would not discover any suspicious bustle on board the sloop. Another shred of fog drifted past them, and then they were deep in a fresh fog bank.

'Thank God!' said Hunter, indifferent to the contrast between this present piety and his preceding blasphemy.

'Hands wear ship,' said Hornblower. 'Lay her on the port tack.'

There was no need to tell the hands to do it quietly; they were as well aware of their danger as anyone. *Le Rêve* silently rounded-to, the sheets were hauled in and coiled down without a sound; and the sloop, as close to the wind as she would lie, heeled to the small wind, meeting the lumpy waves with her port bow.

'We'll be crossing their course now,' said Hornblower.

'Please God it'll be under their sterns and not their bows,' said Winyatt.

There was the duchess still in her cloak and hood, standing right aft as much out of the way as possible.

'Don't you think Your Grace had better go below?' asked Hornblower, making use by a great effort of the formal form of address.

'Oh, no, *please*,' said the Duchess. 'I couldn't bear it.' Hornblower shrugged his shoulders, and promptly forgot the duchess's presence again as a new anxiety struck him. He dived below and came up again with the two big sealed envelopes of despatches. He took a belaying pin from the rail and began very carefully to tie the envelopes to the pin with a bit of line.

'Please,' said the duchess, 'please, Mr Hornblower, tell me what you are doing?'

'I want to make sure these will sink when I throw them overboard if we're captured,' said Hornblower grimly.

'Then they'll be lost for good?'

'Better that than that the Spaniards should read 'em,' said Hornblower with all the patience he could muster.

'I could look after them for you,' said the duchess. 'Indeed I could.'

Hornblower looked keenly at her.

'No,' he said, 'they might search your baggage. Probably they would.'

'Baggage!' said the duchess. 'As if I'd put them in my baggage! I'll put them next my skin—they won't search *me* in any case. They'll never find 'em, not if I put 'em up my petticoats.'

There was a brutal realism about those words that staggered Hornblower a little, but which also brought him to admit to himself that there was something in what the duchess was saying.

'If they capture us,' said the duchess, '—I pray they won't, but if they do—they'll never keep me prisoner. You know that. They'll send me to Lisbon or put me aboard a King's ship as soon as they can. Then the despatches will be delivered eventually. Late, but better late than never.'

'That's so,' mused Hornblower.

'I'll guard them like my life,' said the duchess. 'I swear I'll never part from them. I'll tell no one I have them, not until I hand them to a King's officer.'

She met Hornblower's eyes with transparent honesty in her expression.

'Fog's thinning, sir,' said Winyatt.

'Quick!' said the duchess.

There was no time for further debate. Hornblower slipped the envelopes from their binding of rope and handed them over to her, and replaced the belaying pin in the rail.

'These damned French fashions,' said the duchess. 'I was right when I said I'd put these letters up my petticoats. There's no room in my bosom.'

Certainly the upper part of her gown was not at all capacious; the waist was close up under the armpits and the rest of the dress hung down from there quite straight in utter defiance of anatomy.

'Give me a yard of that rope, quick!' said the duchess.

Winyatt cut her a length of the line with his knife and handed it to her. Already she was hauling at her petticoats; the appalled Hornblower saw a gleam of white thigh above her stocking tops before he tore his glance away. The fog was certainly thinning.

'You can look at me now,' said the duchess; but her petticoats only just fell in time as Hornblower looked round again 'They're inside my shift, next my skin, as I promised. With these Directory fashions no one wears stays any more. So I tied the rope round my waist outside my shift. One envelope is flat against my chest and the other against my back. Would you suspect anything?'

She turned round for Hornblower's inspection.

'No, nothing shows,' he said. 'I must thank Your Grace.'

'There is a certain thickening,' said the duchess, 'but it does not matter what the Spaniards suspect as long as they do not suspect the truth.'

Momentary cessation of the need for action brought some embarrassment to Hornblower. To discuss with a woman her shift and stays—or the absence of them—was a strange thing to do.

A watery sun, still nearly level, was breaking through the mist and shining in his eyes. The mainsail cast a watery shadow on the deck. With every second the sun was growing brighter.

'Here it comes,' said Hunter.

The horizon ahead expanded rapidly, from a few yards to a hundred, from a hundred yards to half a mile. The sea was covered with ships. No less than six were in plain sight, four ships of the line and two big frigates, with the red-and-gold of Spain at their mastheads, and, what marked them even more obviously as Spaniards, huge wooden crosses hanging at their peaks.

'Wear ship again, Mr Hunter,' said Hornblower. 'Back into the fog.'

That was the one chance of safety. Those ships running down towards them were bound to ask questions, and they could not hope to avoid them all. *Le Rêve* spun around on her heel, but the fog-bank from which she had emerged was already attenuated, sucked up by the thirsty sun. They could see a drifting stretch of it ahead, but it was lazily rolling away from them at the same time as it was dwindling. The heavy sound of a cannon shot reached their ears, and close on their starboard quarter a ball threw up a fountain of water before plunging into the side of a wave just ahead. Hornblower looked round just in time to see the last of the puff of smoke from the bows of the frigate astern pursuing them.

'Starboard two points,' he said to the helmsman, trying to gauge at one and the same moment the frigate's course, the direction of the wind, the bearing of the other ships, and that of the thin last nucleus of that wisp of fog.

'Starboard two points,' said the helmsman.

'Fore and main sheets!' said Hunter.

Another shot, far astern this time but laid true for line; Hornblower suddenly remembered the duchess.

'You must go below, Your Grace,' he said curtly.

'Oh, no, no, no!' burst out the duchess with angry vehemence. 'Please let me stay here. I can't go below to where that seasick maid of mine lies hoping to die. Not in that stinking box of a cabin.'

There would be no safety in that cabin, Hornblower reflected—Le Rêve's scantlings were too fragile to keep out any shot at all. Down below the water line in the hold the women might be safe, but they would have to lie flat on top of beef barrels.

'Sail ahead!' screamed the look-out.

The mist there was parting and the outline of a ship of the line was emerging from it, less than a mile away and on almost the same course as Le Rêve's. Thud—thud from the frigate astern. Those gunshots by now would have warned the whole Spanish fleet that something unusual was happening. The battleship ahead would know that the little sloop was being pursued. A ball tore through the air close by, with its usual terrifying noise. The ship ahead was awaiting their coming; Hornblower saw her topsails slowly turning.

'Hands to the sheets!' said Hornblower. 'Mr Hunter, jibe her over.'

Le Rêve came round again, heading for the lessening gap on the port side. The frigate astern turned to intercept. More jets of smoke from her bows. With an appalling noise a shot passed within a few feet of Hornblower, so that the wind of it made him stagger. There was a hole in the mainsail.

'Your Grace,' said Hornblower, 'those aren't warning shots——'

It was the ship of the line which fired them, having succeeded in clearing away and manning some of her upper-deck guns. It was as if the end of the world had come. One shot hit *Le Rêve*'s hull, and they felt the deck heave under their feet as a result as if the little ship were disintegrating. But the mast was hit at the same moment, stays and shrouds parting, splinters raining all round. Mast, sails, boom, gaff and all went from above them over the side to windward. The wreckage dragged in the sea and turned the helpless wreck round with the last of her way. The little group aft stood momentarily dazed.

'Anybody hurt?' asked Hornblower, recovering himself.

'On'y a scratch, sir,' said one voice.

It seemed a miracle that no one was killed.

'Carpenter's mate, sound the well,' said Hornblower, and then, recollecting himself, 'No, damn it. Belay that order. If the Dons can save the ship, let 'em try.'

Already the ship of the line whose salvo had done the damage was filling her topsails again and bearing away from them, while the frigate which had pursued them was running down on them fast. A wailing figure came scrambling out of the after-hatchway. It was the duchess's maid, so mad with terror that her seasickness was forgotten. The duchess put a protective arm round her and tried to comfort her.

'Your Grace had better look to your baggage,' said Hornblower. 'No doubt you'll be leaving us shortly for other quarters with the Dons. I hope you will be more comfortable.'

He was trying desperately hard to speak in a matter-of-fact way, as if nothing out of the ordinary were happening.

as if he were not soon to be a prisoner of the Spaniards; but the duchess saw the working of the usually firm mouth, and marked how the hands were tight-clenched.

'How can I tell you how sorry I am about this?' asked the duchess, her voice soft with pity.

'That makes it the harder for me to bear,' said Hornblower, and he even forced a smile.

The Spanish frigate was just rounding-to, a cable's length to windward.

'Please, sir,' said Hunter.

'Well?'

'We can fight, sir. You give the word. Cold shot to drop in the boats when they try to board. We could beat 'em off once, perhaps.'

Hornblower's tortured misery nearly made him snap out 'Don't be a fool', but he checked himself. He contented himself with pointing to the frigate. Twenty guns were glaring at them at far less than point-blank range. The very boat the frigate was hoisting out would be manned by at least twice as many men as *Le Rêve* carried—she was no bigger than many a pleasure yacht. It was not odds of ten to one, or a hundred to one, but odds of ten thousand to one.

'I understand, sir,' said Hunter.

Now the Spanish frigate's boat was in the water, about to shove off.

'A private word with you, please, Mr Hornblower,' said the duchess suddenly.

Hunter and Winyatt heard what she said, and withdrew out of earshot.

'Yes, Your Grace?' said Hornblower.

The duchess stood there, still with her arm round her weeping maid, looking straight at him.

I

'I'm no more of a duchess than you are,' she said.

'Good God!' said Hornblower. 'Who—who are you, then?'

'Kitty Cobham.'

The name meant a little to Hornblower, but only a little.

'You're too young for that name to have any memories for you, Mr Hornblower, I see. It's five years since last I trod the boards.'

That was it. Kitty Cobham the actress.

'I can't tell it all now,' said the duchess—the Spanish boat was dancing over the waves towards them. 'But when the French marched into Florence that was only the last of my misfortunes. I was penniless when I escaped from them. Who would lift a finger for a one-time actress—one who had been betrayed and deserted? What was I to do? But a duchess—that was another story. Old Dalrymple at Gibraltar could not do enough for the Duchess of Wharfedale.'

'Why did you choose that title?' asked Hornblower in spite of himself.

'I knew of her,' said the duchess with a shrug of the shoulders. 'I knew her to be what I played her as. That was why I chose her—I always played character parts better than straight comedy. And not nearly so tedious in a long role.'

'But my despatches!' said Hornblower in a sudden panic of realization. 'Give them back, quick.'

'If you wish me to,' said the duchess. 'But I can still be the duchess when the Spaniards come. They will still set me free as speedily as they can. I'll guard those despatches better than my life—I swear it, I swear it! In less than a month I'll deliver them, if you trust me.'

Hornblower looked at the pleading eyes. She might be a spy, ingeniously trying to preserve the despatches from being thrown overboard before the Spaniards took possession. But no spy could have hoped that *Le Rêve* would run into the midst of the Spanish fleet.

'I made use of the bottle, I know,' said the duchess. 'I drank. Yes, I did. But I stayed sober in Gibraltar, didn't I? And I won't touch a drop, not a drop, until I'm in England. I'll swear that, too. Please, sir—please. I beg of you. Let me do what I can for my country.'

It was a strange decision for a man of nineteen to have to make—one who had never exchanged a word with an actress in his life before. A harsh voice overside told him that the Spanish boat was about to hook on.

'Keep them, then,' said Hornblower. 'Deliver them when you can.'

He had not taken his eyes from her face. He was looking for a gleam of triumph in her expression. Had he seen anything of the sort he would have torn the despatches from her body at that moment. But all he saw was the natural look of pleasure, and it was then that he made up his mind to trust her—not before.

'Oh, thank you, sir,' said the duchess.

The Spanish boat had hooked on now, and a Spanish lieutenant was awkwardly trying to climb aboard. He arrived on the deck on his hands and knees, and Hornblower stepped over to receive him as he got to his feet. Captor and captive exchanged bows. Hornblower could not understand what the Spaniard said, but obviously they were formal sentences that he was using. The Spaniard caught sight of the two women aft and halted in surprise; Hornblower hastily made the presentation in what he hoped was Spanish.

'Señor el tenente Espanol,' he said. 'Señora la Duquesa de Wharfedale.'

The title clearly had its effect; the lieutenant bowed profoundly, and his bow was received with the most lofty aloofness by the duchess. Hornblower could be sure the despatches were safe. That was some alleviation of the misery of standing here on the deck of his waterlogged little ship, a prisoner of the Spaniards. As he waited he heard, from far to leeward, roll upon roll of thunder coming up against the wind. No thunder could endure that long. What he could hear must be the broadsides of ships in action—of fleets in action. Somewhere over there by Cape St Vincent the British fleet must have caught the Spaniards at last. Fiercer and fiercer sounded the roll of the artillery. There was excitement among the Spaniards who had scrambled on to the deck of *Le Rêve*, while Hornblower stood bareheaded waiting to be taken into captivity.

Captivity was a dreadful thing. Once the numbness had worn off, Hornblower came to realize what a dreadful thing it was. Not even the news of the dreadful battering which the Spanish navy had received at St Vincent could relieve the misery and despair of being a prisoner. It was not the physical conditions—ten square feet of floor space per man in an empty sail loft at Ferrol along with other captive warrant officers—for they were no worse than what a junior officer often had to put up with at sea. It was the loss of freedom, the fact of being a captive, that was so dreadful.

There were four months of it before the first letter came through to Hornblower; the Spanish government, inefficient in all ways, had the worst postal system in Europe. But here was the letter, addressed and readdressed, now safely in his hands after he had practically snatched it from a stupid Spanish non-commissioned officer who had been puzzling over the strange name. Hornblower did not know the handwriting, and when he broke the seal and opened the letter the salutation made him think for a moment that he had opened someone else's letter.

'Darling Boy,' it began. Now who on earth would call him that? He read on in a dream.

'DARLING BOY,

I hope it will give you happiness to hear that what you gave me has reached its destination. They told me, when I delivered it, that you are a prisoner, and my heart bleeds for you. And they told me, too, that they were pleased with you for what you had done. And one of those admirals is a shareholder in Drury Lane. Whoever would have thought of such a thing? But he smiled at me, and I smiled at him. I did not know he was a shareholder then, and I only smiled out of the kindness of heart. And all that I told him about my dangers and perils with my precious burden were only histrionic exercises, I am afraid. Yet he believed me, and so struck was he by my smile and my adventures, that he demanded a part for me from Sherry, and behold, now I am playing second lead, usually a tragic mother, and receiving the acclaim of the groundlings. There are compensations in growing old, which I am dis-covering too. And I have not tasted wine since I saw you last, nor shall I ever again. As one more reward, my admiral promised me that he would forward this letter to you in the next cartel—an expression which no doubt means more to you than to me. I only hope that it reaches you in good time and brings you comfort in your affliction.

I pray nightly for you.

Ever your devoted friend,

KATHARINE COBHAM.'

Comfort in his affliction? A little, perhaps. There was some comfort in knowing that the despatches had been delivered; there was some comfort in a second-hand report that Their Lordships were pleased with him. There was comfort even in knowing that the duchess was re-established on the stage. But the sum total was nothing compared with his misery.

Here was a guard come to bring him to the commandant, and beside the commandant was the Irish renegade who served as interpreter. There were further papers on the commandant's desk—it looked as if the same cartel which had brought in Kitty Cobham's note had brought in letters for the commandant.

'Good afternoon, sir,' said the commandant, always polite, offering a chair.

'Good afternoon, sir, and many thanks,' said Hornblower. He was learning Spanish slowly and painfully.

'You have been promoted,' said the Irishman in English.

'W-what?' said Hornblower.

'Promoted,' said the Irishman. 'Here is the letter: "The Spanish authorities are informed that on account of his meritorious service, the acting-commission of Mr Horatio Hornblower, midshipman and acting-lieutenant, has been confirmed. Their Lordships of the Admiralty express their confidence that Mr Horatio Hornblower will be admitted immediately to the privileges of commissioned rank." There you are, young man.'

'My felicitations, sir,' said the commandant.

'Many thanks, sir,' said Hornblower.

The commandant was a kindly old gentleman with a pleasant smile for the awkward young man. He went on to say more, but Hornblower's Spanish was not equal to the technicalities he used, and Hornblower in despair looked at the interpreter.

'Now that you are a commissioned officer,' said the latter, 'you will be transferred to the quarters for captured officers.'

'Thank you,' said Hornblower.

'You will receive the half-pay of your rank.'

'Thank you.'

'And your parole will be accepted. You will be at liberty to visit in the town and the neighbourhood for two hours each day on giving your parole.'

'Thank you,' said Hornblower.

Perhaps, during the long months which followed, it was some mitigation of his unhappiness that for two hours each day his parole gave him freedom; freedom to wander in the streets of the little town, to have a cup of chocolate or a glass of wine—providing he had any money—making polite and laborious conversation with Spanish soldiers or sailors or civilians. But it was better to spend his two hours wandering over the goat paths of the headland in the wind and the sun, in the companionship of the sea, which might alleviate the sick misery of captivity. There was slightly better food, slightly better quarters. And there was the knowledge that now he was a lieutenant, that he held the King's commission, that if ever, ever, the war should end and he should be set free he could starve on half-pay—for with the end of the war there would be no employment for junior lieutenants. But he had earned his promotion. He had gained the approval of authority, that was something to think about on his solitary walks.

There came a day of south-westerly gales, with the wind shrieking in from across the Atlantic. Across three thousand miles of water it came, building up its strength unimpeded on its way, and heaping up the sea into racing mountain ridges which came crashing in upon the Spanish coast in thunder and spray. Hornblower stood on the headland above Ferrol harbour, holding his worn greatcoat about him as he leaned forward into the wind to keep his footing. So powerful was the wind that it was difficult to breathe while facing it. If he turned his back he could breathe more easily, but then the wind blew his wild hair forward over his eyes, almost inverted his greatcoat over his head, and furthermore forced him into little tottering steps down the slope towards Ferrol, whither he had no wish to return at present. For two hours he was alone and free, and those two hours were precious. He could breathe the Atlantic air, he could walk, he could do as he liked during that time. He could stare out to sea; it was not unusual to catch sight, from the headland, of some British ship of war which might be working slowly along the coast in the hope of snapping up a coasting vessel while keeping a watchful eye upon the Spanish naval activity. When such a ship went by during Hornblower's two hours of freedom, he would stand and gaze at it, as a man dying of thirst might gaze at a bucket of water held beyond his reach; he would note all the little details, the cut of the topsails and the style of the paint, while misery wrung his bowels. For this was the end of his second year as a prisoner of war. For twenty-two months, for twenty-two hours every day, he had been under lock and key, herded with five other junior lieutenants in a single room in the fortress of Ferrol. And to-day the wind roared by him, shouting in its outrageous freedom. He was facing into the wind; before him lay Corunna, its white houses resembling pieces of sugar scattered over the slopes. Between him and Corunna was all the open space of Corunna Bay, flogged white by the wind, and on his left hand was the narrow entrance to

Ferrol Bay. On his right was the open Atlantic; from the foot of the low cliffs there the long wicked reef of the Dietnes del Diablo—the Devil's Teeth—ran out to the northward, square across the path of the racing rollers driven by the wind. At half-minute intervals the rollers would crash against the reef with an impact that shook even the solid headland on which Hornblower stood, and each roller dissolved into spray which was instantly whirled away by the wind to reveal again the long black tusks of the rocks.

Hornblower was not alone on the headland; a few yards away from him a Spanish militia artilleryman on look-out duty gazed with watery eyes through a telescope with which he continually swept the seaward horizon. When at war with England it was necessary to be vigilant; a fleet might suddenly appear over the horizon, to land a little army to capture Ferrol, and burn the dockyard installations and the ships. No hope of that to-day, thought Hornblower —there could be no landing of troops on that raging lee shore.

But all the same the sentry was undoubtedly staring very fixedly through the telescope to windward; the sentry wiped his streaming eyes with his coat sleeve and stared again. Hornblower peered in the same direction, unable to see what it was that had attracted the sentry's attention. The sentry muttered something to himself, and then turned and ran clumsily down to the little stone guard-house, where sheltered the rest of the militia detachment stationed there to man the guns of the battery on the headland. He returned with the sergeant of the guard, who took the telescope and peered out to windward in the direction pointed out by the sentry. The two of them jabbered in their barbarous Gallego dialect; in two years of steady application

I*

Hornblower had mastered Galician as well as Castilian, but in that howling gale he could not intercept a word. Then finally, just as the sergeant nodded in agreement, Hornblower saw with his naked eyes what they were discussing. A pale grey square on the horizon above the grey sea—a ship's topsail. She must be running before the gale making for the shelter of Corunna or Ferrol.

It was a rash thing for a ship to do, because it would be no easy matter for her to round-to into Corunna Bay and anchor, and it would be even harder for her to hit off the narrow entrance to the Ferrol inlet. A cautious captain would claw out to sea and heave-to with a generous amount of sea room until the wind moderated. These Spanish captains, said Hornblower to himself, with a shrug of his shoulders; but naturally they would always wish to make harbour as quickly as possible when the Royal Navy was sweeping the seas. But the sergeant and the sentry were more excited than the appearance of a single ship would seem to justify. Hornblower could contain himself no longer, and edged up to the chattering pair, mentally framing his sentences in the unfamiliar tongue.

'Please, gentlemen,' he said, and then started again, shouting against the wind. 'Please, gentlemen, what is it that you see?'

The sergeant gave him a glance, and then, reaching some undiscoverable decision, handed over the telescope—Hornblower could hardly restrain himself from snatching it from his hands. With the telescope to his eye he could see far better; he could see a ship-rigged vessel, under close-reefed topsails (and that was much more sail than it was wise to carry) hurtling wildly towards them. And then a moment later he saw the other square of grey. Another topsail. Another ship. The foretopmast was noticeably shorter than the maintopmast, and not only that, but the whole effect was familiar—she was a British ship of war, a British frigate, plunging along in hot pursuit of the other, which seemed most likely to be a Spanish privateer. It was a close chase; it would be a very near thing, whether the Spaniard could reach the protection of the shore batteries before the frigate overhauled her. He lowered the telescope to rest his eye, and instantly the sergeant snatched it from him. He had been watching the Englishman's face, and Hornblower's expression had told him what he wanted to know. Those two ships out there were behaving in such a way as to justify his rousing his officer and giving the alarm. Sergeant and sentry went running back to the guard-house, and in a few moments the artillerymen were pouring out to man the batteries on the verge of the cliff. Soon enough came a mounted officer urging his horse up the path; a single glance through the telescope sufficed for him. He went clattering down to the battery and the next moment the boom of a gun from there alerted the rest of the defences. The flag of Spain rose up the flagstaff beside the battery, and Hornblower saw an answering flag rise up the flagstaff on San Anton where another battery guarded Corunna Bay. All the guns of the harbour defences were now manned, and there would be no mercy shown to any English ship that came in range.

Pursuer and pursued had covered quite half the distance already towards Corunna. They were hull-up over the horizon now to Hornblower on the headland, who could see them plunging madly over the grey sea—Hornblower momentarily expected to see them carry away their top-masts or their sails blow from the bolt-ropes. The frigate was half a mile astern still, and she would have to be much closer than that to have any hope of hitting with her guns in that sea. Here came the commandant and his staff, clattering on horseback up the path to see the climax of the drama; the commandant caught sight of Hornblower and doffed his hat with Spanish courtesy, while Hornblower, hatless, tried to bow with equal courtesy. Hornblower walked over to him with an urgent request—he had to lay his hand on the Spaniard's saddlebow and shout up into his face to be understood.

'My parole expires in ten minutes, sir,' he yelled. 'May I please extend it? May I please stay?'

'Yes, stay, señor,' said the commandant generously.

Hornblower watched the chase, and at the same time observed closely the preparations for defence. He had given his parole, but no part of the gentlemanly code prevented him from taking note of all he could see. One day he might be free, and one day it might be useful to know all about the defences of Ferrol. Everyone else of the large group on the headland was watching the chase, and excitement rose higher as the ships came racing nearer. The English captain was keeping a hundred yards or more to seaward of the Spaniard, but he was quite unable to overhaul her—in fact it seemed to Hornblower as if the Spaniard was actually increasing his lead. But the English frigate being to seaward meant that escape in that direction was cut off. Any turn away from the land would reduce the Spaniard's lead to a negligible distance. If he did not get into Corunna Bay or Ferrol Inlet he was doomed.

Now he was level with the Corunna headland, and it was time to put his helm hard over and turn into the bay and hope that his anchors would hold in the lee of the headland. But with a wind of that violence hurtling against cliffs and headlands strange things can happen. A flaw of wind coming out of the bay must have caught her aback as she tried to round-to. Hornblower saw her stagger, saw her heel as the backlash died away and the gale caught her again. She was laid over almost on her beam-ends and as she righted herself Hornblower saw a momentary gap open up in her maintopsail. It was momentary, because from the time the gap appeared the life of the topsail was momentary; the gap appeared and at once the sail vanished, blown into ribbons as soon as its continuity was impaired. With the loss of its balancing pressure the ship became unmanageable; the gale pressing against the fore-topsail swung her round again before the wind like a weathervane. If there had been time to spare to set a fragment of sail farther aft she would have been saved, but in those enclosed waters there was no time to spare. At one moment she was about to round the Corunna head-land; at the next she had lost the opportunity for ever.

There was still the chance that she might fetch the open-ing to the Ferrol inlet; the wind was nearly fair for her to do that—nearly. Hornblower on the Ferrol headland was thinking along with the Spanish captain down there on the heaving deck. He saw him try to steady the ship so as to head for the narrow entrance, notorious among seamen for its difficulty. He saw him get her on her course, and for a few seconds as she flew across the mouth of the bay it seemed as if the Spaniard would succeed, against all proba-bility, in exactly hitting off the entrance to the inlet. Then the backlash hit her again. Had she been quick on the helm she might still have been safe, but with her sail pressure so outbalanced she was bound to be slow in her response to her rudder. The shrieking wind blew her bows round, and it was instantly obvious, too, that she was doomed, but the Spanish captain played the game out to the last. He would not pile his ship up against the foot of the low cliffs. He put his helm hard over; with the aid of the wind rebounding from the cliffs he made a gallant atttempt to clear the Ferrol headland altogether and give himself a chance to claw out to sea.

A gallant attempt, but doomed to failure as soon as begun; he actually cleared the headland, but the wind blew his bows round again, and, bows first, the ship plunged right at the long jagged line of the Devil's Teeth. Hornblower, the commandant, and everyone, hurried across the headland to look down at the final act of the tragedy. With tremendous speed, driving straight before the wind, she raced at the reef. A roller picked her up as she neared it and seemed to increase her speed. Then she struck, and vanished from sight for a second as the roller burst into spray all about her. When the spray cleared she lay there transformed. Her three masts had all gone with the shock, and it was only a black hulk which emerged from the white foam. Her speed and the roller behind her had carried her almost over the reef—doubtless tearing her bottom out—and she hung by her stern, which stood out clear of the water, while her bows were just submerged in the comparatively still water in the lee of the reef.

There were men still alive on her. Hornblower could see them crouching for shelter under the break of her poop. Another Atlantic roller came surging up, and exploded on the Devil's Teeth, wrapping the wreck round with spray. But yet she emerged again, black against the creaming foam. She had cleared the reef sufficiently far to find shelter for most of her length in the lee of the thing that had destroyed her. Hornblower could see those living creatures crouching on her deck. They had a little longer to live—they might live five minutes, perhaps, if they were lucky. Five hours if they were not.

All round him the Spaniards were shouting maledictions. Women were weeping; some of the men were shaking their fists with rage at the British frigate, which, well satisfied with the destruction of her victim, had rounded-to in time and was now clawing out to sea again under storm canvas. It was horrible to see those poor devils down there die. If some larger wave than usual, bursting on the reef, did not lift the stern of the wreck clear so that she sank, she would still break up, for the survivors to be whirled away with the fragments. And, if it took a long time for her to break up, the wretched men sheltering there would not be able to endure the constant beating of the cold spray upon them. Something should be done to save them, but no boat could round the headland and weather the Devil's Teeth to reach the wreck. That was so obvious as not to call for a second thought. But . . . Hornblower's thoughts began to race as he started to work on the alternatives. The commandant on his horse was speaking vehemently to a Spanish naval officer, clearly on the same subject, and the naval officer was spreading his hands and saying that any attempt would be hopeless. And yet. . . . For two years Hornblower had been a prisoner; all his pent-up restlessness was seeking an outlet, and after two years of the misery of confinement he did not care whether he lived or died. He went up to the commandant and broke into the argument.

'Sir,' he said, 'let me try to save them. Perhaps from the little bay there. . . . Perhaps some of the fishermen would come with me.'

The commandant looked at the officer and the officer shrugged his shoulders.

'What do you suggest, sir?' asked the commandant of Hornblower.

'We might carry a boat across the headland from the

dockyard,' said Hornblower, struggling to word his ideas in Spanish, 'but we must be quick—quick!'

He pointed to the wreck, and force was added to his words by the sight of a roller bursting over the Devil's Teeth.

'How would you carry a boat?' asked the commandant.

To shout his plan in English against that wind would have been a strain; to do so in Spanish was beyond him.

'I can show you at the dockyard, sir,' he yelled. 'I cannot explain. But we must hurry!'

'You want to go to the dockyard, then?'

'Yes—oh, yes.'

'Mount behind me, sir,' said the commandant.

Awkwardly Hornblower scrambled up to a seat astride the horse's haunches and clutched at the commandant's belt. He bumped frightfully as the animal wheeled round and trotted down the slope. All the idlers of the town and garrison ran beside them.

The dockyard at Ferrol was almost a phantom organization, withered away like a tree deprived of its roots, thanks to the British blockade. Situated as it was at the most distant corner of Spain, connected with the interior by only the roughest of roads, it relied on receiving its supplies by sea, and any such reliance was likely, with British cruisers off the coast, to be disappointed. The last visit of Spanish ships of war had stripped the place of almost all its stores, and many of the dockyard hands had been pressed as seamen at the same time. But all that Hornblower needed was there, as he knew, thanks to his careful observation. He slid off the horse's hindquarters—miraculously avoiding an instinctive kick from the irritated animal—and collected his thoughts. He pointed to a low dray—a mere platform on wheels—which was used for carrying beef barrels and brandy kegs to the pier.

'Horses,' he said, and a dozen willing hands set to work harnessing a team.

Beside the jetty floated half a dozen boats. There was tackle and shears, all the apparatus necessary for swinging heavy weights about. To put slings under a boat and swing her up was the work of only a minute or two. These Spaniards might be dilatory and lazy as a rule, but inspire them with need for instant action, catch their enthusiasm, present them with a novel plan, and they would work like madmen—and some of them were skilled workmen, too. Oars, mast and sail (not that they would need the sail), rudder, tiller and balers were all present. A group came running from a store-shed with chocks for the boat, and the moment these were set up on the dray the dray was backed under the tackle and the boat lowered on to them.

'Empty barrels,' said Hornblower. 'Little ones—so.'

A swarthy Galician fisherman grasped his intention at once and amplified Hornblower's halting sentences with voluble explanation. A dozen empty water breakers, with their bungs driven well home, were brought, and the swarthy fisherman climbed on the dray and began to lash them under the thwarts. Properly secured, they would keep the boat afloat even were she filled to the gunwale with water.

'I want six men,' shouted Hornblower, standing on the dray and looking round at the crowd. 'Six fishermen who know little boats.'

The swarthy fisherman lashing the breakers in the boat looked up from his task.

'I know whom we need, sir,' he said.

He shouted a string of names, and half a dozen men

came forward; burly, weather-beaten fellows, with the self-reliant look in their faces of men used to meeting difficulties. It was apparent that the swarthy Galician was their captain.

'Let us go, then,' said Hornblower, but the Galician checked him.

Hornblower did not hear what he said, but some of the crowd nodded, turned away, and came hastening back staggering under a breaker of fresh water and a box that must contain biscuit. Hornblower was cross with himself for forgetting the possibility of their being blown out to sea. And the commandant, still sitting his horse and watching these preparations with a keen eye, took note of these stores too.

'Remember, sir, that I have your parole,' he said.

'You have my parole, sir,' said Hornblower—for a few blessed moments he had actually forgotten that he was a prisoner.

The stores were safely put away into the stern-sheets and the fishing-boat captain caught Hornblower's eye and got a nod from him.

'Let us go,' he roared to the crowd.

The iron-shod hoofs clashed on the cobbles and the dray lurched forward, with men leading the horses, men swarming alongside, and Hornblower and the captain riding on the dray like triumphing generals in a procession. They went through the dockyard gate, along the level main street of the little town, and turned up a steep lane which climbed the ridge constituting the backbone of the headland. The enthusiasm of the crowd was still lively; when the horses slowed as they breasted the slope a hundred men pushed at the back, strained at the sides, tugged at the traces to run the dray up the hillside. At the crest the land became a track, but the dray still lurched and rumbled along. From the track diverged an even worse track, winding its way sideways down the slope through arbutus and myrtle towards the sandy cove which Hornblower had first had in mind—on fine days he had seen fishermen working a seine net on that beach, and he himself had taken note of it as a suitable place for a landing party should the Royal Navy ever plan a descent against Ferrol.

The wind was blowing as wildly as ever; it shrieked round Hornblower's ears. The sea as it came in view was chaotic with wave-crests, and then as they turned a shoulder of the slope they could see the line of the Devil's Teeth running out from the shore up there to windward, and still hanging precariously from their jagged fangs was the wreck, black against the seething foam. Somebody raised a shout at the sight, everybody heaved at the dray, so that the horse actually broke into a trot and the dray leaped and bounced over the obstructions in its way.

'Slowly,' roared Hornblower. 'Slowly!'

If they were to break an axle or smash a wheel at this moment the attempt would end in ludicrous failure. The commandant on his horse enforced Hornblower's cries with loud orders of his own, and restrained the reckless enthusiasm of his people. More sedately the dray went on down the trail to the edge of the sandy beach. The wind picked up even the damp sand and flung it stinging into their faces, but only small waves broke here, for the beach was in a recess in the shoreline, the south-westerly wind was blowing a trifle off-shore here, and up to windward the Devil's Teeth broke the force of the rollers as they raced along in a direction nearly parallel to the shore-line. The wheels plunged into the sand and the horses stopped at the water's edge. A score of willing hands unharnessed them and a hundred willing arms thrust the dray out into the water—all these things were easy with such vast manpower available. As the first wave broke over the floor of the dray the crew scrambled up and stood ready. There were rocks here, but mighty heaves by the militiamen and the dock-yard workers waist-deep in water forced the dray over them. The boat almost floated off its chocks, and the crew forced it clear and scrambled aboard, the wind beginning to swing her immediately. They grabbed for their oars and put their backs into half a dozen fierce strokes which brought her under command; the Galician captain had already laid a steering oar in the notch in the stern, with no attempt at shipping rudder and tiller. As he braced himself to steer he glanced at Hornblower, who tacitly left the job to him.

Hornblower, bent against the wind, was standing in the stern-sheets planning a route through the rocks which would lead them to the wreck. The shore and the friendly beach were gone now, incredibly far away, and the boat was struggling out through a welter of water with the wind howling round her. In those jumbled waves her motion was senseless and she lurched in every direction successively. It was well that the boatmen were used to rowing in broken water so that their oars kept the boat under way, giving the captain the means by which, tugging fiercely at the steering oar, he could guide her through that maniacal confusion. Hornblower, planning his course, was able to guide the captain by his gestures, so that the captain could devote all the necessary attention to keeping the boat from being suddenly capsized by an unexpected wave. The wind howled, and the boat heaved and pitched as she met each lumpy wave, but yard by yard they were struggling up to the wreck. If there was any order in the waves at all, they were swinging round the outer end of the Devil's Teeth, so that the boat had to be carefully steered, turning to meet the waves with her bows and then turning back to gain precarious yards against the wind. Hornblower spared a glance for the men at the oars; at every second they were exerting their utmost strength. There could never be a moment's respite—tug and strain, tug and strain, until Hornblower wondered how human hearts and sinews could endure it.

But they were edging up towards the wreck. Hornblower, when the wind and spray allowed, could see the whole extent of her canted deck now. He could see human figures cowering under the break of the poop. He saw somebody there wave an arm to him. Next moment his attention was called away when a jagged monster suddenly leaped out of the sea twenty yards ahead. For a second he could not imagine what it was, and then it leaped clear again and he recognized it—the butt end of a broken mast. The mast was still anchored to the ship by a single surviving shroud attached to the upper end of the mast and to the ship, and the mast, drifting down to leeward, was jerking and leaping on the waves as though some sea god below the surface was threatening them with his wrath. Hornblower called the steersman's attention to the menace and received a nod in return; the steersman's shouted 'Nombre de Dios' was whirled away in the wind. They kept clear of the mast, and as they pulled up along it Hornblower could form a clearer notion of the speed of their progress now that he had a stationary object to help his judgment. He could see the painful inches gained at each frantic tug on the oars, and could see how the boat stopped dead or even went astern when the wilder gusts hit her, the oar blades pulling ineffectively through the water. Every inch of gain was only won at the cost of an infinity of labour.

Now they were past the mast, close to the submerged bows of the ship, and close enough to the Devil's Teeth to be deluged with spray as each wave burst on the farther side of the reef. There were inches of water washing back and forth in the bottom of the boat, but there was neither time nor opportunity to bale it out. This was the trickiest part of the whole effort, to get close enough alongside the wreck to be able to take off the survivors without stoving in the boat; there were wicked fangs of rock all about the after end of the wreck, while forward, although the forecastle was above the surface at times, the forward part of the waist was submerged. But the ship was canted a little over to port, towards them, which made the approach easier. When the water was at its lowest level, immediately before the next roller broke on the reef, Hornblower, standing up and craning his neck, could see no rocks beside the wreck in the middle part of the waist where the deck came down to water level. It was easy to direct the steersman towards that particular point, and then, as the boat moved in, to wave his arms and demand the attention of the little group under the break of the poop, and to point to the spot to which they were approaching. A wave burst upon the reef, broke over the stern of the wreck, and filled the boat almost full. She swung back and forth in the eddies, but the kegs kept her afloat and quick handling of the steering oar and lusty rowing kept her from being dashed against either the wreck or the rocks.

'Now!' shouted Hornblower—it did not matter that he spoke English at this decisive moment. The boat surged forward, while the survivors, releasing themselves from the lashings which had held them in their shelter, came slithering down the deck towards them. It was a little of a shock to see there were but four of them—twenty or thirty men must have been swept overboard when the ship hit the reef. The bows of the boat moved towards the wreck. At a shouted order from the steersman the oars fell still. One survivor braced himself and flung himself into the bows. A stroke of the oars, a tug at the steering oar, and the boat nosed forward again, and another survivor plunged into the boat. Then Hornblower, who had been watching the sea, saw the next breaker rear up over the reef. At his warning shout the boat backed away to safety—comparative safety—while the remaining survivors went scrambling back up the deck to the shelter of the poop. The wave burst and roared, the foam hissed and the spray rattled, and then they crept up to the wreck again. The third survivor poised himself for his leap, mistimed it, and fell into the sea, and no one ever saw him again. He was gone, sunk like a stone, crippled as he was with cold and exhaustion, but there was no time to spare for lamentation. The fourth survivor was waiting his chance and jumped at once, landing safely in the bows.

'Any more?' shouted Hornblower, and receiving a shake of the head in reply; they had saved three lives at the risk of eight.

'Let us go,' said Hornblower, but the steersman needed no telling.

Already he had allowed the wind to drift the boat away from the wreck, away from the rocks—away from the shore. An occasional strong pull at the oars sufficed to keep her bows to wind and wave. Hornblower looked down at the fainting survivors lying in the bottom of the boat with the water washing over them. He bent down and shook them into consciousness; he picked up the balers and forced them into their numb hands. They must keep active or die. It was astounding to find darkness closing about them, and it was urgent that they should decide on their next move immediately. The men at the oars were in no shape for any prolonged further rowing; if they tried to return to the sandy cove whence they had started they might be overtaken both by night and by exhaustion while still among the treacherous rocks off the shore there. Hornblower sat down beside the Galician captain, who laconically gave his views while vigilantly observing the waves racing down upon them.

'It's growing dark,' said the captain, glancing round the sky. 'Rocks. The men are tired.'

'We had better not go back,' said Hornblower.

'No.'

'Then we must get out to sea.'

Years of duty on blockade, of beating about off a lee shore, had ingrained into Hornblower the necessity for seeking sea-room.

'Yes,' said the captain, and he added something which Hornblower, thanks to the wind and his unfamiliarity with the language, was unable to catch. The captain roared the expression again, and accompanied his words with a vivid bit of pantomime with the one hand he could spare from the steering oar.

'A sea anchor,' decided Hornblower to himself. 'Quite right.'

He looked back at the vanishing shore, and gauged the direction of the wind. It seemed to be backing a little southerly; the coast here trended away from them. They could ride to a sea anchor through the hours of darkness and run no risk of being cast ashore as long as these conditions persisted.

'Good,' said Hornblower aloud.

He imitated the other's bit of pantomime and the captain gave him a glance of approval. At a bellow from him the two men forward took in their oars and set to work at constructing a sea anchor—merely a pair of oars attached to a long painter paid out over the bows. With this gale blowing, the pressure of the wind on the boat set up enough drag on the float to keep their bows to the sea. Hornblower watched as the sea anchor began to take hold of the water.

'Good,' he said again.

'Good,' said the captain, taking in his steering oar.

Hornblower realized only now that he had been long exposed to a winter gale while wet to the skin. He was numb with cold, and he was shivering uncontrollably. At his feet one of the three survivors of the wreck was lying helpless; the other two had succeeded in baling out most of the water and as a result of their exertions were conscious and alert. The men who had been rowing sat drooping with weariness on their thwarts. The Galician captain was already down in the bottom of the boat lifting the helpless man in his arms. It was a common impulse of them all to huddle down into the bottom of the boat, beneath the thwarts, away from that shrieking wind.

So the night came down on them. Hornblower found himself welcoming the contact of other human bodies; he felt an arm round him and he put his arm round someone else. Around them a little water still surged about on the floorboards; above them the wind still shrieked and howled. The boat stood first on her head and then on her tail as the waves passed under them, and at the moment of climbing each crest she gave a shuddering jerk as she snubbed herself to the sea anchor. Every few seconds a new spat of spray whirled into the boat upon their shrinking bodies;

it did not seem long before the accumulation of spray in the bottom of the boat made it necessary for them to disentangle themselves and set about, groping in the darkness, the task of baling the water out again. Then they could huddle down again under the thwarts.

It was when they pulled themselves together for the third baling that in the middle of his nightmare of cold and exhaustion Hornblower was conscious that the body across which his arm lay was unnaturally stiff; the man the captain had been trying to revive had died as he lay there between the captain and Hornblower. The captain dragged the body away into the stern-sheets in the darkness, and the night went on, cold wind and cold spray, jerk, pitch, and roll, sit up and bale and cower down and shudder. It was hideous torment; Hornblower could not trust himself to believe his eyes when he saw the first signs that the darkness was lessening. And then the grey dawn came gradually over the grey sea, and they were free to wonder what to do next. But as the light increased the problem was solved for them, for one of the fishermen, raising himself up in the boat, gave a hoarse cry, and pointed to the northern horizon, and there, almost hull-up, was a ship, hove-to under storm canvas. The captain took one glance at her—his eyesight must have been marvellous—and identified her.

'The English frigate,' he said.

She must have made nearly the same amount of leeway hove-to as the boat did riding to her sea anchor.

'Signal to her,' said Hornblower, and no one raised any objections.

The only white object available was Hornblower's shirt, and he took it off, shuddering in the cold, and they tied it to an oar and raised the oar in the maststep. The captain saw Hornblower putting on his dripping coat over his bare ribs and in a single movement peeled off his thick blue jersey and offered it to him.

'Thank you, no,' protested Hornblower, but the captain insisted; with a wide grin he pointed to the stiffened corpse lying in the stern-sheets and announced he would replace the jersey with the dead man's clothing.

The argument was interrupted by a further cry from one of the fishermen. The frigate was coming to the wind; with treble-reefed fore and maintopsails she was heading for them under the impulse of the lessening gale. Hornblower saw her running down on them; a glance in the other direction showed him the Galician mountains, faint on the southern horizon—warmth, freedom and friendship on the one hand; solitude and captivity on the other. Under the lee of the frigate the boat bobbed and heaved fantastically; many inquisitive faces looked down on them. They were cold and cramped; the frigate dropped a boat and a couple of nimble seamen scrambled on board. A line was flung from the frigate, a whip lowered a breeches ring into the boat, and the English seamen helped the Spaniards one by one into the breeches and held them steady as they were swung up to the frigate's deck.

'I go last,' said Hornblower, when they turned to him. 'I am a King's officer.'

'Good Lor' lumme,' said the seamen.

'Send the body up, too,' said Hornblower. 'It can be given decent burial.'

The stiff corpse was grotesque as it swayed through the air. The Galician captain tried to dispute with Hornblower the honour of going last, but Hornblower would not be argued with. Then finally the seamen helped him put his legs into the breeches, and secured him with a line round his waist. Up he soared, swaying dizzily with the roll of the ship; then they drew him in to the deck, lowering and shortening, until half a dozen strong arms took his weight and laid him gently on the deck.

'There you are, my hearty, safe and sound,' said a bearded seaman.

'I am a King's officer,' said Hornblower. 'Where's the officer of the watch?'

Wearing marvellous dry clothing, Hornblower found himself soon drinking hot rum-and-water in the cabin of Captain George Crome, of His Majesty's frigate *Syrtis*. Crome was a thin, pale man with a depressed expression, but Hornblower knew of him as a first-rate officer.

'These Galicians make good seamen,' said Crome. 'I can't press them. But perhaps a few will volunteer sooner than go to a prison hulk.'

'Sir,' said Hornblower, and hesitated. It is ill for a junior lieutenant to argue with a post captain.

'Well?'

'Those men came to sea to save life. They are not liable to capture.'

Crome's cold, grey eyes became actively frosty—Hornblower was right about it being ill for a junior lieutenant to argue with a post captain.

'Are you telling me my duty, sir?' he asked.

'Good heavens, no, sir,' said Hornblower hastily. 'It's a long time since I read the Admiralty Instructions and I expect my memory's at fault.'

'Admiralty Instructions, eh?' said Crome, in a slightly different tone of voice.

'I expect I'm wrong, sir,' said Hornblower, 'but I seem to remember the same instruction applied to the other two— the survivors.'

Even a post captain could only contravene Admiralty Instructions at his peril.

'I'll consider it,' said Crome.

'I had the dead man sent on board, sir,' went on Hornblower, 'in the hope that perhaps you might give him proper burial. Those Galicians risked their lives to save him, sir, and I expect they'd be gratified.'

'A Popish burial? I'll give orders to give 'em a free hand.'

'Thank you, sir,' said Hornblower.

'And now as regards yourself. You say you hold a commission as lieutenant. You can do duty in this ship until we meet the admiral again. Then he can decide. I haven't heard of the *Indefatigable* paying off, and legally you may still be borne on her books.'

And that was when the devil came to tempt Hornblower, as he took another sip of hot rum-and-water. The joy of being in a King's ship again was so keen as to be almost painful. To taste salt beef and biscuit again, and never again to taste beans and garbanzos. To have a ship's deck under his feet, to talk English. To be free—to be free! There was precious little chance of ever falling again into Spanish hands. Hornblower remembered with agonizing clarity the flat depression of captivity. All he had to do was not to say a word. He had only to keep silence for a day or two. But the devil did not tempt him long, only until he had taken his next sip of rum-and-water. Then he thrust the devil behind him and met Crome's eyes again.

'I'm sorry, sir,' he said.

'What for?'

'I am here on parole. I gave my word before I left the beach.'

'You did? That alters the case. You were within your rights, of course.'

The giving of parole by captive British officers was so usual as to excite no comment.

'It was in the usual form, I suppose?' went on Crome. 'That you would make no attempt to escape?'

'Yes, sir.'

'Then what do you decide as a result?'

Of course Crome could not attempt to influence a gentleman's decision on a matter as personal as a parole.

'I must go back, sir,' said Hornblower, 'at the first opportunity.'

He felt the sway of the ship, he looked round the homely cabin, and his heart was breaking.

'You can at least dine and sleep on board to-night,' said Crome. 'I'll not venture inshore again until the wind moderates. I'll send you to Corunna under a flag of truce when I can. And I'll see what the Instructions say about those prisoners.'

It was a sunny morning when the sentry at Fort San Anton, in the harbour of Corunna, called his officer's attention to the fact that the British cruiser off the headland had hove-to out of gunshot and was lowering a boat. The sentry's responsibility ended there, and he could watch idly as his officer observed that the cutter, running smartly in under sail, was flying a white flag. She hove-to within musket shot, and it was a mild surprise to the sentry when in reply to the officer's hail someone rose up in the boat and replied in unmistakable Gallego dialect. Summoned alongside the landing slip, the cutter put ashore ten men and then headed out again to the frigate. Nine men were laughing and shouting; the tenth, the youngest, walked with a fixed expression on his face with never a sign of emotion—his expression did not change even when the others, with obvious affection, put their arms round his shoulders. No one ever troubled to explain to the sentry who the imperturbable young man was, and he was not very interested. After he had seen the group shipped off across Corunna Bay towards Ferrol he quite forgot the incident.

It was almost spring when a Spanish militia officer came into the barracks which served as a prison for officers in Ferrol.

'Señor Hornblower?' he asked—at least Hornblower, in the corner, knew that was what he was trying to say. He was used to the way Spaniards mutilated his name.

'Yes?' he said, rising.

'Would you please come with me? The commandant has sent me for you, sir.'

The commandant was all smiles. He held a despatch in his hands.

'This, sir,' he said, waving it at Hornblower, 'is a personal order. It is countersigned by the Duke of Fuentesauco, Minister of Marine, but it is signed by the First Minister, Prince of the Peace and Duke of Alcudia.'

'Yes, sir,' said Hornblower.

He should have begun to hope at that moment, but there comes a time in a prisoner's life when he ceases to hope. He was more interested, even, in that strange title of Prince of the Peace which was now beginning to be heard in Spain.

'It says: "We, Carlos Leonardo Luis Manuel de Godoy y Boegas, First Minister of His Most Catholic Majesty, Prince of the Peace, Duke of Alcudia and Grandee of the First Class, Count of Alcudia, Knight of the Most Sacred Order of the Golden Fleece, Knight of the Holy Order of Santiago, Knight of the Most Distinguished Order of Calatrava, Captain General of His Most Catholic Majesty's forces by Land and Sea, Colonel General of the Guardia de Corps, Admiral of the Two Oceans, General of the cavalry, of the infantry, and of the artillery"—in any event, sir, it is an order to me to take immediate steps to set you at liberty. I am to restore you under flag of truce to your fellow-countrymen, in recognition of "your courage and self-sacrifice in saving life at the peril of your own".'

'Thank you, sir,' said Hornblower.